BLESSEDLY BOUND

AN ELEMENTAL WITCH TRIALS NOVEL

BOOK ONE

LUCRETIA STANHOPE

Acknowledgements

As with all magical creatures, (well maybe not all, but many, a lot, more than a few, probably enough to make it a norm) I have a wonderful power of three that keeps me strong. My editors, beta readers and those who make it possible for me to put one word behind the other, commas in the right places, if there is such a beast as a properly placed comma (this is a bigger issue than you might imagine) and to have the faith in myself needed to create from the soul. They also add infinite joy to my life, and chocolate, they give chocolate. So, in alphabetical order, because, seriously, as much as I love these three people, they would wonder why their names were in any other order. That's why we can't just do nice things. Andrew, Jamie, and Toneye, thank you from the bottom of my sparkly soul.

Chapter One

Gwen glared at her raven Lewis, who watched her from his perch. "You can help me or mind your own business."

"Will it be my business when you lay freezing in a snowstorm?" His words whispered in her mind.

With her last step out of the main room and into the hall she inhaled a full breath. They discussed his concerns already, more than once. Her focus remained steady as she opened the door, unshaken by the flourish of feathers when Lewis flew by her face. It didn't bother her anymore, not like it used to. Over time she came to understand it as the equivalent to a child's temper tantrum.

The wood boards of the porch creaked under her weight. With a tug she closed the door and ended the stream of warmth from inside, along with the debate. The siding rose waist high and the screen blocked much of the snow. Regardless, the temperature pierced the extra layers she wore.

Lewis watched as she struggled with the outside door.

She shoved her shoulder against it a few times. The high snowdrift caused it to need more muscle than Gwen's small stature could give.

The raven changed to his man form, shoved the door open, and shifted back before he took flight into the night.

"Thank you." Her words filled the emptiness around her.

With her head turned so that the chill didn't slap her face, she walked down the steps into the storm. The wind swirled the fluffy new snow in a way that made it hard to see. The deeper into the chilling white she walked the more she needed to use memories, awful memories, and instinct to guide the way. Her eyes scanned for Lewis as she fought the snow in the direction of the tree line, toward where she knew they discovered her grandmother.

Dead. Burned.

Gwen tried not to think about her first few days at the manor. Awful days filled with tales of what the police found. The local sheriff told those tales with indifference. The disconnection in his voice and eyes made sense for police officers, but made her uncomfortable. Those days, and those words stayed raw and fresh in her mind.

Still in her first week, her clothes remained in suitcases, and she didn't feel anything other than confused. She tried to understand what happened, why it happened, or where she belonged. Every day felt like a blur of crime scenes, police, details she never wanted to hear, and a manor that she didn't, and may never feel at home in.

The sound of snow as it crunched under her feet became background music to those memories, while her mind drifted to the first day she walked the grounds alongside the police officers.

Her thoughts broke.

A warm spot grew from the coldness and wrapped around her. The whistle of the wind stopped. The smell of burned pine, death, and ice mingled together in the air like a macabre barbecue. She knew she stood in the right spot.

The trees appeared as dark shadows of some unknown monsters reflected against the white snow. She turned away from the imagined monsters toward the manor she couldn't see anymore. An isolated sense of dread washed over her. She drew in a deeper breath, the air dried her throat. Every exhale formed a cloud before it faded, sucked into the void she felt.

Her face shivered, teeth chattered, and fingers felt numb. The urgency to get on with her attempt at a vision pulled her from her drifting thoughts. To delay any longer meant a real risk of frost bite.

A flash of black cut through the snowy air. Lewis.

She pulled off her gloves, reached her hands out to the rough bark, and rested her bare palms on the burnt tree. The tree where her grandmother died.

Bound and burned.

Her feet slid out of her shoes and dug into the icy layers. As a reflex they recoiled. It took all of her will to force them deeper. Her toes wiggled through the snow while she ignored both the wind that cut through her clothes and the hot pin pricks of freezing flesh on her feet.

At first it was easy to dig away the new fluffy flakes, and then it took some extra effort as she worked at the older, more compressed layers. She did not register that she hit the soil under her feet until her mind took her back to the near past.

Sometimes past visions came in manageable snippets, and other times she felt transported. This time she felt the tug of a transport. She hoped for that when she decided to take her chances in the snowstorm in order to use the waning moon to aid her.

A breeze blew. The air carried on it had a dry warmth. She looked up, stars above her sparkled in the dark night sky.

It must be a summer night, she thought. *No, it can't be.*

She inhaled the scent of char and let her mind focus. Warmth surrounded her again. From where? The air itself was cold, a winter night, but with a warm breeze.

Her eyes opened wide.

Fire.

Fire burned in front of her. As the flames grew higher, they scorched her skin. She struggled to back away from the flames but found she couldn't move. Her eyes looked down. Everywhere she looked she saw dancing shades of yellow and orange. She wrestled against the rope that held her bound, tied to a tree.

"Burned at the stake." She heard the words echo in the night, followed by laughter.

She pushed aside the hot and pain as she tried to see who the laugh came from. Her eyes scanned the flames that licked closer to her. The wicked laugh filled her head. Sweat beaded on her forehead. The heat made it hard to concentrate. She needed a glance, a glimpse, anything she could link to.

Brown eyes flashed in front of her. She couldn't see anything else, her mind refused to piece together anything other than brown eyes. She saw no face. Even the voice sounded genderless.

"Now you will burn, witch," the same voice said.

The flames reached higher. She heard herself screaming. Two distinct sets of screams rang out, her own and her grandmother's. The heat swallowed her thoughts. She smelled the unmistakable smell of skin on fire and singed hair. Things started to black out as consuming pain enveloped her.

As soon as her consciousness closed to the fire, she felt cold. Her hands strained to grip the snow beneath them as she lay sprawled on the ground.

Her eyes opened again to see the ivory world replaced by crimson. She looked down, and said a prayer that the ropes would burn so she could flee from the heat and pain.

Blackness came again. Coldness woke her again.

Again, her eyes opened to heat and fire. She tried to back out of the past, but flames continued to cook her skin.

Her eyes closed. She felt clammy. The sweat on her skin froze in the arctic air.

"Lewis," she managed to say before the flames sucked her back.

When she started to return again she felt warmth, not heat. She felt movement. Someone carried her in their arms. The wind still howled, snow swirled. Too weak to do anything more, she rested against the familiar body of Lewis.

The next time she opened her eyes, she saw the main room inside the manor. She felt the comfort of a soft blanket and heard the crackle of the fire.

Lewis perched on the chair to the right of the couch she rested on. He watched in silence.

"Thank you." She sat up, and leaned back on the pillows.

"You could have died," he said, still as a voice in her head.

She licked her chapped lips. "I need to know. You know I only had one night to do this before the moon phase changed."

"Was it worth it?"

"Any little bit that can help me find out who did this to grandma is worth anything."

"You were hurt."

"Yes. Burned." She held out her arms, her eyes examined the unmarred flesh. "You healed them already?"

"Of course I healed them. You knew she was burned, what have you learned?" His words started out soothing but became an annoyance as he chastised her.

Gwen rubbed her hands together. "She was burned alive. I learned why she was killed that way. She was not burned after being killed some other way. They, whoever killed her, put her to death as a witch."

"Did you see who did it?"

"No, I saw brown eyes, and heard a crazy laugh."

"Brown eyes, and how exactly is that useful?"

"I can't be sure. It's something."

"It is not something worth dying for in a snowstorm."

Gwen laid her head back and closed her eyes. They already argued about this before she went outside. She didn't have the desire to do it again. "Thank you, was what started this conversation. How about you just say you're welcome and we call it a night?"

"Welcome," he said and proceeded to preen. She interpreted that as ravenspeak for, 'this is not worth my time.'

"Lewis?" Her eyes remained closed.

"Yes, my witch?"

"What can pull me into the past?"

"Did you feel out of control?" He changed forms and sat beside her on the couch.

"I did. Whatever it was, with the eyes, it kept pulling me back every time I tried to come back to here." She opened her eyes when she felt him sit.

He looked at her, his thin brows creased with the same concern that was in every one of the sharp features of his face. His dark brown eyes, rimmed in black, looked back at her, also concerned. His hand reached down and stroked her hair, that glistened as deep a black as his own.

She tried to hide her own fear as he studied her with intensity. He didn't stay in the form of a man often, not since they realized they shared a deep, inappropriate desire for each other. Magical partners did not entertain such an attraction. In all his forms, he only consisted of magical energy. It could not happen. She felt a twinge of sorrow at the thought of their agreement that he would stay in the form of a raven, unless an absolute need for him to be otherwise arose.

"I don't feel any magic on you. No links or residue." His brows uncreased.

"Was I in danger do you think? I've never felt like things noticed me before when I look in the past."

"They shouldn't have noticed you. It should have been like watching a film. It engaged you?" he asked, in a tone riddled with concern.

"Yeah, you don't think I could have called something here somehow? Maybe I wasn't seeing the past, maybe some supernatural being was showing me something?"

"Nothing seemed extraordinary from here. You looked no different than any other time you have had visions. I didn't feel any magic in the air aside from yours." His features wrinkled more as he thought.

"Are we safe now?" She sat up a little more.

"Yes, of course, lay down and rest. I will get you something hot to drink and add wood to the fire before I shift back."

As she watched him walk away, she felt that he knew more than he let on. Lately, the wedge between them grew in size at a rate that alarmed her. She could tell something about the night rattled him. Not only did it show in his eyes, but he shifted forms. What had startled him enough to do that?

When he came back, he handed her a cup of hot chocolate and then tossed wood on the fire.

"What scared you?" she asked after she took a sip of her drink.

"You screaming, to start with." He turned back to her. "I never want to hear you hurting."

"No Lewis, what scared you enough that you are here, now, like this?"

"I wanted to touch you and make sure there was nothing on you that needed magic to remove it." He looked away in what she read as an attempt to avoid eye contact.

"You are lying. I thought as my familiar you had to help me."

"I do. I will always do what is best for you."

Those words stung as she remembered the argument about him and her never being together.

"Yes, well make sure in protecting me you also keep me aware of the dangers too."

"It sounds like a witch, voodoo maybe, or a demon," he said. "A demon is not something either of us needs to be tangling with."

"Why would a demon burn grandma at the stake?"

"I don't know, and I am sad you had to see that."

"I lived it, bound and burned. It was awful and painful."

He sat down and took her in his arms. "I'm so sorry you had to feel that. Please stay away from that spot. It is clearly still active with something."

"For now, but I will not stop looking for answers. You must understand that. If you know something, you can save me some work."

He didn't answer. They both let the needed conversation transition into silence as she drifted to sleep in his lap. While she slept, he considered what happened in the snowstorm. He wondered which of his buried secrets would surface, and what else might happen as a result.

Chapter Two

Gwen lingered in the cab of her truck. Her eyes followed the wiper blades as they tried in vain to keep the windshield clear of snow. It reflected her effort to brush aside the sadness she felt at knowing she could have met her grandmother.

The rubber blades gave a squeaky protest as if to say, 'at least we're still trying.'

"Great, now inanimate objects are mocking me," she said to the empty cab, and turned off the ignition. The blades stopped mid-swipe. "Now who is trying?"

The victory over the blades felt hollow. Like she did. She always wanted a family. How could Lizzy leave her granddaughter alone?

The cab started to lose its warmth as soon as she turned off the engine. She needed to face the town. Face the people who knew her grandmother better than she did.

She meant to visit the day she arrived. Sidetracked by a mixture of sadness, police, and the flood of questions, both from her own mind and the local sheriff, she never made time. The snow and wind that whistled outside lengthened her postponement. Roads she already found narrow became more of a challenge to navigate.

She imagined herself stuck alone at her estate, and wanted to get some yarn and groceries.

She pulled her purse off the floorboard. Meeting new people made her nervous. Historically, as soon as she felt close to someone they moved away, pushed her away, or worse died. Even Lewis, who shared a magical bond with her, pushed her away.

Her fingers ran over the leather strap of her bag, as images of nights alone in her apartment came unwelcome to the surface of her mind. Would it be the same there? Her alone in that big old manor? Or would she make a connection?

"Time to find out," she said to herself.

Her hand hesitated on the door handle.

She remained in the cab of her truck a moment as she gathered her nerve to navigate the icy walkway. Growing up in Louisiana, she lacked experience with ice and the kind of weather currently plaguing the small town in northwestern Kansas.

The ball of yarn with the word Yartist in the window tempted her enough to get out and brave the slippery sidewalk.

She pushed the door open.

The little yarn shop would be her reward for facing both the snow and her own personal demons.

A warm blast of air from the shop greeted her as a welcomed reward for successful navigation of the treacherous path. The scent of freshly brewed coffee teased her with the promise of comfort. She secured the door against the elements and turned to find a tall, thin woman stood nearby.

Friendly hazel eyes studied Gwen. The wrinkles around Kathy's mouth reflected many gentle smiles that preceded the one she now wore. "Oh dear, you must be Lizzy's granddaughter. Striking family resemblance. Come, I have coffee to warm you. I was hoping to meet you soon." The woman tucked her long brown and gray hair up in a bun she held in place with a knitting needle. "I'm Kathy, this is my shop. How do you like your coffee? Today I have a hazelnut blend."

Gwen couldn't help but smile back and feel nourished emotionally by Kathy, who seemed to overflow with kindness. "Gwen, I'm Gwen, it's nice to meet you. I'll have sugar and cream if it's no trouble." She looked around at all the tidy little baskets, filled with yarn of various colors and thicknesses.

Kathy waved off the idea before she turned around to get a cup of coffee. "We have a knitting room in the back. Come, sit, we must chat. The little bell will ring if anyone comes in."

"Wonderful, thank you. Please don't let me keep you from anything." Gwen took the cup Kathy offered her, and followed her to a small archway in the back-right corner of the store.

"Oh, dear heavens, keep me? You will soon learn, if you stay. You will stay, won't you? This is where you come for coffee, yarn, to sit a spell and hear all the gossip you ever need. Due to the weather our regulars are not here right now, but typically this room would have at least three ladies."

Gwen walked in behind Kathy, who switched the light on.

Shelves lined the walls, some holding yarns, others holding tubs with assorted craft supplies. While she listened to Kathy talk about the regulars as if she should know them, her eyes flicked to three posters on the walls. They depicted cute mice playing with yarn balls. It added to the cozy 'her kind of place,' feeling. "Sounds lovely. I meant to come sooner. As soon as I saw a yarn shop. I knit. The distraction would be good for my nerves, but I didn't bring any supplies."

"Bless your heart it would. How are you holding up? We loved Lizzy so much. Sweet as a button. Here every Wednesday for our group. We meet to knit, for charity. You are more than welcome to come. We meet every Wednesday after I close, at six." Kathy slid into a seat and nodded for Gwen to do the same.

Gwen smiled, then sat down. While she found it sweet, the fast-paced talking overwhelmed her. Subdued best described her chats with Lewis, when he came around. He didn't care for idle chat. She felt outmatched. "That sounds great. Once I get settled."

"Of course. Awful. How are you up there, banging around all alone? Did you meet your neighbor yet?" Kathy asked.

"You mean Sebastian?" Gwen took a small sip of her coffee before continuing. "No, I keep trying to meet him. He has documents for me, but he is hard to pin down. I guess I really haven't pressed him. I just don't feel up to that yet."

"Oh, do meet with him. He was Lizzy's best friend. Didn't come to town much at all, but Lizzy always told stories about him."

"Do you think he might know more about what happened?" Gwen ran her finger along the handle of the cup.

"If anyone would. He saw her every day from what I gather. Didn't Curtis, I mean, Sheriff Curtis, have anything to tell you?" Kathy asked as her brows pinched together.

Gwen frowned. "No, seems they have no leads yet. I didn't, well I didn't know Lizzy. I'm just feeling a bit lost."

Kathy sipped her coffee. "Well, I will talk with Curtis at dinner. He is always at Mel's Diner. When you have time, stop in there. I know Mel has been eager to meet you too. I just can't imagine anyone not liking Lizzy, much less hurting her. Kind, generous, a good, good soul."

"Do you know why my mom left?" Gwen felt forward to ask so soon, but it played on her mind.

Kathy looked away toward the door. "No honey, Lizzy never spoke about anything sad. You talk to Sebastian, he would know."

"I will," Gwen said, and finished her coffee. "Can I get some fingering yarn? I think I want to make a lacy wrap."

"Of course, and you don't forget about next Wednesday. I'll save you a seat. There will always be a seat here for you. All the ladies will be so excited. It's been hard looking at her empty chair." Kathy frowned briefly, before smiling again.

"Lizzy knitted? She came here?" Gwen said, unable to hide her surprise as she caught up with what Kathy said when they first sat down.

Kathy gave a small chuckle at Gwen and repeated herself. She added some more details. "I wish you knew her. She was such a sweet creature. Every Wednesday, we knit for charity, she was always first to sign up for everything. Knitted beautiful lace. Just gorgeous delicate things. Your mom was learning too when she was a little girl."

Gwen smiled at that and walked with Kathy to pick out some lacy blue yarn for her wrap. After several squeezes, Gwen settled on some alpaca that Kathy said just arrived.

"Thank you. I will see you Wednesday." Gwen wrapped the top of her bag over and peered out the window, happy to see the snow momentarily stopped.

The walk to the car and drive to the grocery proved uneventful, much to her pleasure. She loved that the store didn't have more than a few people. While she walked the aisles, she thought about her visit with Kathy. She felt excited about what the next week could hold and struggled to recall the last time she felt that way. Her mind played out happy, but impossible scenes of Lizzy as a person, and as a grandmother, while she tossed things in her cart.

Safely back in the truck, she looked at her phone. The clock read almost five, more time slipped away from her and Kathy while they chatted than she thought. Thinking back, she realized they probably walked the store looking at yarn just as long.

Before she started driving she decided to call Sebastian, not sure why she put it off. Shortly after she arrived in town she made a few tries with no answer and gave up. She told herself she would deal with it all later. Later kept getting pushed back but she needed to handle all the finer details. That would mean planning a memorial, which in all probability topped the reasons why later never happened. As before, his phone rang with no answer. This time she left a short message with her number.

She didn't sense Lewis when she arrived back at the manor. Since she wouldn't have his help, she smiled that the salt he laid kept the path mostly free of snow. She brought in the things that needed to be put away immediately and left the rest for later.

She added more wood to the fire and turned her attention to the dwindling stack of wood beside the fireplace. A frown formed while she contemplated if the stack would hold out until Lewis returned. The pile outside just needed carried in, he chopped it before he left. Due to the weather, she decided to give him more time before she dragged it in herself.

Settled on the couch, she pulled out her needles and new yarn. The feeling of the yarn in her hands melted away any remaining tension. The sound of the clicking needles punctuated her thoughts. Considering how much Kathy implied everyone loved Lizzy, Gwen struggled to imagine who would burn her alive.

Over the years, Lewis told Gwen very little about her family. She knew Lizzy and her mother both practiced witchcraft. Could another witch have done it? Or even a demon, as Lewis suggested.

Her phone rang and she looked at the screen to see Sebastian's number.

"I am free this evening," he said after they exchanged hellos. His voice sounded smooth with a hint of something exotic. Mediterranean, she guessed.

"Oh, sure if you are up for the weather. I don't mind waiting until tomorrow when the sun is out and it's warmer." She didn't want him making a special trip out in the nasty cold to meet with her.

"I am afraid my days are accounted for. Tonight then?"

She agreed and they hung up. Her hands quickly finished the stitches in her current row of knitting. After she set the project down, she made her way to the kitchen to start a fresh pot of coffee before adding the last few pieces of wood to the fire.

"Lewis?" As she expected, he did not respond. She did not use magic to reach him. Adding wood to a fire did not fall into a summon-able emergency.

She wondered if she should have agreed to a meeting with a strange man, alone. Kathy said he and Lizzy shared a deep friendship. That should make him safe. While she felt cheated she never got to know Lizzy, she liked the idea someone who knew her intimately lived next door. She imagined Sebastian as a gentle, frail older man that came over for tea and long chats. That picture gave her comfort and eased some of her worry about the late-night meeting.

She walked over to the door and cracked it opened. Even though the snow stopped and the wind let up, the cold remained bitter. She closed the door quickly. Her eyes looked at the fire that dwindled and threatened to extinguish. She frowned. She would need more wood before Lewis came home. The large room demanded a fire, and she didn't want it chilly when Sebastian arrived. Not after he faced the weather to meet with her.

She tugged on her heavy coat, thick gloves, and hat, before she headed off to the side of the house to gather more logs. Her hands hurt from the cold almost as soon as she stepped outside. Between her fumbling frozen fingers, and the weight of the wood, she found she could only manage one piece at a time. Rather than opening the door for each trip, she started a small pile of logs just outside the front door.

"Go inside." The smooth voice she recognized from the phone call as Sebastian danced in the air.

She turned to see a man approaching behind her. He stood at least a foot taller than her five foot four and looked down at her with piercing blue eyes. The rest of his features remained hidden from both her sight and the cold. She started to protest, but he cut his eyes at her and she changed her mind.

On the porch, she grabbed a piece of wood off the stack. She carried it inside and tossed it on the fire. While she waited for Sebastian, she tugged off her jacket, gloves and hat. She rubbed her hands together in an effort to get the feeling back in her fingers.

When the door opened again, Sebastian walked in with his arms full of wood. He walked over to the empty spot beside the fireplace, and stacked it neatly.

"Thank you, I'm sorry you had to…" she started to say.

"No worries." His eyes looked her over.

She tried to maintain a smile even though the intensity of his gaze made her blush.

He looked at her as if he wanted to memorize every detail about her. When he pulled off his hat and scarf, he revealed a face she did not anticipate. She expected to see a man two generations older than her. Instead, an entrancing young man closer to her age, no older than mid-thirties stood in front of her. His flawless face embodied the sensuality of his smooth voice.

She looked away and took a step back as she blushed again. She wanted the distance as a buffer against the embarrassing and inexplicable attraction she felt to the stranger.

Sebastian pulled off his jacket and walked it to the hook by the front door as if he knew his way around. As Lizzy's best friend, Gwen expected as much.

"I made coffee if you'd like." Her eyes watched as he moved with an unnatural grace.

When he stepped closer, his chestnut hair danced across his shoulders.

Too perfect, she thought. Like her Lewis. Magical. Standing nearer, she felt that he put off the same magical feeling Lewis did.

She looked at his eyes again and noticed the thick black rim outside of the cobalt blue, just as with Lewis. Could he have been Lizzy's familiar, not just a friend? Could she even ask that? Aware she looked at him too long and with too much attention, she focused her eyes on the fire.

"Thank you, but no." His eyes lingered on hers. "When you have warmed up, we can get to business."

"Of course. I'm sure you have plans. I appreciate you coming over."

"No plans, after business I look forward to talking with you. If you will allow me to monopolize your evening."

His voice danced across her ears and the scent of man mixed with sandalwood filled the air between them. *Yes, please monopolize me*, she thought. "I had no other plans."

"Lovely." He walked over to a chair just beside the couch.

She didn't notice his bag when he came in. He pulled out some papers from the side of it and looked up at her.

"What are we doing first?" Despite losing all her family, she never had any estates to deal with before.

"I'm going to leave several documents with you that you will need to read and sign. Most are so I can have things transferred to your name and release funds. In the meantime, should you need anything, anything at all, you have but to ask. There is a fund for such occurrences at your disposal." He paused and watched her face. He frowned a little and then carried on. "There is a copy of the will. You will also find her final wishes, which I can help you with as much as you need."

She tried to smile but the thought of making final arrangements took her to dark places. It made her realize again she never could get to know Lizzy. Never.

"How about I take this whole stack of nasty papers and leave them in the office for you. Then we can talk of lighter things?"

She nodded and followed him, watching as he put everything on the desk in the office she barely looked in before. Most of her days were spent in the main room since she did not feel at home enough to explore yet.

As they walked back to the main room and the warmth of the fire, she noticed he radiated a warm, comforting feeling himself. Again, she wondered what sort of magical creature shared her space, and if they should have waited to meet when Lewis could join them.

She did not get a feeling of danger from him. Her instincts told her the opposite. She felt a natural pull toward him. It felt like she knew him. Like they shared a link already.

She smiled, sat on the couch, and tried to resist the urge to ask him about magic. The look in his eyes as he watched her said he also had something on his mind that he held back.

Chapter Three

"How are you settling in?" Sebastian asked. His eyes lingered on Gwen's full lips while she answered.

"I haven't, not really. I mean I found where the needed rooms were, but I haven't explored." She looked over to see him watching her. "I'm still sleeping here, on the couch," she said, with a sigh as punctuation.

He brought his attention away from the soft curves on both Gwen's face and body and looked at her eyes, mortified. "Sleeping on the couch? That won't do. Lizzy would have both our heads. Let me show you the other rooms. I can give you a little history and help you settle on a better place to rest. We can talk about other things while we explore."

"It's not so bad." She gave him a half smile. "I don't want to be a bother. I can explore later."

"You are no bother. Where else am I to find such charming company?" Her smile captivated him.

She studied him closer with her deep brown eyes. "Were you her familiar?"

His eyes twinkled and a smile formed at the corners of his mouth. "No, but your senses are sharp. I am sure her familiar is in mourning before being chosen for his next witch."

"But you are like my Lewis?"

"Lewis, I assume is your familiar?" he asked. Gwen nodded and he continued. "Where is Lewis tonight?" He found it unusual that she was alone, among other things.

"Off doing whatever it is guides do when not practicing magic." She shrugged. "You didn't answer my question."

"No, I'm sorry. I was like your Lewis. I am..." He paused a moment before he continued. "Retired."

She frowned at his answer. "Did you know Lizzy well?"

He stood and reached out a hand. "Yes, very well. She was my best friend in this world. Come, unless I have made you uncomfortable, let me show you around your home."

She took his hand to stand. The warmth of his touch against her palm buzzed. She pulled her hand back and followed him across the room. "Why did my mom leave?"

"You don't start small, do you? Don't you want to know her favorite food or thing to do on a Sunday night?" he asked as they entered the room to the right. "This, by the way, was her favorite room in the whole house. If you look up on a clear night, you can see every star in the sky."

She stood beside him, and looked through the glass ceiling at the black sky with its twinkling stars. The thought of Lizzy loving that room made her smile since it drew her too. Lounge chairs and a swing she rocked in earlier in the day lined the outer edges of the room.

"We will find journals upstairs that tell all about your family history. Good and bad. I can tell you, or you can read from Lizzy's own words. Either way." He turned to her and saw doubt and fear in her eyes. "Know that she loved you. She loved you and your mother both deeply."

She felt herself caught in his gaze again. "You have captivating eyes."

His smile grew. "You do say what is on your mind. Beautiful trait, that fits you well."

"Sorry, I have never had much of a thought to mouth filter."

His smile remained. "No apologies. Let's find you a room."

They walked back to the main room where he added a log to the fire, before they walked up the stairs.

She barely ventured up the stairs herself. What few doors she opened revealed rooms filled with covered furniture. Part of her still did not want to face snooping in her grandmother's things.

He opened the first door. "This is a guest room, one of many. Lizzy did like to entertain. Most of the rooms were made up like this, just in case a guest needed to stay. The weather here can be changeable. How does it feel to you?"

She looked at him puzzled. "Feel? Okay, I guess."

"You are filled with magic as Lizzy was. Does this room speak to you?" Patience showed in his tone and presence.

She looked around, took a few steps deeper in the room, and then turned back to him. "I'm not that kind of witch. I weave magic, and I get visions. Mostly I have to touch something."

His brows creased but he didn't say anything. He knew that under the surface, Gwen held power far beyond spell-casting. He could feel her magic pulse. It reached out to him each time they stood close. He stepped into her space and closed his eyes. Her vibrations almost felt to him like an adolescent just before their gifts unwound. That should not be the case with her. Not with her blessings and not as a woman. He needed to talk with Lewis.

"If this room gives you no feelings, let's move on." He decided not to talk about magic with her until he found out from Lewis why she seemed oblivious to her capabilities.

They walked into several more rooms, none of which gave her any feelings. He could tell the next room they walked in felt different to her.

"What was this room?" she asked.

He walked in behind her and pulled a sheet off a white crib in the corner. "Feel like home? This was to be your room."

"It did feel different, warmer." She looked around the room.

"It should, we already blessed this room to comfort you, many years ago."

A fireplace dominated one wall and a large window took up much of the outside wall. She walked over and opened the curtain. Despite the darkness, she could see it looked over the side yard toward the forest.

"I can swap one of the guest beds with the crib if you like? There is already a dresser and nightstand." He pulled the sheets off the furniture to show her. "There is a white sleigh bed in the third room we saw." He walked over and pulled a sheet off a mirror on a white painted base.

"It's all lovely." She ran a finger over the shiny white dresser, and then walked to the mirror.

In the reflection, she saw her tired eyes with dark circles. The drab brown sweater she wore clung to her at the chest and waist, making her feel frumpy. That feeling grew when she saw his beautiful face appear behind her in the reflection.

"Beautiful," he said, watching her in the mirror.

She stepped away. "If Lewis gets home soon maybe he can help with the bed. You can't alone."

"I could, but we can finish the tour and see what happens."

If all familiars shared the unnatural strength Lewis did, she assumed he probably could move a bed by himself with little effort. The next room they walked into belonged to her mother. Sebastian watched as she walked around and looked at things.

"Did you know mom well?" she asked.

He watched her pretend to be interested in the furniture. "I did, fairly well, yes."

"What was she like?"

"As sweet as Lizzy. All the women I've known in your family have beautiful souls."

"Why did she leave? If my family is so sweet, what were we running from?" Gwen turned to him with a look that longed for knowledge.

"The past, sweetheart. The dark past was catching up with you. Are you sure you wouldn't rather read about it?"

Gwen looked down. Maybe it would be best to read it, rather than hear it from a stranger. Of course, she didn't know Lizzy any better than Sebastian.

She walked over to the wall and pulled a sheet off a painting. It depicted a beautiful wooded scene with a castle in the center. She looked closer at the details and saw all sorts of fairies and creatures in the wooded part. "This is beautiful."

He stepped closer to her and looked at the picture too. "Thank you. I painted that for your mother many moons ago. She always wanted her very own castle, it was the best I could do to make that wish come true."

She turned to him again. "You painted this? It is stunning." She paused before asking, "Were you my mom's familiar?"

"Yes, I did paint it, and no, I was not. I haven't had a witch to guide in a very long time."

She noticed his presence bristle. "I feel like I should know you. Like we already do know each other."

His eyes said he understood. "Peculiar, isn't it?"

They walked to the last room on the floor. All the surfaces wore a slight layer of dust instead of sheets like the other rooms.

When her eyes landed on the painting above the fireplace, she knew why everyone said she looked like Lizzy. The resemblance in the eyes and lips stood out even though Lizzy looked taller and thinner than Gwen. Long gray hair framed her face. Her soft and gentle eyes held Gwen's attention.

"Did you paint this as well?" Gwen studied the details of the painting.

"I did, I tried to capture her spirit, but there is no way to give due justice to such a beautiful, gentle soul."

She could tell how much he cared for Lizzy by the way he depicted her. "It's lovely. You must have loved her greatly to have painted her with such attention to detail."

"Perhaps you will sit for me in time."

Gwen tried to ignore the sensual tone in his voice. "I'm not painting material."

"I will show you otherwise." He walked over and placed a hand on the large chest at the foot of the bed. "In here are the journals I mentioned." He rubbed his fingers together.

Gwen felt a rush of magic and heard a click as the chest unlocked. "Can you teach me that?"

"Lewis can."

Gwen knelt at the chest and reached inside. She pulled out a dress. Her mind flashed to a gazebo on a lake. She saw a wedding. She couldn't make out distinct faces but she felt happiness.

Happiness and joy.

She opened her eyes to see Sebastian looking at her with his deep blue eyes. "I saw a gazebo."

He enjoyed the sensation of her magic wash over him and then dissipate before he responded. "I will take you there as well. No doubt you saw your grandfather?"

"No, I didn't see any faces. I felt happy. They were very happy."

The sparkle came back to his eyes. "Oh yes. The love of a lifetime."

Gwen smiled at him. "Is the gazebo here?"

"Yes, it is on your side of our lake. It will be where we have the services."

"We have a lake?"

"We do."

Her excitement vanished and she frowned as she thought of the services. "I'm not sure I can do this. How do you say goodbye to someone you never got to say hello to? How can I even make a service for her when I didn't know her?"

"You don't have to do it alone. You have Lewis, and now you have me. Lizzy wanted her memorial to be a celebration. If it is too hard for you, I will arrange it all. That way you can celebrate her life just as she wanted."

"Thank you." She gently laid the dress back in the chest.

"The journals are in the bottom of the chest. There may be more upstairs in the altar room as well." When he spoke of the altar room, he smiled.

"I meant to ask you about that. The upstairs is locked."

"Yes, she didn't leave it unlocked. The key will be in her nightstand." He stood, and walked over to the nightstand. He slid opened the drawer and fished out a key.

"Were you up for more tonight? It is getting late," she said, not sure what hours he usually kept, or if he even needed sleep. Lewis never did.

"You are looking a little sleepy." He stepped closer and scanned her eyes. "Did you need to take a break and warm back up?"

"Maybe, yes," she said, and stepped back. She did not want to get caught in his nearness, scent, or gaze again. The magnetism between them made her wonder if witches and familiars always felt that way. She did with Lewis. That ended in awkwardness.

Back downstairs, she made her way to the kitchen to start more coffee. When she walked out to the main room, he had already added more wood and stood by the now roaring fire.

Sensing her, he turned and watched her hips as she walked over and sat her cup on the mantel. When she stood beside him at the fire rubbing her hands together, the scent of roses filled his area. He closed his eyes and breathed her in deeply. Just under the roses he could smell a faint hint of soap that lingered from her morning bath, coffee, and woman. He found the mixture an intoxicating cocktail. He opened his eyes and tried to ignore the pull he felt.

"The lake was her favorite place. We shared many beautiful nights there." He oriented the moment away from uncomfortable to casual. "Your grandfather built the gazebo and your mother fed the ducks in the summer."

She picked up her mug and sipped her coffee. "I would like to see it. When you are free again can you show me the lake and upstairs? I will have papers ready for you too."

"I am occupied tomorrow, but I can come by Saturday night at sunset."

The tension in her face from thinking about the memorial eased. "Perfect, thank you."

"Did you get to go to town yet?" he asked.

She nodded. "A little. I stopped at the grocery and yarn shop. Kathy is sweet."

"Kathy is charming. In fact, everyone you meet in town will likely be charming. Do make time to eat at Mel's. She makes divine food from what I have been told."

"I will very soon. I'm feeling a bit better after tonight. It's been so overwhelming."

"I imagine so."

Gwen sat her coffee back down and looked toward the door. "I'm sorry Lewis is not in yet. I know he would like to meet you. It can't be often you meet another familiar. I mean, I haven't met another witch before." She paused and looked at him with serious eyes. "Why would someone want to burn her like that?"

"I wish I knew. She didn't make enemies. I didn't feel magic that night."

"Were you here?"

His face took a solemn look and he shook his head. "Not at the house. I was at the lake, painting. By the time I saw the fire…" He stopped and drew in a deep breath. "I was here as fast as possible."

"I'm sure you were. If you didn't sense magic, then you think it was a person. A regular person?"

He looked at the fire in front of them. "It's what my instincts say."

"Is there anyone, anyone at all that didn't like her that you know of?"

"She never mentioned anyone. All her stories of town were always happy. I never heard her use an unkind word about anyone."

They puzzled a little more over who might have wanted to hurt Lizzy before they shifted to lighter things. Gwen talked about the yarn she bought and listened as he talked about the latest painting he worked on. She started to get sleepy and they agreed to explore the rest another night.

Sebastian left to make his way home. He felt uneasy that her familiar remained gone, considering the unsolved murder and her dark family history.

At his house, he paced his study a little while and decided to shift and wait for Lewis. While he waited, his mind drifted to Gwen. He knew her as an unborn baby before her mother left. He knew he was fated to be a part of her life. Help her with magic. Be a mentor.

He should not feel the type of attraction he felt toward her.

She spoke to him in ways no woman ever did. Ways that made him understand why a familiar would give up all their magic to be a human.

Chapter Four

Lewis landed on the porch and instantly sensed another presence. His wings stretched and his head turned. He scanned the night and spotted the wolf sat to his right, watching him with intense blue eyes. It sat totally still as Lewis looked it over. The coat of the large wolf had a lot of brown, and gold, with dark fur close to the face and down the back.

Strong magic emanated from the creature. He knew it was Sebastian. The legend. The familiar to many powerful witches. The familiar cherished by witches and familiars alike right up until he killed his own witch. After that, the council of witches and collective of familiars agreed to his banishment, forever. Lewis knew the story even before his assignment to Gwen. The collective expanded his knowledge of Sebastian due to his links to Lizzy. They felt he might pose a danger to Gwen or try to alter her fate. He expected to meet him sooner.

"Sebastian," Lewis said on the wind.

"Lewis, I presume. We need to talk."

Lewis stretched his wings. He knew it would happen eventually, but after his long miserable night, a talk with Sebastian held no appeal. He shifted to a man and opened the door.

Sebastian trotted over and shifted just inside the house.

They both looked to Gwen who slept soundly on the couch.

Sebastian nodded toward the stairs and walked up them with Lewis following behind.

Once they were alone Sebastian said, "Gwen has decided on a room. Would you like to help me set up a bed for her while we talk?"

"Quaint." Lewis followed him to the room. He didn't like the idea that Sebastian spent the night alone with Gwen. He needed to be away, it couldn't have been put off. "I do hope you don't plan on befriending my Gwen as you did Lizzy."

"I leave plans to the fates."

"No, you don't. I know who you are."

Sebastian cut his eyes at Lewis and then turned his attention to moving the crib into one of the other rooms. He assumed all familiars knew of him, and probably the worst of the details about what happened. He decided not to argue that point right then. "Is there a reason you leave your witch alone in a time of need?"

"Let's set a boundary while we are just starting out, shall we?" Lewis cocked his head and gave Sebastian a hard look. "How about you never question what I do with my witch? Let's not pretend there is not a reason you don't have a witch of your own."

Sebastian used the time it took to move the crib into a spare room to let the sting of those words roll off. They needed to talk about Gwen, not his past. "I understand your misgivings regarding me and my past. I have no ill will toward any witch or familiar. Regardless of what you may have been counseled to believe, I will never be a danger to either," he said when he came back in the room.

Lewis laughed. "I wonder the opinion your last witch would have on the truth of those words."

The words hung in the air, making it feel thick. Sebastian tried not to let images of his witch, Anne, enter his mind. "Those boundaries you spoke of; they should also extend to my last witch. You do realize that while I think what happened to Lizzy has no supernatural ties, there are very real threats to Gwen that do. They are supernatural, dark, and extremely dangerous to her."

"If you are referring to her family curse, I am aware and have it well in hand."

"There is no well in hand with that woman." Sebastian dragged in the mattress.

Lewis followed him with the box spring. "I get you were some sort of beloved something to Lizzy, and to her familiar. I do not hold you in such high esteem. To me you are just another risk to shield Gwen from."

"You smell of magic, dark magic," Sebastian said bluntly, after he arranged the frame of the bed in the center of the wall. He wondered why a familiar would practice dark magic.

"Stay out of it." Lewis flung the box springs and mattress on the frame. "Where are the linens Jeeves?"

Sebastian took a deep breath and walked out to the linen closet. He returned with the sheets and a comforter. "Very well Lewis. We all have our secrets to keep. Why is Gwen not trained?"

"I would repeat, stay out of it. Did Lizzy know? Did she know what you are?"

"Of course she did. She and I were dear friends, we held no secrets from each other."

Lewis wrinkled his nose. "She may have chosen to ignore what you are, but Gwen won't. Did you tell her?"

"It didn't come up. I don't find it makes for good idle chatter."

"No, I don't imagine it would. You know when she realizes you are a monster she won't hold you as close as Lizzy did."

Sebastian paused to look at him. "Is that what worries you? Is this about what you have done? Will she think you are a monster?"

"Don't deflect. No magic I practice will ever make me into what you are. You are the thing nightmares are made of."

Sebastian nodded his head, ceding to that for now. He knew he was a monster and a nightmare to some. "She is more than a seer or caster. You do realize the power she can command, don't you?"

"Yes," Lewis said, sounding agitated. "You need to leave that to me. You will do good to assume I know what is best for my witch."

"She's defenseless as a child."

"She is never defenseless with me." His voice filled with a strange mix of uncertainty and pride.

"While this may be true, you assume I am a danger to Gwen, yet I was here all night. She was defenseless. Had I been the monster you fear I am, she wouldn't be resting peacefully downstairs."

Lewis clenched his teeth. "I will consider it a blessing from the great mother that your monster didn't come out to eat her tonight."

"I consider it reckless. This room needs wood," he said and walked out. He could feel things teetering on one of the two of them crossing lines that would end up in some sort of magical showdown. He did not want that. Gwen did not need that.

When he crossed the main room, he paused again to watch Gwen. Even sleeping she radiated magic, restrained, untrained magic. Unleashed, he could only imagine her magnificence. His eyes lingered on her face. He wondered how much her magic affected the draw he felt to her and if Lewis struggled against it too. None of his witches commanded power like her. Witches like her were mythical.

Once Sebastian stocked the room with wood he looked to Lewis who still held a face full of defiance. He could sense Lewis had a newness to his soul, new and vulnerable to influence. Her power and past demanded a more experienced hand. He wondered why they would pair one so reckless and new with a witch like Gwen.

"What else?" Lewis asked.

"I'm sorry we started this out as we did. I should have been less confrontational. Just as I will be here to help Gwen through this, I will also be here for you in any way you need."

"If I have need for you, trust times will be desperate. Stay away from me and we will be just fine."

"Lewis, whatever you think you need to do for Gwen, dark magic is not the answer."

Lewis walked out of the room. "Stay away from me and leave training Gwen to my judgment."

Sebastian knew he needed to leave. He could smell the dark lingering on Lewis. The familiar scent made him worry more for Gwen than before.

When Sebastian arrived home, he sat in his study, watched the fire burn, and puzzled over the night. A few things unsettled him, but he wouldn't have time to consider them before the morning came. He slowly made his way to his room and closed the door. He bolted it shut before he laid down.

Lewis stood in the main room and watched Gwen sleep. He hated that he missed her first meeting with Sebastian. He walked over and rested a hand on her forehead. There was no magic residue, good or bad. Her sleep felt peaceful, dreams sweet. He added more wood to the fire and left again.

He wanted to stretch his wings and allow the wind to blow away the lingering dark magic.

Chapter Five

Two neon signs flashed at Gwen. One sign, the larger one, read Mel's with bright white and red bulbs hung in the center. The other, a small tube twisted into the word diner, sat just to the right of the larger one. She planned her trip at brunch because she wanted a quiet moment to meet Mel, who Kathy spoke so highly of.

She turned the truck off and tugged her coat closed before she made a dash toward the door. A lovely blast of warm air wrapped around her when she stepped inside. The smell of bacon and eggs, mixed with a hint of fresh coffee teased her senses.

Gwen looked around as she undid the zipper on her coat.

The inside felt bigger and more open than the outside made it appear. She found the classic white, black, and chrome look welcoming. She walked between the larger tables on the right and the booth styled seats that lined under the window on her left. Over the bar, she could see an opening that Gwen assumed looked in the kitchen. The huge black and white clock that hung on the wall in front of her read ten forty-five.

Gwen walked to the counter in the back and sat at a stool.

Before she even settled in, a woman with a larger than life presence came out from the kitchen door. Her curls almost glowed in a shade of copper red only achieved by dying over white hair. Gwen guessed her to be over sixty by the depth of the creases that formed around her smile and at the edges of her friendly brown eyes.

"Little Lizzy!" the woman said in a shrill tone. She moved around the counter with a speed that startled Gwen, considering she carried a hefty weight on her tall frame.

Before she knew what happened, Gwen found herself engulfed in the woman's soft embrace. She breathed in the smell of bacon, coffee, and baby powder.

"Oh, stand up, stand up let me look at you." The woman tugged Gwen from the stool and took both of her hands.

Gwen let the woman keep a hold of her hands as she looked at her. "Mel?" she asked, sounding timid.

"Yes, yes, dear. I am so glad you made it safe. You need food, let me make you something. What do you love dear?" Mel looked at her with an expectant expression.

"I'm Gwen," she said, and smiled at Mel. Like with Sebastian and Kathy, it felt like she already knew her.

"Of course you are. Our Lizzy told us all about your sweet face. Coffee? Pie, did you eat breakfast yet?"

"I, umm, coffee, yes, and no pie. I'm really a cake type but I haven't had breakfast yet."

Mel shook her head and tsk'ed at Gwen. "Just like Lizzy, always too busy to eat. I'll sort that out for you. Lizzy always had waffles and fruit. I can whip you up french toast if you like, your mamma loved that, or do you have a favorite?"

"French toast, that would be delicious."

Mel walked Gwen to a booth and sat her down with a cup of coffee while she disappeared in the back to cook. When she returned, she carried a plate stacked with several slices of powdered french toast. She sat the plate down and grabbed a bottle of syrup.

"How are you, sweetheart? Do you need anything up there? I can send you with some leftovers from the morning shift."

"Oh, thank you, no. I'm fine. Well, still trying to figure out things really."

"I imagine. It is so shocking. I keep expecting Lizzy to walk in here with her smiling face."

Gwen chewed a bite and swallowed, savoring the meal she apparently needed. The sweetness of the powdered sugar and syrup soothed her soul. Mel cooked it exactly how she liked it, crisp on the outside and chewy in the middle. "This is delicious, thank you."

"You are so welcome. You bring yourself here anytime your tummy rumbles."

Gwen saw nothing but love and friendliness in Mel's face. She continued to eat and listen to Mel talk about Lizzy, and how much she loved her.

The door opened and a little bell chimed, drawing Mel from her latest tale. "Excuse me, darling," she said, and stood up. "Curtis. Sit yourself down. Coffee and cheese danish?"

"You know it," Curtis said, and sat in the booth across from Gwen.

Gwen knew him as the indifferent sheriff who spent so much time at her place, and asked her a million questions the day she arrived. Mel disappeared and returned with his things before leaving again to tend to lunch preparations.

"I hoped to see you again, Miss Hensley," Curtis said after swallowing a bite of his danish.

Gwen looked into his friendly, coffee colored eyes. She figured him close to Mel's age based on the lines in his hard, tanned features. His hair was neatly trimmed, sandy blonde, and peppered with gray. The rugged handsomeness of his features matched his aloof style.

"Just Gwen will do," she said, and kept eating her toast.

"Do you have time for a chat, Miss Gwen?" he asked between bites.

"I do, did you have news?"

"I'm sorry, I can't tell you more right now. Have you settled in?"

She gave him a puzzled look. "Sure, did you want to chat about me settling in or is there something new about the case?"

"Both, did you know William, your grandfather?"

"No, I never knew any of my family. I only have the very vaguest memories of my mother." She watched him over the top of her cup as she sipped her coffee. His face didn't give away anything he might be thinking. She assumed all police officers could do that.

"Who all have you spoken with in town about the case?"

"No one really, I've only met Kathy and Mel."

His face never changed. "I should have something I can tell you soon. Try not to worry." He finished his drink before he stood. "Thanks Mel, see you for dinner, love," he yelled out as he left.

While Gwen found his brief visit a little odd, she found most everyone there a little odd, mostly in a good way. She wondered if his address for Mel was just a case of friendly town-speak, or if they had some sort of relationship.

She smiled at the thought of the clashing of Mel's vibrant personality and his stoic attitude.

Mel came back in. "Did you need a refill? I'm about to get hit with the lunch rush."

"No, I'm good, let me just check out." Gwen stood and grabbed her purse.

"Oh heavens, you don't have to rush off."

"I need to make a few more stops before I head home," she said, and walked to the counter. She paid Mel before asking, "Did you know William too?"

"Of course. If you want to find out more about your family, try, Mike, at the library. Aside from gossip and opinion you can get from anyone else, Mike is working on family histories for the predominate families in town, like yours."

"Oh, thank you," Gwen said and left.

She followed the directions on her phone a few blocks off main street to the library. The parking lot sat mostly empty, probably staff cars she assumed with it being the middle of a work and school day.

She walked inside and smiled at the blast of heated air that she already came to love when she walked into shops around town.

The scent of books added to the warm, welcoming feeling. In her mind, she could almost hear the sound of an old book opening and sending out its welcoming scent. She smiled as she walked over to the front desk.

The older lady who stood at the desk looked at Gwen over reading glasses that perched precariously on the end of her long nose. The severe bun the woman wore made Gwen wonder how she didn't have a crippling headache.

"Can I help you?" the woman said in a flat tone, neither warm or cold, but somehow fitting of the librarian.

"Yes please. Mel said that Mike might be able to help me with some questions I have?" Gwen said, in a hushed voice while offering a friendly smile.

"Who may I say is calling?"

"Gwen, Gwen Hensley."

The woman gave her a harder look. "Yes, I see that now. Just a moment, Miss Hensley." The woman picked up her phone and pressed a button. "Sorry to bother your lunch but there is a *Hensley* here to see you."

Gwen thought the way she said 'a Hensley' almost made it sound like a dirty word.

The woman hung up the phone and looked to Gwen. "He will be right out," she said, and looked back down at her work, excusing Gwen without saying a word.

Gwen hoped her own face didn't reflect her shock. She put on her best smile as she walked over and started looking at the display of books nearest the counter. The books had all been wrapped in brown paper and the display read *blind date with a book*. On the brown wrapping a brief description was given. She smiled at the idea.

Gwen stood reading a book description when she felt eyes on her. She turned around to see who she assumed was Mike. He didn't look like a historian or librarian to her. He looked very apple pie, tall with an athletic build and neatly cut light brown hair. His steel gray eyes looked at her in a way that she interpreted as annoyed.

His gaze made her want to take in the town gossip rather than his researched facts.

She quickly sat the book down. "I'm sorry to interrupt you. Mel suggested I might be able to get some information from you."

He continued to eye her and then turned and started to walk away. "Follow me please."

She walked with him to an office and he closed the door behind them.

He sat down at a desk that had a lot of stacks of papers and documents of various heights. There was a bowl of soup in front of him. "If you don't mind, I will eat while we talk. What can I help you with, Mrs. Hensley?"

"Miss, just Gwen, please." She looked around the small office as she sat down. There were a few shelves that were just as haphazardly crammed with documents as the desk. "Thank you for seeing me. It seems I came on a bad day. I can make an appointment if that would be better," she said, feeling like she annoyed him just by showing up.

"No, I am afraid I am always busy. Those of us who have to work don't have free days to traipse around town. Today has already been disturbed by a visit from Curtis, drilling me about you and yours and now…" He paused and smiled. "Now, what is it I can do for you?"

"Why was Curtis here?" she asked, shocked at that revelation.

"I assure you I don't know."

"I, well, I just wanted to get a little history on William and Lizzy."

"I don't have much. I am sure if you are nosing around enough you will discover that I was trying to compile a history, and Lizzy was being…" He paused and took a sip of his soup. "Difficult."

Gwen looked shocked at the first unpleasant word she heard spoken about Lizzy. It was an odd word choice and made her wonder what sort of things he meant by difficult.

"I'm sorry. I just wanted to know what happened to William, and how it might be related to what happened to Lizzy."

"I will tell you what I told Curtis. I can't see a link. Everyone knows William was killed on duty by an addict who panicked. He is in jail, now, forever."

Mike ate his soup while Gwen wondered why Curtis would focus on that angle. Surely the whole in jail thing eliminated that suspect. She looked at Mike's eyes to see if he held anything back but they only showed his annoyance.

"I'm sorry to have bothered you. I am also sorry for whatever issues you have had due to my family." Gwen stood to leave. She felt uncomfortable around Mike. "I'm still learning about them myself, but if I can help with your project, please let me know."

He looked up at her, his eyes softened for a second before he looked back down at his desk. She assumed she would love the library as much as the yarn shop, being a book lover. After her brief visit she changed that assessment. As she walked out toward her car, the woman at the desk didn't even bother to look up or say goodbye.

The cold air outside felt more comforting than the cold feeling Gwen felt inside the building.

While she drove home she puzzled over why Curtis asked her about William, if everyone knew he died in the line of duty. How could it be related, and why did it matter what she or some librarian knew about him? Too bad the librarian wasn't friendly enough to help her answer those questions.

As soon as she got home, after adding wood to the fire, she turned on her laptop and started searching for information on William Hensley. She found a void of information before he arrived in town. She easily ran across the articles about him and Lizzy getting married, having Winnie, her mother, and his death.

She even got a result of an interview with the junkie several years later. He claimed to have never owned a gun and that he did not shoot William. The best she could tell, they found his fingerprints on the unregistered gun. The case was very circumstantial and he only confessed under duress or so he claimed later.

"Hmm," she said, and looked up to see Lewis standing at the fire.

"Hmm, what?" he asked as he turned to her. "Did you see the room we set up for you?"

"Room?" She stood, walked over, and stood beside him.

"Yes, my witch, Sebastian said you picked it and so we made it yours." He smiled as she turned and started toward the stairs.

"What did you make of Sebastian? Isn't he fantastic?" she yelled over her shoulder.

He snorted and walked up behind her. "No, not fantastic. Moderately tolerable."

"Grouchy, you won't believe the day I've had." She opened the door to see her room. "Oh Lewis, it's perfect."

He smiled as she hugged him and then started a fire while she related all that happened. "Do you think that Mike had something to do with Lizzy?" he asked.

"I don't, he seemed annoyed but not murderous. It just seems odd that William should even be part of the questioning. I want to talk to the junkie."

"What for?" Lewis looked at her with wide eyes and a wrinkled nose.

"Closure, to see what he might add to the puzzle."

"Sweetheart, with all you have been through, do you really think you need to be facing your grandfather's murderer? It won't help solve what happened to Lizzy, that man is in jail."

"Well, it might. The prison isn't too far off." Gwen sat on the bed and noticed a stack of books on the nightstand. "What are these?"

"From Sebastian, isn't he fabulous?" Lewis said, his tone mocking her own.

She frowned at him and opened one. "Wow, Lizzy's journals!"

She forgot all about the prison and the odd day as she laid back and started reading while Lewis rubbed her feet. She sunk deep in the reading and didn't even question why he kept his human form.

Chapter Six

"Lewis." Gwen peeked in each room she walked by as she looked for him.

On Saturday, most everything in town closed so she spent the day reading journals while Lewis made some minor repairs. He worked at locating and stopping drafts to help with the battle against the cold, which felt more like a war in the huge old house.

Lewis smiled at hearing her excited voice. "In here, my witch," he said from the dining room.

She paused when she stepped inside and felt his magic. It always took more magic to hold his human form and she enjoyed the way it buzzed in the air.

"Did you find the draft?"

"Drafts, yes, some, not all. What has you so excited?" He watched her face as she hovered in the door frame.

"Did you know that my family has some voodoo connection?"

Lewis reached out and placed his hand on the table as his reality started to spin. He struggled to keep form. "I…" He closed his eyes, trying to find balance.

Gwen crossed the huge room and made her way around the table.

She reached out to offer any magical support she could give. "What is it?"

Lewis pulled himself back from the darkness that crept into his mind. "I think I've been in this form too long." He sat down in the chair beside them.

"Well, shift back. You scared the daylight out of me. The drafts will be there when you are feeling better. Can I help you?" She absentmindedly ran her fingers through his hair.

"Where… who told you about a voodoo connection? Is this more about that junkie?"

"I read it in the journals. I'm not done yet, but I found out that it has something to do with why Lizzy came here."

Sebastian, Lewis thought. "I think we have enough of a mystery with who would want to hurt Lizzy at the moment, don't you?"

"Lewis, did you hear me? Voodoo? She was running from something, someone, maybe they killed her." She paused and looked down at him. Her brows creased as she saw something in his eyes.

He shifted and sat perched on the chair.

"What the actual hell Lewis? Why did you do that for? What are you hiding?"

Lewis flew from the room with Gwen following.

"Lewis? What is it?"

"Gwen, leave it alone. Please." His voice whispered in her mind.

"What, the journals? Lizzy? William? What do you know? You tell me damn it." She followed him out of the room and stopped in the main room. She watched him as he preened "Did you know about Lizzy? This whole time? My whole life?"

"Yes, Gwen. I told you before, I have been watching your soul since before you were born."

She held on to the edge of the couch, feeling her anger boil up. "Why didn't you tell me? I could have known her."

"I do everything through the lens of what is best for you." His voice rang in her head as almost angry.

"Best for me? To be alone in a shitty little hovel when I had family?" Gwen didn't wait for an answer. She stormed out of the room and into the glass room. She pulled the door closed behind her.

She paced the room in an effort to get her feelings to come back in control. The view from the room was stars and an empty, dark sky. Tugging her jacket closed, she walked across the room, then opened the outside door, and walked into the night. The cool air wrapped around her as if trying to put out the fire that burned inside her from the anger she felt.

As she walked and put distance between her and Lewis, she started to feel better. How could he have not told her? How could it ever be best for her? He knew how alone and desperate she felt in the city.

The sound of crunching snow gave way to the sound of breaking sticks as she realized she walked into a forested area. She looked up, seeing a strangely comforting webbing of bare tree limbs. They looked like woven sticks covering her view of the night sky. Each crunching footfall washed away a little of her anger. By the time she came to the edge of the woods, she didn't feel angry anymore.

As far as she could see in front of her a white blanket of snow covered the ground. She saw no house, no woods, no lake. She felt truly alone. The barren whiteness crashed in around her as she let the sadness hiding under her anger wash over her.

Her whole life seemed to float from one loss to the next. She counted on Lewis as her only constant, the only certainty in her life. Lewis provided her grounding when things shifted. If he could lie to her and keep important things secret from her, how could she believe he loved her in any way? The hollow feeling welled up and she sobbed openly. She wailed at the emptiness inside and around her. As the tears rolled down her face, the sky cried with her. Little drops turned to snow as they fell on her face.

Sebastian stood at the edge of the clearing. Her unhappiness and the magic it called on filled the night and beckoned him to her. He watched in awe as the sky responded to her sorrow. Little beads of despair turned to frozen drops that clung to her hair. They looked like pearls on the black strands. Even in her absolute sadness, he found her more beautiful than anyone he ever laid eyes on before.

Her sobs still came in waves. She felt the weight of his coat wrap around her shoulders.

"Come inside," he said.

His voice broke the silence and she turned to him. She looked up into his deep blue eyes and saw a sadness that matched her own.

"I don't want to," she managed to say more as a squeak. "Show me the lake. I need to feel happiness."

"You are cold to the core," he said, his voice smooth and tender. "Let me warm you first."

She nodded, knowing he meant to use magic. She relaxed as he wrapped his arms around her. She felt his usual warmth and then felt something different. A warm tingle raced across her skin and seemed to sink inside of her. Not only did she feel warmer, her sadness seemed eased as well. His arms felt strong and safe.

She tilted her head up, looking at him. His pale skin made a striking contrast against his dark hair and the night sky. "Thank you," she said, barely above a whisper.

He still held her tight against him, feeling protective. When he looked at her he saw the fragile emotions that danced in her eyes. The feelings that stirred in him made him feel uneasy. Being a magical creature he never entertained such feelings. He felt stunned by how easily a glance at her awakened them.

He looked away and turned, smoothly tucking her under his arm. "The lake awaits."

She didn't respond. Instead she walked in silence with him, enjoying the warmth of his closeness in the bitter cold. When they came out of the woods she saw a large lake with a huge gazebo on one side.

They walked over to a small pit with a fire already burning.

She rubbed her hands together over the flames. "You did this?"

"I assumed we would need the fire. I did promise to show you the lake."

"Can I ask you something?"

"You can ask me anything, mi belleza."

"Why would a familiar lie to their witch?"

He stepped next to her by the fire. "That may be best answered by Lewis. I am sure he only did what he felt was needed."

"What was Lizzy running from?" She kept her eyes on the fire.

"You've been reading?"

"Yes, and apparently there is something bad, something related to voodoo. Something Lewis knows."

Sebastian sighed. "It won't touch you if I can help it."

"Was that what killed Lizzy?"

"No."

"You sound so sure." She looked at him puzzled.

"I am sure. I would have been able to sense that. If not before, then after."

She looked out over the lake. "It feels peaceful here."

"Always."

"What happened to William?"

"He was shot while arresting a junkie. It was a local tragedy."

"Was his family local?"

"William's?" he asked.

"Yes."

He shook his head. "He didn't have family as far as I know. That was one thing he and Lizzy bonded over. They were alone in this world."

"Was he a witch?"

"No, and Lizzy kept him as shielded from that as possible."

The wind blew and Gwen stepped closer to the fire. "Was the sheriff here for that? Curtis?"

"Yes, he was the deputy under William, why?"

"He asked me about William, and that makes me think somehow there is a connection I am missing. I was hoping to find it in the journals, but I got sidetracked by the whole voodoo thing. Then I realized Lewis lied. I don't even feel like I have my feet on the ground now."

Sebastian turned to her and looked in her eyes, again seeing the sadness creeping in. He frowned. "When things get to be too much, please call me. I can give answers. I can stop the spinning and I can also take this sorrow." He reached out and placed a finger on her cheek.

As he ran his finger on her face she felt her mood lighten. She watched as her sadness appeared in his eyes. "You took it? Just now, that easily?"

He smiled warmly and she watched as he held out a hand. A small gray ball formed just above his opened palm and he blew it. Both of them watched as it floated away.

"Can you teach me that?" she asked, amazed.

"I could, but Lewis should," he said, and turned back to the fire.

"I don't think Lewis likes when I do anything magic, even spells."

Sebastian frowned again. "Why don't we go inside and look at papers, get you something warm to drink, and explore the top floor?"

As they walked back to her house, Sebastian kept her under his arm, protecting her from the cold and symbolically from the hardships attacking her from all sides.

"How do you know where we are going?" she asked as they walked.

"Animal instincts," he said in a playful tone.

"What is your true form?"

"Now? It is a man."

"Okay, what is your animal form," she asked and then paused. "Why is it a man now? Are you still able to shift?"

"I am and I do not very often. It's complicated."

"I gathered as much from what I have read so far."

He paused and looked at her with an eyebrow arched. He planned to tell her if she didn't sense what he was soon. He didn't think with all that had been on her mind, it was the best night. "How about we just agree there is more to this big bad wolf than howling at the moon."

"Really," she said, and stopped to look at him more closely.

At times she felt she could see the raven in Lewis. She searched Sebastian for signs of his wolf. She watched his jaw tighten and felt an urge to kiss his face.

He enjoyed the feeling of her eyes on him. He enjoyed her closeness. He enjoyed her entirely too much. When her hand reached for his face, he closed his eyes and relished the sensation of her touch. He allowed all his senses to focus on her, breathing in her scent, feeling her touch, feeling the hint of uncertainty just before she pulled away.

"I can see you as a wolf," she said, and waited for him to start walking again before she fell in step beside him.

When they walked in the door, Lewis quickly shifted and looked at them both with narrowed eyes. "Where have you been?"

"At the lake," Gwen said.

"At the lake? It is single digits outside." He cut his eyes to Sebastian. "She isn't like us, you know. That kind of cold is dangerous."

"She isn't as fragile as you think. I kept her warm." Sebastian narrowed his eyes in return.

"*She* is standing right here." Gwen walked over to the fire.

"With all that is happening, I would think you would understand the wisdom of not carelessly using magic here," Lewis said.

"Keeping her warm isn't careless, it's prudent."

"Let's try keeping her inside where altering the temperature can be done without magic."

"Let's try speaking to her." Gwen walked to the office before returning with the papers for Sebastian.

He took the papers and sat down, looking them over. "These look perfect. I will call tomorrow with arrangement details. Leave it to me. I will leave you two to yourselves." He gave Lewis a forced smile before he stood and turned to walk out.

Gwen found she still didn't want to face Lewis. She closed her eyes, sighed, and walked upstairs to read a little in the journals before she drifted off.

Chapter Seven

"Lewis, what is happening between us?" Gwen asked as she sipped her coffee.

"There are some things we just can't talk about. Please, I would ask that you stop prying into your family's past too."

"Prying?" Her face froze in disbelief. "I am trying to find out who killed Lizzy."

"You should leave that to the sheriff."

She could not believe what she heard from Lewis. Lewis her familiar, her only friend and someone not very long ago she considered herself in love with. "What are you so afraid of me finding out? Just tell me. I love you, anything that happened we can get through. Together, like always."

"No. Please, my witch, stop prying."

She finished her coffee and walked to the kitchen to make another cup. "Whatever you are hiding, I will find out. I won't stop 'prying' until I know what Lizzy was running from."

"I wish you wouldn't. It has nothing to do with what killed her." He followed behind her.

"How would you know that? Do you know who killed her?"

"Of course not," he said, sounding shocked. "Try Sebastian for that."

"He doesn't know."

"Maybe he just isn't telling you."

"One of you is keeping secrets. What do you have against him?" Her hands wrapped around the coffee cup, letting it warm them.

"He's dangerous."

"Why would you say that?"

"Hasn't Mr. Honesty told you about his monstrous secret?"

"That he is a wolf? He's no more dangerous than you. He is a familiar for goodness sake. Historically and naturally speaking, wolves and ravens work well together. Odin had both at his side."

"No, he 'was' a familiar. You are not Odin, and I will not likely be working together with him on anything. That aside, his wolf isn't what you need to worry about."

Her eyes narrowed and her forehead creased. "What?"

"Ask him about what he is."

"I will, whatever. I need to make some notes. Next week is going to be so busy." Gwen walked over to the kitchen miscellany drawer, pulled out a tablet, and started to scribble down things she wanted to do.

Her list contained things like: go to the knitter's group, plan the remembrance celebration, visit the prison, and explore upstairs. On the other side of the page she made notes about the people she met. She circled the name Mike, and hesitated before writing down Sebastian. While she didn't really view him as a suspect, something about him set off Lewis and she planned to ask him about his secret.

Lewis went back to making repairs while she found out all she could off the internet about visiting hours, and what she would need to do in order to get approved for a visit at the prison. It didn't seem very high security and regardless, she knew she would pass any background checks.

She downloaded the needed forms and even looked up the prisoner information. Her eyes filled with tears as she looked at his picture, at his eyes, and wondered what sort of person shoots someone in cold blood, rather than facing a drug charge?

It made her happy that most everything could be done online and what couldn't, would be done onsite after her approval as a visitor. She gathered everything and filled in forms for the rest of the afternoon, before sending the packet back to the facility to start the approval process. It looked to her like there would be a delay, because as a self-identified family member of the victim her paperwork would go through a liaison.

When her phone rang it startled her, but she felt a wave of happiness to see Sebastian calling. After exchanging hellos, she asked what day he planned on having the remembrance.

"That's tricky. Lizzy wanted it to be a nighttime celebration. The reverend Lizzy requested is in service Monday, and Sunday, Mel is opened late on Friday and Saturday, Kathy has group Wednesday. That leaves us with Tuesday or Thursday. Did you have a preference?"

"Tuesday seems soon, unless you want next Tuesday or this Thursday. Oh really, if you are planning it, you would know best how much time everyone needs."

He responded to the tension in her voice. "Sweetheart, everyone will drop everything for this. Why don't we try Thursday? I don't want this hanging over your head as a worry. It will be beautiful and I will handle all the details."

"What do I need to do?" she asked.

"If you must do something, you can arrange with Mel to cater the event. I will get Linda from the hotel to arrange invitations. She used to be a party planner and will love the challenge. I know who Lizzy would want for the music and I will arrange the bartender. It will be a party as Lizzy would have wanted."

"Thank you." Gwen sounded choked up as she thought about saying goodbye to Lizzy in such a final way.

"Are you alone? Do you need someone there?"

"No, no, Lewis is around somewhere."

Sebastian kept control of the sigh he felt coming. Lewis remained a mystery to him. Lewis did not belong as the guide to a witch like Gwen, not that he guided her. "How has your day been?"

"Good I guess. I was looking into what I needed to do to visit the prison."

"That doesn't sound like a very nice way to spend the day."

"No, maybe not," she said, and walked over to the fire. "I was going to look upstairs today, did you want to?" she started to ask but stopped, feeling embarrassed to ask him any more favors.

He hesitated because he didn't know what to think about what he felt around her, and he wanted time to make sure his emotions stayed in check. He expected a magical tug between a witch and a familiar, but this felt different, passionate, and he never felt that with a witch, or any human. With the amount of time he endured trapped in a human form, he assumed he experienced every human emotion. That no longer rang true.

Did her being an elemental witch have anything to do with it? He never worked with or even stood near one before. They were very rare, very powerful, more connected to forces of nature, and as such creatures like him. It didn't help that her powers hummed under the strain of being bound somehow.

Recklessly untrained. He still needed to talk more with Lewis about that.

"Sebastian?"

"I'm sorry, my mind was drifting. If you don't mind, I have things I must attend tonight."

"Did you want me to wait for you? To explore?"

"Of course not. It is a very magical place, take Lewis, let him explain to you what things are."

"He may not want to."

Sebastian tapped his fingers on his leg. "If that is the case, call and I will make time."

She sensed his preoccupation and didn't press the issue. "I will, thank you. Thank you for everything. I will call Mel Monday. Let me know if you need me to do anything else."

They hung up and she walked out of the room. She followed her senses to Lewis, who she found standing in the glass room, staring off at the night sky.

She walked up behind him and stood just to his side. "I'm going to the third floor. There is supposed to be magic things there. I would like if you would come with me," she said, looking up at the stars.

Lewis took in a breath. His kind existed on the joy derived from teaching witches how to use magic. It gave them purpose. That conflicted with the most important vow he made, not to teach her. He could feel the binding he placed around her gifts starting to unravel, probably due to stress, and it wouldn't help that Sebastian possessed such strong magic so close to her. Everything about Sebastian brought danger.

"Of course, my witch." He took her hand and they walked up the stairs.

When they reached the top floor, she pulled the key from her pocket and unlocked the door.

"Where did you find that?" he asked.

"Sebastian found it in Lizzy's room."

He nodded, of course he did.

They entered the top floor to see one large room. It looked to her like most of the walls had been taken out, with the exception of what looked like a few small supply rooms, no bigger than closets at the far end. Random support beams broke up the space. Gwen assumed since the ceiling was so high, that the attic floor had been removed, except for the small loft along the far wall.

"It's massive," she said, and let his hand go as she walked into the room.

Lewis followed closely behind her, feeling the room still held a vibration from past magical activities. It all felt like harmless, light, earth magic to him. He didn't think he needed to perform a cleansing. It would all dissipate over time.

Shelves lined most of the walls. They held books, loose papers, jars of powder, herbs, and candles. He knew a ton of questions would soon come and he needed to decide just how much he wanted to lie to protect her. He already did much worse than lie. To keep this pinned down, he needed to get Sebastian on board. The thought of telling him his reasons made him shudder.

Gwen sensed his tension. "Are you okay tonight, Lewis?"

He nodded. "Yes. This is just not how I wanted us to work. This isn't the kind of magic you use."

She stopped at the altar and looked down at the floor. The remains of white powder sprinkled the boards around her in what was left of a circle. "What's this?"

"Protection circle. It's for when you work with magic and need to keep things in or out of your area."

"Why don't we ever do that when I work?" She could sense his tension growing.

"You don't work that kind of magic. Your weaving barely puts off any magical pulse, it wouldn't attract anything."

"Attract?"

"When you work strong magic, it can catch the attention of things on this and other realms. It's best to leave things like that to stronger witches." Insinuating she wasn't a strong witch was hard to do. Deep down, he felt pride that he was given such a rare treasure to guide. As soon as he was presented with either her safety or her magic, there hadn't been a dilemma. He would always choose her safety, even if it meant she never did more than parlor tricks with her magic.

"Was Lizzy a strong witch from what you knew?" Just asking made her angry. That he knew about Lizzy before she died, increased the unease between them.

"She was stronger than many, yes."

She walked over to the altar and started to reach for a stone.

"Don't touch things. You don't know what she was working on." He hoped if he used a stern tone, fear might nip her curiosity.

"She only practiced white magic, right?"

"As far as we know."

She turned back to him and in a tone harsher than she meant, said, "Well what would a stone like that be used for?"

"Many things, each stone has different properties, it could have been used to bind something unwanted, and you handling it wouldn't be wise."

"Will you teach me how to…" she paused, turned around, and looked at things before she continued. "Use any of this?"

"When the time is right. If necessary," he said as firmly as he could. He wished she would just walk away from the room, the house, and everything even remotely connected to her family.

Gwen closed her eyes and reminded herself she loved Lewis. She let out a deep breath and walked over to the loft. She climbed the stairs and found a small window looking toward the west with a huge window seat. It looked like a peaceful place to sit and think.

"Anything interesting up there?" Lewis shouted up.

"No, nothing for you to worry about. It looks like it is just a place to sit and think. You can go now." She hoped her tone gave him a clue how she felt about his resistance to teach her.

Lewis hated that lately he needed to push her buttons. He didn't see another option. He couldn't teach her any magic, not yet. What he needed was another night away. A night to explain to Fannie the deal they made needed an adjustment. He never foresaw her at the manor, stumbling into magic, and worse, stumbling into Sebastian whose presence tugged at her own magic. A dark smile filled his face, maybe Fannie could use voodoo to take Sebastian out of the equation. He pushed the thought away. So far, everything he did he could justify as protecting her, letting his emotions get involved would change that.

"I won't be far if you need me," he called up.

"Unless I have magic questions," she said to herself as she heard him walk out and close the door.

She lost track of time while she sat at the window, staring out into the night, wondering about what Lewis was hiding. Why did his tension pulse so strong, and how was it connected to her family?

When she couldn't form any clearer thoughts, she made her way downstairs to read a little in the journals before bed.

She started getting heavy eyes as she read about Lizzy contemplating sending her mother, Winnie, away. They bound her first so someone named Fannie couldn't find her.

Who is Fannie?

The next paragraph woke her up as she read it over and over.

Even if we can bind Winnie, could we begin to bind little Gwen? She is so powerful for one not even born yet. How can we mask them? They must go before it is too late. Sebastian thinks we can protect them here, but I fear Fannie would devour them both.

Chapter Eight

"Talk to me, you are pulsing a dangerous amount of anger." Lewis followed Gwen to the kitchen.

Sleeping on the revelation did not ease her anger one bit. The time actually made it grow. "Lewis, I suggest you leave me the hell alone." She picked up her phone and dialed Sebastian. "Please call me when you can," she said to his machine.

Lewis knew who she called. He also knew she wouldn't hear from him anytime soon. Not until sundown. "You want to go learn things upstairs? Is that what this is about? We can go learn some new spells if it is that important to you. I can teach you how to cast a circle. Whatever you want."

She spun around and looked him in the eyes. "Answer me carefully Lewis. Like our relationship depended on it."

He nodded, feeling her energy pulling his magic. He needed to rebind her before she unraveled.

"Can I be a powerful witch?" She waited, her eyes wide with anger.

He sucked in a breath.

"Yes or no only," she added.

His eyes closed as he said, "yes," barely above a whisper.

"Will you tell me why you kept that from me? Yes or no, only."

His eyes pleaded with her not to ask.

She bit the edge of her mouth. "Who is Fannie?"

At that, he started to shift as he struggled to hold his form.

"We clearly need to talk, now," she said, and poured herself a cup of coffee. "You can tell me these things and I will try my best to forgive your secrets. Or I can read more and learn them on my own with no such forgiveness."

"Gwen, please, it is dangerous knowledge that you want. I wouldn't keep things from you to be spiteful, ever, I love you. I love you more than I can express."

"You don't love me enough to be honest. That isn't very much at all."

The anguish he felt showed on his face. "Can I have time? Can you stop reading, stop asking, and stop practicing magic for just a few days? Please Gwen, it could mean your life."

"Do you know who killed Lizzy, or Winnie." Her tone was demanding.

"I do not know who killed Lizzy. Her debt was paid by her mother."

"I don't understand. You know who killed my mother?"

He slowly nodded yes.

"I, I, you need to go somewhere now. Anywhere but my space. Go outside, upstairs, I don't care where you go as long as it is away from me."

Lewis walked away, sensing her tension ease when he did. He needed the space too. He needed to see Fannie again. The box was opened and he would need to make new arrangements for Gwen's debt.

Gwen knew she told him to leave, but it startled her to sense he did leave. She didn't feel him near, not upstairs, not outside. Something felt very wrong. She called Sebastian again, this time she left a clear message about what happened and why she needed to talk to him.

The size of the house, which only recently started to feel open and airy, suddenly felt like a huge, empty cavern. The emptiness around her threatened to make her weep, so rather than sulking at home, she got ready and made her way to town to make the arrangements with Mel.

Only a few customers from the morning rush remained when Gwen arrived at the diner. Mel rushed over to greet her as soon as she walked in.

"Gwen! Sit, sit, what can I feed you?" Mel asked, and then hugged her. "How are you, child?"

Gwen smiled. She imagined, with such an over-the-top friendly personality and appearance, everyone smiled at Mel. "I'm good, and you?"

"Always good. What are you eating? Coffee?"

"Coffee and a danish?"

"Cheese? Raspberry and cheese?"

Gwen let out a happy sigh. "Raspberry and cheese, please."

Mel vanished and returned in a flash with a danish and coffee.

Gwen set at the bar and watched as Mel wiped things down and started getting ready for the lunch rush.

"Mel, would you be able to cater a remembrance celebration for Lizzy?" Gwen felt the words stick a little.

She sipped her coffee, glad Sebastian offered to arrange everything else. She felt like she might get overwhelmed just thinking about this small part. She reached out and felt the laminate counter under her hands in an effort to ground herself.

"Would I? Don't be silly, of course I would. When are you planning it for, dear?" Mel did not stop her work while they talked.

"Sebastian thought Thursday?"

"Okay, do you have a rough idea on numbers, sweetie?"

Gwen looked to her notes and told Mel the estimate Sebastian told her. "That's give or take. He thought Linda would know more and wanted to make sure we did not forget anyone."

"I will contact Linda. That's so like him to do this for Lizzy. You know he and William were close too." Mel gave her a sympathetic look and brought her another danish.

"I get the feeling everyone here is close. I love it, feels like it was home."

"You are home, honey. We are all glad you came back. You tell Sebastian he can count on me. Let me know if you need anything else." She wiped a few more things and then spun around. "Are you going to drag Sebastian to the festival? We have missed him the last few years."

"Festival?" Gwen said, and sipped some of the hot coffee.

"Oh, you know with everything else, well, I just assumed Kathy filled you in... no it isn't Wednesday. I bet Wednesday the girls tell you all about it. Never mind that. Listen to me. You must come to the festival and bring Sebastian. He needs to get out more. Man like that all alone..."

Mel paused. She smiled as she watched Gwen eat and sip her coffee. "Anyway, it isn't this coming weekend or next, but the weekend after that and you have to come. Friday is a late start after arrival and set up, mostly it is just rides and a parade in the evening. Saturday is the bizarre, you wouldn't believe the fabulous odd vendors that come, followed by the auction, ask Kathy about that, darling. Sunday there is a livestock show, and when all the out-of-towners leave we have a dance, a square dance. It is a hoot."

"I wouldn't dream of missing it," Gwen said, meaning it. She dug in her purse and pulled out a checkbook. "Let me leave you a deposit so you can get supplies for Thursday."

Mel and Gwen talked a little more about what would be needed, and then Gwen left with a full belly and happy heart.

She looked down at her phone, wondering when Sebastian might call. He did say he had other things to do, plus there was the hundred things he agreed to do for her, between settling the estate and planning the celebration.

When Gwen got home, the house still felt like an empty cavern. Lewis remained elusive. After making herself some soup for lunch, she walked upstairs and took the journal she read in to the loft. She reread the paragraph about her being powerful, and let her mind wonder why Lewis would want to keep that from her.

Gwen startled awake when her phone rang. She looked out the window to see darkness. She fished her phone from her pocket as she stretched her neck, rubbing the ache that sleeping sitting up caused.

"Are you okay?" Sebastian asked, concerned from the messages she left during the day.

With her brain still foggy, she thought back to what she said, what happened with Lewis, and started to cry. "No, no, I am not."

"I am coming over," he said.

"I'm in the loft, it's unlocked," she said, and hung up.

She wiped the tears from her eyes and tried to look as presentable as possible. While she felt certain Sebastian wouldn't judge her either way, she didn't want to totally fall apart. The blow of losing Lewis as a rock when she needed him most in that role, wiped her out both physically and emotionally.

She stood up and started looking over the room below her. After a few minutes, the door opened and Sebastian walked toward her in long, graceful steps. He always seemed so together, she wondered what he must think of her. He witnessed her crumbling to pieces since the day they met.

He felt her eyes on him and looked up, his smile warm. He could feel her sadness, feel her uncertainty, and feel that she was teetering dangerously on the edge of her magic unraveling in a very unsafe way. If that much power unleashed in a rush, it could devastate her. Lewis should have slowly worked on it with her since she was a child.

"I'll come down," she said, sounding stronger than she felt. "I made arrangements with Mel."

He watched as she climbed the stairs, and made his way to the other side of the room. "What happened?"

Her lips pursed as she tried to say it without bursting into tears. "He lied. I've lost my rock, just when the storm seems to have started raging."

Sebastian closed his eyes and took in a deep breath. She needed a friend, a guide, and someone to get her through this. Everything else he felt, he quickly shoved down and took her in his arms.

When she stopped crying she looked at him with red eyes, her lashes wet.

He felt a mixture of sadness and admiration. "What do you need?"

"To know. I need to know. What happened to Lizzy? Why were we, me and mom, sent away? What was she running from? Am I able to do more than Lewis taught me? Who is Fannie? What is all this stuff? Why do you scare him?"

He took a few measured breaths. "I am going to make as much clear as I can. I promise to always be honest with you, but you know in doing so, the gulf between me and Lewis grows."

"Did he ask you not to tell me about those things?" she asked, looking at him puzzled.

"I would rather we just didn't discuss Lewis. I would never want to be a reason for tension between a witch and their familiar."

She nodded, it made sense he would have some loyalty to his own kind, even if they didn't like each other. "Do you know who killed Lizzy?"

"No, you asked me that already." He took her hand and walked toward the center of the room.

"But you do know who she was running from."

He helped her to sit, before sitting down beside her on the floor. "I do."

"What is this powder made of?" she asked, looking around them, remembering Lewis said protection of some sort.

"It depends on what it was used for. This was mostly salt. Salt is wonderful for keeping in or out dark things."

She ran her fingers through the powder, feeling the crystals and trying to imagine Lizzy sitting there with them. "Did you work magic with her?"

"Not as a rule, occasionally, yes. I blessed your room. I helped bind your mother before she left."

"Why did she need bound?"

"So that Fannie couldn't follow her."

49

Gwen looked at him with sharp eyes. "Did you try to bind me? It said in the journal Lizzy didn't think I could be bound. You wanted us to stay?"

"I did not try to bind you. As you probably read, I thought better of it."

Her brows furrowed. "Do you still think whatever we ran from is following me?"

"Yes, I do, and I still think you can handle it. Easily."

"Wait, if you didn't bind me then it could have followed us, mom, it killed her. I gave it a way to find her?"

"Don't," he said, and held her hand in his. "You were not even born yet and thinking like that is not helpful right now." His eyes filled with worry.

She knew that if she radiated some magic trail, whatever they tried to shield them from followed her right to her mother. "Fannie, is she a voodoo lady?"

He looked at her, seeing she needed to hear it then and with honesty. "Yes, she is a voodoo queen, and I won't kid you, she is a powerful lady."

"She is related to this debt? My family made some deal with her family?"

"With her."

"Lizzy did?"

"No, well before Lizzy's time. Lizzy was the first who refused to pay the debt."

Gwen furrowed her brows. "Good for her."

He smiled. "I agree. Lizzy was a strong woman, a powerful witch and had the soul of an angel. The debt was more than she was willing to pay."

"Sebastian, can you teach me? Would you?"

Sebastian felt his breath catch. It seemed like there wasn't enough air in the room. Did he dare? Could he teach her in the way she needed with these underlying feelings of desire? She needed a guide and Lewis didn't want to be that, whatever the reasons, but could he? "That is a request with huge implications."

"I'm sorry. It was presumptuous. It seems like I have known you forever and I realize we have only just met." She looked away.

"No," he said, shaking his head. "That is not why I hesitate. I worry for the bond you need with Lewis. I worry for the price you might pay for aligning with me. I would without reservation be your mentor, mi belleza, if I thought it best for you."

Frustration filled her features and voice. "What are the implications? Can't you just show me simple things?"

"You are not just a simple witch and that has to be considered when teaching you anything."

"What is it that makes me so special? I don't feel very special."

"I will teach you if you decide that you can't learn from Lewis, but I would implore you to give him a chance. There is a bond with him that I can't have with you, one you will need."

"The thoughts we share you mean?"

"Yes, that, the ability to summon him and the ability to share power."

She looked at him like she was hearing it for the first time. "Try something simple. Show me how you took my sadness the other night."

He chuckled. "That is only something simple because you are so special. It is actually quite advanced." He took her hand and placed it on his face. "Look at my eyes. See the sadness behind them?"

"Yes," she said, and frowned at having missed how much sadness reflected back at her.

His tone became deep and serious. "Now this is very important. When you start to feel it, stop. I have too much sadness for you. Make it your intention to pull just a little into your fingers. I need you to stop it at your hands, do not bring it into you."

Gwen looked at him and nodded, even though she didn't know exactly what he meant. The more she looked and saw the sadness clouding just behind his beautiful eyes, the more she wanted to get it right. She thought about the kindness he showed her. How tender and comforting he was, and made it her intention to be the same for him.

Suddenly she felt nauseous as a deep soul crushing sadness washed over her. Her instincts screamed at her to run away but her body felt frozen in pain. The pain in her mind stabbed like nothing she felt before.

Her eyes filled with tears and he pulled her hand away.

She folded into a ball and wept. Her shoulders heaved as her body fought to keep the sadness from setting in. She cried so deeply she started to hyperventilate. Sweat beaded on her forehead and she started to shake. She rolled over and started to dry-heave.

His voice was faint in the distance but darkness encased her.

"Look at me." His voice grew louder.

She felt his hand on her chin as he made her look at him. There was a flash of blue eyes. Another wave of sadness that felt like a broken heart and a deep betrayal started to fold in on her.

Peace washed over her. The blackness lifted.

"You took way too much. That is a danger with one so strong. We should start with something less, well, just less," he said and took her in his arms, rocking her.

"But you took it back? All that, it was horrible," she said once she felt more gathered.

"It is mine; I can carry it. We need to start smaller I believe."

"I've never felt so sad," she said, and reached for his face again.

He reached up, stopping her. "Nor do I want you to again."

"When I get stronger, better at it, can I take it from you?" she asked, as she wiped her tears, and then brushed her hands through her hair.

"No. I earned that. Why don't we practice a few things you might find more useful?"

Sebastian showed her how to unlock the door like she asked. He taught her to manipulate things with intentions, and much to her joy, how to share happiness.

It was late when they finished and he lingered a bit, hoping to see Lewis, but eventually gave up.

Before leaving, he checked the doors and peeked in to see her soundly sleeping. She accomplished more in one night than he imagined she could. Teaching her made him feel magical again. That Lewis did not want that felt wrong.

As he made his way home, the good feelings from the night with her switched to dread. The dangers still lingered and she needed a lot more instruction.

Chapter Nine

Gwen woke to an empty house. By midday, it took a great deal of restraint not to summon Lewis. She never worried before when he stayed away but since he left on such a bad note, she felt uneasy about him being gone so long.

She pulled out of her drive and headed for town, deciding a day out would be better than staying in and worrying. As she drove, she saw an opening and assumed it was for Sebastian's house. She rang his number but got no answer, as usual, and hung up, not leaving a message. She decided she would grab him a thank you gift in town, that would give her a reason to stop in on the way back.

She really didn't even know what she wanted to do in town. What she did know was she didn't want to be home alone. She parked at the end of main street and walked along the sidewalk, looking in the various shop windows. The sound of her feet crunching in the occasional frozen-over snow pile was strangely soothing.

She passed the yarn shop, a barber shop, a hardware store and a nursery on the right side, and then she turned off and strolled a few side streets before having dinner at Mel's. Only a few tables didn't have people happily eating. She like the idea of disappearing in the large group to avoid

Curtis. She didn't want to face him, his odd questions, and his hard eyes. Something about him made her edgy. A lot of things. The way he looked at her with his suspicious cop eyes. The matter of fact way he talked about her grandmother's death. The fact she couldn't get a read on his emotions.

Before she left, Mel told her where she could get craft supplies and she made a fast stop to put together a gift of painting supplies for Sebastian. It wasn't the most creative gift, but it gave her an excuse to see him again. While she shopped, she realized she did want to see him again for no other reason than to see him.

She called again as she pulled in his drive and still got no answer. Her nerves keyed up as she walked toward the huge house. She rang the bell and waited a minute before deciding she should just leave a message. He always returned her calls and came by when she asked.

She only took a few steps toward her truck when a hard, cracked voice said, "Can I help you?"

She turned to see a tall, thin man. His thick gray hair seemed bright compared to his pale skin. His sunken eyes were a sharp, dark brown, and looking at her with a stern glare.

"I was here to, to see Sebastian," she said, stammering.

"He is unavailable; might I tell him who called?"

She figured him for a butler or some sort of help. "I'm Gwen. I will just call later," she said, and took a step back.

"Miss Hensley. I am sorry I didn't recognize you. Please come in. I have some papers to ask you about," he said, and stepped back, opening the door fully.

She hesitated. "Is Sebastian here?"

"He will be available in an hour or so. We can sort out the bank papers while you wait."

She nodded and stepped in, looking around. The spiced scent in the air reminded her of an Indian market. The hall had rich tapestries and beautiful, colorful oriental carpets covered marble floors.

"Your coat," the man said, and reached out a hand to take her coat, which he hung by the door.

She followed him to a library, lined with shelves of neatly arranged books.

He walked to the desk in the center of the room and shuffled some papers.

"This one needs signed, and I need a blank check so that I can set up the transfer," he said, and pushed a paper toward her.

She looked it over and signed her name at the bottom. "I'll give Sebastian a check when I leave. I left my purse in the truck." She smiled.

"Of course." He walked out, with her following behind. "There is a fire in his study if you would like to wait in there. Did you want me to take your things?" he added, nodding at the bags she carried.

"That would be lovely, and I can manage the bags."

She followed him down a long hall, to a large open room with deep burgundy walls. An oversized high-back chair faced a huge window. A small table sat beside it. A few longer tables with books and lamps on them occupied the walls between the shelves.

"Would you like anything while you wait?" he asked, and then tossed a few logs on the already burning fire.

"No, thank you." The smell of sandalwood escaped from the fabric when she sat down. She could almost feel Sebastian next to her as she breathed it in.

When she heard the door close, a feeling of being trapped washed over her. She walked over to the window and opened the curtains to remedy the little bit of claustrophobia she felt. She paced, more and more nervous about being in his house with each passing minute. How would he view her visiting there? He might have old fashioned ideas that didn't include a woman making an uninvited visit to a man's house.

The nervousness passed when the door opened and she saw his smile. She saw no judgment, just his usual friendly features. His beautiful eyes examined her, making her wish she dressed better for his scrutiny.

"To what do I owe this lovely surprise?" His voice was as smooth as ever and he looked even more perfect than before.

"I was in town and, I brought you something. I wanted..." she paused and her honesty kicked in. "I wanted to see you." She watched as his eyes seemed to glimmer an even deeper blue.

"I find every little thing about you breathtaking." He repaid her honesty with some of his own.

She blushed and couldn't concentrate on making words. Instead, she reached out, handing him the bag.

He looked inside and smiled, thanking her. "Are you feeling better tonight?"

"Yes and no. Lewis is gone again. Still. He never came home last night."

He frowned deeply and rubbed his fingers together. "Can you summon him?"

"I didn't want to since it wasn't an emergency. We fought and I guess I just feel responsible if something happens."

"I have an idea." He took the bag in one hand and her hand in the other.

She enjoyed the warmth of his grip as his fingers laced in hers. The grasp of his smooth hand felt strong, yet tender.

When they walked out of the room, the man that let her in stood waiting at the end of the hall. They walked over to him and Sebastian reached out, handing him the bag.

"Yardley, please take this to my studio. We will be in the east room. We are not to be disturbed."

The man took the bag and nodded "Yes Sir," he said, and walked off.

She walked with Sebastian down another hall and at the end, they came to an even larger room with a huge fireplace on the far wall. A lounger sat in front of the fireplace. The brown colors used to decorate the room gave it a soothing feeling. He walked over and tossed a few logs on the fire.

He nodded to the lounger and she sat down, watching as he walked over and sat beside her. The smooth elegance of his movements captivated her.

"We've had a very serious start to what should be a much more relaxing friendship. Please sit back. I would like to hear more about you."

She looked at him, puzzled.

"Tell me about Louisiana, jobs you've worked, your neighbors' dog, your favorite color, what topping you need on your pizza? We can return to more serious things after Thursday."

She smiled at him and allowed herself to sink back into the cushions as she started with what she liked on her pizza. Sometime between her first job and him learning to paint, she ended up relaxing against him.

They continued to chat and as she listened to him talking about when he first met Lizzy, they both became more comfortable. By the end of the night, her head rested in his lap and his fingers twirled her hair. She fought to keep her eyes opened as his words became a soothing song that lulled her to sleep.

Sebastian noticed she drifted in and out while he talked and that made him happy. She needed to relax and he liked that she found his company calming. He couldn't remember ever entertaining at his house and enjoyed the way her sweet scents mingled with the familiar aromas of home. He could tell she had used a different shampoo as the roses smelled subtler, he hoped it wasn't a permanent change. That thought made him realize again what he felt around Gwen exceeded the usual magical pull. He pushed the thought away. After Thursday for more serious things.

He kept talking and twirling, thinking and watching her face. As he noticed the other night at her house, even sleeping she took his breath away.

When he felt her drift to a deep sleep, he concentrated more on the magical vibration she put out. It struggled against something.

Bound.

He knew Lewis didn't want her taught, but it stunned him to think of a familiar binding his own witch. He found the carelessness of the bindings even more shocking. Her power pressed dangerously at the amateur spell.

After Thursday, if Lewis did not give him a good reason, he planned to tease the binding off himself. She did not need a surge of power to add to her problems.

Sebastian sensed Lewis before he knocked and gently scooted out from under Gwen. He made sure she stayed asleep before he walked out, and shut the door behind him.

In the hall, Yardley greeted him. "Sir, there is a guest in your study. He insisted. I'm sorry."

"That's quite all right." He walked past him toward the study.

As soon as he stepped in the room, he could smell Fannie on Lewis. He fisted his hands at his sides and pursed his lips together. "Evening."

Lewis turned, taking in Sebastian's aggressive posture and tone. "Why is Gwen here?"

"She didn't want to be alone. The better question is, why was she alone?"

"I had to attend to things."

"I smell what you attended to. I don't want to know what you have been doing. That is your business. However, I won't have you connecting that woman to this area."

"I will do whatever is needed to protect Gwen."

"You don't honestly think Fannie would hesitate to take her, no matter what you have done for her, do you?"

"I have to believe that. I have made sacrifices you will never understand to protect her."

Sebastian closed his eyes and took in a breath. "I would understand. You don't need to work with or for her. I don't care what she has threatened you with, we can put an end to this whole thing."

Lewis shook his head. "No, she will take her. Do you know what happens when she does that? Eternity. An eternity of suffering. Gwen can't face her. Gwen is a new soul, a sweet new soul. Fannie is evil, centuries old, and stronger than even you. It's a debt, it must be paid. I have paid it; I will continue to pay it. I love Gwen, you wouldn't understand."

"You keep saying I wouldn't understand; you know what I have done. You know I understand hard choices. I also understand bad choices and their eternal implications. Don't end up like me." Sebastian softened his posture.

Lewis stayed rigid. "We are not going to be friends. Please don't teach her. I have agreed to only teach her spells. She can't learn anything else, especially not how to call the elements."

"It won't be so simple. She can call the elements with her emotions. You can't keep that bound. Your bindings are breaking already."

"If you want to help me then make them more effective, make them stronger. You can do that."

He shook his head and narrowed his eyes. "You want me to bind her? She is the most magnificent creature I have ever felt and you want me to wrap that up and throw it away? I wouldn't do it when Lizzy asked, Lizzy who I adored, and now you think I will because you made an empty promise to that vile hag Fannie?"

Lewis felt himself getting shifty.

"Relax, please. I am not your enemy here, Fannie is, always has been. I won't let her hurt you either," Sebastian said.

Lewis laughed. "You don't understand. It's too late for me. I'm hers."

Sebastian stepped back and looked at him, sniffing the air and watching Lewis as he shifted a little before getting solid again. "You made a bond with that?" The words spat out of his mouth. "Let me cleanse it, now, before she settles in deep around your soul."

"No, that would mean a confrontation now. Gwen is not ready. Let her bury the pain with Lizzy. Let me think. This bond has allayed her concerns and bought time."

Horror washed over Sebastian. "No, no, this bond has put us all at risk. You are fighting her now? Is that why you can't hold a form?"

Lewis nodded. "She wants to see you, see us."

Sebastian wanted to curse, wanted to hit him, but knew it wouldn't help. "Come." He walked out, heading for his altar room.

"What are we doing?" Lewis asked, following behind, while still fighting off the push he felt coming from Fannie.

"You need a gris gris from me, something of equal power to block this vision she is trying to use."

"You want me to let you curse me?" Lewis asked, and stepped back.

Sebastian kept walking. "No, I am going to make a charm just to protect you from her seeing through your eyes. She will sense it as she senses it now, you fighting her."

Lewis paused. "Why are you helping me?"

"Gwen. Like you, I am doing it for Gwen."

"This doesn't change us."

"This changes everything."

They walked into the room and Lewis asked no questions as Sebastian prepared the talisman. He didn't want to know what fluids and powders Sebastian used or why. When Sebastian finished, he gave Lewis a small charm attached to a string.

"Who taught you voodoo?"

"Fannie," Sebastian said flatly, looking at Lewis with hard eyes.

Lewis looked at him, believing him and not wanting to ask more.

"Now that you are connected to her there are other things we need to consider. I don't have time tonight. I must go as you know, but tomorrow, while Gwen is at the yarn group we need to talk more. Please don't contact Fannie again."

Lewis agreed and thanked Sebastian, even though he still felt a deep dislike for him. They walked out to where Gwen slept and said goodnight.

She drove home with Lewis. On the way, neither said anything. A silent understanding hung between them as they let their love wrap around each other's thoughts.

Chapter Ten

"I'm sorry," Lewis said, after listening to Gwen rant, rage, and finally cry about what happen between them. "I promise it will be better. I will be better."

Gwen wanted to believe him. She needed to believe him. She avoided him all day, but didn't want to leave out with things still so bad. Not after how awful she felt, thinking that something bad happened to him. "Please Lewis. I don't need words. Help me. Teach me. Be here for me like you used to be."

"I will, my witch." He kissed the top of her head.

She felt a little better about her and Lewis. They would still have to reconcile what happened. The lies and years lost. Her glance lingered on him a bit longer before she left for town.

The bell chimed when she walked in to the yarn shop. The smell of fresh coffee greeted her, wrapping her in warmth, and chasing away the cold of the night air.

She barely made it in the door before Kathy walked over.

"Gwen, I am so glad you came! The ladies are already here, you can join them and I will be back when the shop closes in just a few." Kathy walked back toward the coffee pot. "Cream and sugar, right?"

"Thank you." Gwen took the cup before she walked back to the small room.

Four sets of eyes greeted her when she stepped in. All of them studied her with equal interest.

"Ladies, this is, Gwen. I have to close up, but you can get her started," Kathy said, before she left to tend the shop.

Two ladies, twins Gwen assumed, who looked to be older than seventy, clicked their knitting needles without even looking at them. Both cocked their heads with white, perfectly curled hair and small reading glasses before they both said, "Gwen," in a shrill tone.

"I'm Pat, and this is Pam," one of them said. The different colored shirts helped Gwen distinguish between them. Pat wore blue and Pam wore green. "Sit down honey," Pat added.

Gwen sat next to a thin blonde who wore her hair in a tight bun. Harsh lines outlined her features. She looked over Gwen with hazel eyes. "I'm Linda. I run the hotel, just past Mel's."

"Linda, so nice to meet you. Sebastian told me about you."

Linda smiled. "He is such a charmer. I have all of your guests settled, RSVP'd, and I turned over the list to Mel."

"Thank you so much."

"No need honey. I'd do anything for that man, with his voice, and we all loved Lizzy." She smiled and winked at Gwen.

"Huh." The woman across from Gwen let out a strange sound.

"Don't you mind Trisha," Pam said. "She's feeling a little grumpy."

Gwen smiled at the short plump woman. She wore all black and had pitch black hair. Gwen guessed her the youngest of the ladies at around fifty. To accent her black, she wore a lot of bright yarn accessories and very bright makeup. Gwen imagined it might be gaudy on someone else, but she wore it well.

"I'd not be grumpy if you and that sheriff would leave my boy alone, and don't you be assuming we 'all' loved Lizzy," Trisha said, not even looking up from her knitting.

"Easy, Trisha, now's not the best time," Pat said, and reached over, patting Gwen's hand.

"I'm sorry, your son is?" Gwen asked.

Trisha kept knitting as she spoke. "Mike's my boy. Smartest boy in town. Best looking, too. He is a good boy, don't know nothing about killing."

"Oh, at the library, yes, very handsome." Gwen couldn't understand why her visiting him made him upset enough to tell his mother. Mel suggested it after all. *Mother's boys*, she thought, *that explains his temperament.*

"Smart too," Trisha said, in a defiant tone.

Kathy came in, winked at Gwen, and sat down. "Of course, we all agree Mike is the smartest, most handsome bachelor in town. Did they show you the pattern, sweetie?"

Gwen shook her head, no.

Kathy rolled her eyes. "Okay we have the festival coming up."

"Mel said to ask you about the auction," Gwen said.

Kathy laughed. "Yes, we are making a blanket to auction for the soup kitchen. Everyone has been making squares, and I will sew them all together. I'm afraid we are running later than usual and still have six squares unassigned."

Kathy got up and retrieved a box that had some completed squares. "These are the done ones. This is one Lizzy made." She handed a pink square with a white heart in the middle to Gwen. "This one too." Kathy handed her another square.

Gwen held the squares and fought back tears. As she rubbed the fabrics between her fingers her lips twitched.

Kathy stood behind her and rubbed her back.

"I can make squares quickly," Gwen said, when she felt more composed.

"Look here," Kathy said, and showed her the graph of the remaining squares. "Which did you want to start tonight?"

"Let me see the chart for this one." Gwen pointed to the one that would go opposite to Lizzy's heart square.

"Perfect, I'll get the chart and yarn for that one." Kathy walked back to the shelf and grabbed the supplies.

While everyone knitted, Gwen listened to them chat. She learned that the festival accounted for twenty percent of the town income each year, the paper boy had a knack for hitting puddles, and Pat and Pam found a notice on their door that their neighbor complained about their barking dog. There also seemed to be an issue with the trashcans not being set upright on trash day. It made Gwen happy to hear about normal problems. It even amused her that each time Trisha opened her mouth, she either complained, or praised Mike.

When the night wound down, Gwen took three of the squares and supplies while Pat, Pam and Linda each took one of the other three. Trisha said she had too much to do at home. Everyone hugged, gave air kisses, and left with promises to see Gwen at the remembrance.

Gwen hung behind to buy some needles and more yarn after everyone left. Kathy gave Gwen her cellphone number in case she needed anything before the remembrance.

"It's going to be okay sweetheart. Mel and I will be there early to help set up. Sebastian already called with the final numbers, and we have tables and whatnot."

"Thank you," Gwen said, and hugged her before she got in her truck.

Lewis perched on the gazebo railing. Sebastian stood beside him, his eyes scanned the lake. Since they were both familiars they did not need Lewis to shift for them to communicate. Lewis tried to stay in his raven form so he could use all his magic to keep Fannie at bay. He still didn't care for Sebastian, but he did get the feeling that if anyone could help him protect Gwen, it was him.

"It seems a strange coincidence that you trained under Fannie and came to live next door to where Lizzy ran to for sanctuary," Lewis said.

"I've considered that. I know the fates have a sense of humor, but I don't think it was coincidence either. Whatever role Fannie envisioned I might play in helping her get her hands on Winnie, didn't happen. She has underestimated my will many times."

"You want revenge on her for something? Did she have anything to do with your last witch?"

Sebastian pressed his lips together. "She did. My revenge is not important. I am not a vengeful soul. Gwen is what matters now."

"But I thought it was the undead."

"Yes, it's more complicated. Being what you are, you know that magical creatures often work together when it suits them."

Lewis felt shifting vibrations come from Sebastian. "I promised to leave that to you and I will. What do you have in mind for Gwen?"

"First, she needs a friend. I will be that. She needs a mentor. You should be that. She can face Fannie. I promise you that. I would never suggest anything I thought she couldn't handle. If you need a mentor, I can be that as well."

"But Fannie is strong. Have you felt her power recently?"

Sebastian turned to the bird and watched him while he pondered what exactly Lewis promised her. "I know what Fannie can do. Why do you imagine she never made contact with Lizzy or Winnie's guides?"

"I... she wasn't owed?"

"She was owed. That is why she took Winnie after Gwen was born, as I warned she would." He rubbed his fingers together while he thought. "She didn't fear Winnie or Lizzy."

"She doesn't fear Gwen."

Sebastian turned to him and looked at him, shocked he hadn't realized at least that much. "Yes, she does. Do you really think she needs you as a power boost? Why do you think she would link with you?"

"To keep an eye on us. Keep tabs on my promises." The raven stared at Sebastian with his black eyes.

"No, she knows against Gwen, she loses. She has seen it in her nasty juju rituals. She knows her end will be at Gwen's hands, and she is scared. That is why we can't rely on her waiting for Gwen to have the next generation. She wants Gwen dead before her visions come to pass."

"But why link with me, why chase Gwen? Gwen wouldn't even know her, wouldn't chase her."

"If Gwen faces her, counting on your boost and that goes to Fannie, what then? A shock and misstep, something Gwen doesn't see coming. Imagine the heartbreak Gwen would have, finding out when she needed you most that you belonged to that woman. The woman who killed her mother."

Lewis felt like his whole world came crashing down. "How could I not see that?" he asked more to himself. "Can I make this right?"

"I'm not sure how to undo what she did with you. I can link with Gwen, the boost would be great, more than enough to counter what could happen to Gwen emotionally."

"She's my witch. You can't do that. I don't want her to do something like that. It was awful. To make the link, we had to sacrifice…"

Sebastian cleared his throat and waved his hand. "Stop. I don't want to know who or what you sacrificed. I can make a charmed bond. Nothing deep like what you did. No sacrifices, nothing that dark. It can be removed after Fannie is gone."

"A charm? Like what you gave me? No real link?"

Sebastian sighed. "I don't want your witch. Not like that."

Lewis considered his options. 'Not like that,' didn't escape him. "Can we not tell her why? Can I please have time to think of how to undo this? I don't want to lose her trust, or her love."

Sebastian frowned. "I don't want to lie to her, ever. It goes against who I am."

"Can you just not volunteer it? Like with your secret. I will lie."

"She may forgive whatever you have done, but if you keep this lying between you, her forgiveness will run out." He looked back at Lewis.

"Please, can I trust you?"

His eyes closed for a long moment. "You want to know if I am trustworthy and I am to prove this by lying?"

"Just let me talk to her. I will suggest you and her, and the charms. I will suggest the lessons, and make plausible reasons that don't involve what I did."

Sebastian pressed his lips and nibbled the edge of his bottom lip while he thought.

He could feel the desperation in Lewis to keep his deeds covered. He also knew they wouldn't stay buried. "If she asks."

"Cross that bridge when we get there."

"And we are a 'we' now?" Sebastian asked and then huffed.

"If you hurt her with your magic lessons or dirty blood."

Sebastian almost laughed at how quickly the small truce was already reduced back to threats. "She needs to know about my 'dirty blood' before any connection is made. Full consent will be needed."

"If you tell her that, she will never want to link with you. She won't even want to look at you again. You are a monster remember?"

"You will find things are not that black and white. I will tell her what I am, after tomorrow night. When I feel she is ready, not before." The sadness that always lingered in his eyes deepened.

"Suit yourself, I would suggest you not at all."

"I would think as soon as her mind is not so distracted she will sense it anyway. Her senses are keen."

Lewis changed tones and with an almost childlike innocence asked, "Have you ever trained an elemental witch?"

"No, Gwen is the first I have ever seen. It is something magical just to be near her." His mind easily drifted to how her presence felt and he smiled as the memories danced across his thoughts.

"You feel that, when she is near?" Lewis asked.

"Of course I do. I am sure anything magical she gets close to feels it as well."

"Did you know she will be able to call more than one?"

"Yes, a rare and beautiful treasure." Sebastian's eyes sparkled when he thought about her power.

Lewis felt a mix of pride and trepidation. "Fannie will know if she starts commanding any of the elements."

"Yes, she will. It won't matter." Sebastian looked behind them. He let his senses reach out and felt the approaching magic. "Gwen is almost home, shall we?"

"What are we doing?"

A warm smile formed on his face. "Tonight? You are going to sit with her, listen to her tell you about yarn and things like that. I am going to paint."

"Paint?" Lewis asked, sounding baffled.

"Yes, I told you not to worry. I will paint and make sure things are ready for tomorrow. More intense things are coming, enjoy the rest while you can. We still have a killer to be wary of. One thing at a time. I've lost my best friend and would enjoy a night to reflect before I say goodbye."

After they left the lake, Lewis went to the house. He stood by the roaring fire and pushed out as happy a vibration as he could.

"Lewis, hello." It startled her to see him waiting on her.

"How was your night?" He took her bags and set them by the couch.

She watched him with narrowed eyes. "Good, you are acting weird. What happened?"

"Nothing happened. I just wanted us to have a nice night."

"I see. Let me get a coffee." She walked to the kitchen to start a pot. "What is up, really?"

He joined her in the kitchen. "Nothing. I love you and I haven't been acting like it. Tell me about your night."

She cut her eyes at him in exaggerated disbelief. Even though she didn't know why he acted so attentive, she didn't fell any malice or dishonesty. She relaxed, sipped her coffee, and told him about her night. She decided not to ask about why he stayed gone so long. She knew he would lie and didn't want that to ruin the night.

Chapter Eleven

The warmth of sun shining on Gwen's face made her smile as she drove toward the lake. Sebastian arranged everything, but wasn't able to be there to help with the setup. He told her he would arrive before things got underway just after dark. She wondered what he kept his days so busy with, but more than that, looked forward to the comfort of his presence.

She parked and got out of the truck.

Mel and Kathy rushed over to greet her with hugs and kind words.

"Sweetie, I had the band boys set up the food tables just there." Mel pointed toward tables just to the right of the fire pit.

"Perfect," Gwen said, surprised by how small her own voice sounded.

Kathy smiled at her in a way that told her she looked as worn out as she felt.

Gwen didn't realize just how emotionally drained facing the day made her until she stood there trying to think of what needed to be done. "The extra chairs you wanted are in my truck." Gwen turned to start unloading.

In no time, the three ladies arranged the remaining chairs. The band ran through their sound checks in front of the fire.

It surprised Gwen how much it warmed the area.

Just when she started to feel like she wanted to run home, she felt Lewis wrap himself around her thoughts. She looked up to see him watching her, perched on a tree that hung over the lake. She smiled over to him and thanked him silently. He whispered his love to her mind and she took comfort from the warmth she felt from inside.

As cars started to arrive, she joined Kathy who introduced her to the short, round, balding preacher. She spoke to Father George on the phone, but didn't picture him quite like he actually appeared. Regardless of his size, his friendly eyes and voice gave her a lot of comfort.

Gwen stood at the back of the chairs along with Father George, Kathy, and Mel, who stayed close for support and greeted people as they arrived. All the kind words and tender handshakes became a blur as she started to feel overwhelmed again.

As the night fell, she felt like the darkness would suffocate her.

The air around her changed, her despair seemed to ease. Her eyes drew to a tall older man who approached in long, graceful strides.

He put out familiar energy that tugged at her. His hair was pulled back in a neat gray ponytail peppered with streaks of brown. When his eyes locked on hers and she stared into those deep-blue pools she held her breath. He told her he needed to glamour his age since people knew him for many years, but she never imagined such a drastic effect. He aged well. Even appearing to be late in his sixties, she found him gorgeous.

He said a few words to Father George and then hugged Kathy and Mel before sliding between Kathy and Gwen. When he took her hand in his, she felt her tension melt away.

"Sorry to not be here sooner," he whispered. His nearness tickled her senses.

She didn't say anything, but squeezed his hand instead.

Once everyone arrived and took a seat, Sebastian walked with Gwen to the front center seats. He stayed close, his arm protectively over her shoulder.

Each time she started to feel overwhelmed, a warmth radiated from him and she felt her emotions ease.

He agreed to let her experience the grief she needed to, but he also promised to not let it overcome her. Both promises were kept.

When she looked at him she could see sadness behind his eyes. Some of the sadness he took from her, but she knew he mourned the loss of the special friendship he shared with Lizzy. She sat a little closer and used the technique he taught her to let the comfort she took from him wash over them both.

When he felt her share the peace with him, he cocked his head and arched an eyebrow while smiling at her. Trained or not, he found her magnificent.

She got up and said a few prepared words. There was a numb feeling as she said her formal goodbye to the grandmother who she never got the chance to know.

A few others spoke and when Sebastian did, every one wept. Gwen heard the emotion in his voice, and saw the pain in his eyes.

Lewis told her before that they felt things differently, deeper, and she wished she knew some way she could help him.

Once the services concluded, things shifted and music started. Everyone helped fold chairs and people started eating, and dancing.

Mel walked over to Gwen and Sebastian and smiled at him as her eyes took him in. She boldly asked him to dance and Gwen stepped back. She grinned as the two swayed together, moving toward the dancing couples. The happiness in the air soothed her.

Gwen made her way over to the food tables and munched on some cheese and vegetables while she watched everyone enjoying themselves. It seemed surreal to her as she stood there, with friends surrounding her, and a home in the distance.

She didn't even realize that while she munched, she walked back to the gazebo. Her eyes locked on the photo and the box that contained Lizzy's remains.

Now that the majority of the people were in the area by the band, a chill filled the air. She tugged the shawl she wore tight around her shoulders. The feeling of the finality of things wrapped around her and sunk in. Her eyes filled with tears and she openly sobbed.

She barely started to cry when she heard thunder crack in the distance. Seconds later, she felt Sebastian rapidly nearing.

He stood behind her and put his hands on her shoulders.

She let him pull some grief away before she turned to look at him. "I need to feel this."

"Of course, and when the celebration concludes I will stay with you while you cry it out. However, no one here needs to get stormed on, nor do they need to see the display that is likely to happen."

"Did I do that? The thunder, and the other night with the snow?"

He nodded and held her too him. "So much sadness, it breaks my heart."

"But how?" she asked. "I'm still just a seer."

"You are…" he started to say, but stopped when he sensed someone else walking toward them.

Kathy walked up. "You two okay?" She looked at the embrace and sadness in both of their expressions.

"Sure." Gwen turned and accepted Kathy's open arms. "Why don't you and Sebastian have a dance. I need a minute; I'll be right there."

"You sure." He looked at her with concern evident in his eyes.

She nodded and watched as they walked away. Once alone, she eyed the picture closer. She could see happiness in the eyes. If she believed what Sebastian told her about Lizzy, she would want her to have a good time.

She walked to the picture and reached out to touch it. "I will get you justice."

When she returned to the people dancing by the fire, a feeling of happiness hanging in the air washed over her. She closed her eyes and let the music speak to her. She swayed slowly at first, maneuvering in and out of the crowd comprised of both couples and single dancers like herself. Even though she felt eyes on her, she didn't pay them any mind. She also felt Lewis in her mind. He danced with her thoughts. She welcomed his mental hug and returned it as she shared the moment with him.

She relaxed so deeply, it startled her when a hand reached out, taking hers.

"May I?"

She opened her eyes to see Sheriff Curtis standing in front of her, and flashed him a warm smile. "Delighted."

He gave a slight bow and pulled her closer to him. He put an arm around her waist and held her hand as they danced. His eyes seemed dark and full of what she took for judgment as he looked at her. "I understand you've been trying your hand at my job," he said in her ear, so she could hear him over the music.

She looked at him, puzzled.

"Got calls from Mike, who was upset about you disrupting him at work, and a colleague at the prison. I should have told him to deny your request."

Her mouth opened. "On what grounds?"

"On the grounds that you need not worry your sweet little heart over killers. Leave that to me. I will make an arrest very soon."

At first, the whole 'sweet little heart' remark offended her, but then the arrest news struck her and she sucked in a breath. "An arrest. Really"

He smiled and his eyes softened. When he smiled, she could see why both Mel and Kathy seemed to have eyes for him. "Really, I won't suffer a murderer in my town."

"Who?" She looked around. The thought of her killer at the celebration for Lizzy made Gwen feel dizzy. She tightened her grip on his hand.

"That, dear, is why you leave such matters to those with harder nerves. I won't be making any statements until the arrest is made. You wouldn't want them to walk on some sort of procedural misstep, now would you?" His tone removed any admiration she just felt for the man.

"Yes, I may need to sit down." She wrapped her arm around his and let him lead her to a chair.

Once she sat down, things started to seem more stable.

"You need a drink? Water or something?" He tried to be soothing but missed the mark.

"No, it just startled me to think they, her killer, could be here with us."

"It's always who you least expect." He looked across the lake and his voice sounded as if his mind already drifted to something more important than her.

She creased her brows. "That's not helpful to think about."

He chuckled softly. "I guess not, that may be why I always let my deputy handle delivering fragile news."

While she agreed with him, she did feel better. His bedside manner and its awful inappropriateness actually eased her nerves. "I'm alright now, thank you, Sheriff. I'm glad you are getting closer to closing this."

"Sheriff, everything okay?" Sebastian walked up. His eyes searched Gwen's face for the answer.

"Yeah, little lady got overwhelmed is all." Curtis looked past Sebastian as he spoke.

Gwen couldn't control her wrinkled nose or the rise of her lip on one side.

Only Sebastian noticed.

Curtis stared back at something by the fire.

Sebastian winked at her and looked over toward the fire, but didn't see anything that looked off. People danced and seemed happy, as they should. "I've got the little lady under control if you want to get back to the party," Sebastian said.

Curtis nodded and walked off.

They both looked at each other with smiles that indicated laughs brewed just under the surface.

Sebastian walked over and took her hands, helping her stand. The air between them grew heavy and they locked eyes. There was no one there, no music, no sadness, just each other. Their hands laced together and the connection seemed deeper than merely holding hands.

Sebastian released her hands and put one of his on the small of her back. He knew the time to explore those attractions would come later. "Would you honor this old man with the last dance, little lady?"

"If you never call me that again," she said, as they walked back to the fire.

Once she was in his arms, the comfort she always got from him mingled with the attraction she often felt when they spent a moment too close to each other. She thought he noticed it as well, since they both seemed to pull away when it happened.

"Is that magic?" she whispered in his ear.

The sound of her sweet voice and the heat of her breath against his skin made him have to concentrate on not missing a beat.

"Magical, but not magic." He tried not to nuzzle noticeably as he spoke.

She sighed and rested her head on his chest as the song continued.

It ended too soon for either of them. Someone with a question about where to plug in something wrangled Sebastian away almost as soon as the song finished.

As the night wore on, the crowd thinned. Gwen watched as the last of the people there ate and chatted. She smiled when she saw Mel walking over.

"You want help loading your truck, sweetie? There are so many leftovers too. I'll load them in my van, but I'm going to follow you home and leave them with you. You won't have to worry with cooking for ages."

"Thank you, I'm alone here, so if you want to take most of the leftovers to the soup kitchen, that would make Lizzy happy," Gwen said, as she thought about all that food and how much would spoil if she kept it.

Mel started to tear up. "You are so much like her, sweet Gwen. Come tell me what you can manage honey," she said, and they walked together to the food tables.

Gwen picked a few days' worth of meals and some deserts, all of which she put in the cab of her truck. She helped Mel load her van with the rest.

Most of the crowd left, all stopping to hug Gwen and remind her to come to this or that in town as soon as she felt up to it. Kathy and the Yartist group stayed after everyone, helping pick up trash and fold tables and chairs.

With everything sorted, Gwen thanked them and promised to see them on Wednesday.

"You could bring your neighbor," Trisha said, watching Sebastian as he helped with the last of the loading of things into trucks and trailers.

Kathy laughed, and Pam and Pat agreed.

"I don't think he knits," Gwen said and smiled at them.

"I'll bet he would if you were teaching," Kathy said, looking to Gwen.

"Her?" Pat asked, and laughed. "He's old enough to be her grandfather. I'll teach him."

Pam laughed. "I don't think I could hold my needles still if he was around."

Kathy laughed hysterically. "I don't think any of us could, even Gwen," she managed to say between laughs.

Sebastian walked up smiling. "Ladies, what have I missed?"

Suddenly everyone stopped laughing and turned several shades of red.

He cocked his head and looked to Kathy who shrugged.

"These lovely ladies were just discussing knitting needles," Gwen said, hardly able to contain her laughter.

"Needles?" He looked puzzled.

"Needles," Kathy said, and then laughed again.

They all laughed, even Trisha, and Gwen felt the last of her anxiety about fitting in wash away.

Once everyone left, Gwen stood at the fire, and looked out over the lake. She felt Sebastian as he came up and stood beside her. His hand laced in hers. Lewis appeared at her other side, also lacing his hand in hers. They both allowed her to feel sadness as they made a combined effort to shield what she sent out from being picked up by other creatures.

Gwen sobbed. As she became lost in grief, the winds howled in agony. Lewis was surprised by the amount of power that surged from her. When her tears flowed, snow was carried on the howling winds, and Sebastian wrapped her in warmth.

They let her express her grief until she had no more tears and the snow and winds died down.

Lewis gathered her in his arms and Sebastian drove them in her truck back to her house where they sat by her while she drifted off, exhausted. Sebastian and Lewis both felt the weight of the implications of her ability to summon not one but two elements simultaneously.

Chapter Twelve

"Company," Lewis said, and started out of the room.

Gwen sipped her coffee and looked at Lewis through sore, puffy eyes.

Once alone, she stood and stretched before making her way to the door.

She opened it just as Curtis was about to knock.

His face was emotionless. "You look awful. Can I come in?"

She ran her fingers through her hair. *His usual charmless self*, she thought. "Yesterday was a hard day. What's going on?" She looked at him with a puzzled and somewhat annoyed expression.

He frowned at her as she stood blocking the door. "I wanted to get here and talk to you before…" He paused and looked toward the driveway. "I've made an arrest."

"You did?" She started to step back.

The sound of tires fighting against the gravel and snow drew her attention. Gwen watched as Trisha parked, flung opened her car door, and hurried toward them.

Curtis made a slight growling sound. "I hoped she wouldn't…" he started to say as Trisha stepped up.

She stood in the small space between them. "Gwen, you tell him he is wrong." Trisha sobbed. Her eyes, usually made up in bright but perfectly applied makeup were bare, pink, and puffy, much worse than Gwen's.

Gwen stepped back to let them both inside. "Come in, I'll make coffee."

Curtis looked at her, almost showing an emotion. "Trisha, you shouldn't be here."

Gwen pulled her in, waited for him to step inside, and shut the door. "It's freezing, go sit by the fire. Do you want coffee?"

Trisha nodded and walked over to the fire.

Curtis took off his hat and followed Gwen to the kitchen. "I tried to get here sooner." He took the cup she offered, and sipped it slowly. "I can make her leave if you would like."

"Make her leave? What is going on?" she asked, as she poured out the other two coffees. She lifted her cup, inhaled it and sighed, content for a moment.

"I was trying to tell you. We arrested Mike this morning."

Gwen sat her cup down without taking a sip. The coffee spilled a little on the counter. "Mike?" She walked over and got a rag. "Mike?" She swept the rag over the small spot repeatedly. "The librarian, Mike, Trisha's boy?"

"It is always the quiet ones." He shook his head as he stared off at the cabinets.

"But that can't be right. Why would he?" Her hand held the rag as she wiped mindlessly. "I didn't get the feeling he would hurt anyone."

He turned his head sharply. "I follow facts Miss Hensley, not feelings."

"Facts? What facts?"

"I can't discuss all that with you. You know that." The look he gave her said he found her question ridiculous.

Gwen got the impression he found everyone below him. "Poor Trisha," she whispered and picked up the cups.

She walked out, set them on the table and hugged Trisha. She didn't know his facts, but Mike as a killer didn't feel right.

Curtis must have missed something.

Trisha clearly lived for her child and Gwen felt her heart break to see her such a mess.

"You tell him Gwen. My baby couldn't, he just couldn't. Curtis, you screwed up." She looked at him with hate.

"Have your coffee," Gwen said gently. She helped Trisha to sit down.

"I'm sorry, Trisha. I told you, you should be arranging a lawyer not harassing Miss Hensley."

"She's not harassing me," Gwen said. She tried hard not to take a defiant stance. Sheriff or not, he sure did grate her the wrong way.

Trisha finished her coffee and stood to leave. "I'm sorry. I need to go," she said, sobbed a little, and made her way for the door.

Gwen followed her out. She lingered on the porch concerned and watched as Trisha got in her car. Once she pulled off she turned to Curtis. "Will she be okay, you think?"

"Yes. She is a stronger woman than you would think. You should come inside, it's cold." He put his hand on the door and waited for her to do what he said.

She slowly stepped inside and looked at him while she tried to let it sink in. "Mike? Because Lizzy wouldn't help him with his silly history? That doesn't seem like murder motive." Gwen's brows furrowed and she sat down on the couch.

"I can't say ma'am. What do you imagine might be a good reason?"

"Well none I guess, but certainly something more than that. You have something more than that on him, don't you?"

"Do you need me to call someone for you?" He took the last sip of his coffee while he scanned the room as if looking for a crime clue somewhere.

She wondered if he always looked for out of place things. It unnerved her. "Can I see him?" She looked up at him and waited for an answer.

His face hardened even more as he shook his head slowly. "Mike? No, you may not."

She rubbed her head at the temples. Yes, he had been the only person to say a bad word about Lizzy, but it didn't seem that extreme. She ignored the sheriff and pulled out her phone. After getting no answer she left a message for Sebastian.

Curtis eyed her, then frowned. "You going to be okay? I do have work to do."

She nodded and stood to walk him out. "Curtis, Sheriff," she said, as he started down the steps.

He slid his hat on and turned around. "Ma'am."

"Thank you."

He nodded and walked to his car.

As soon as she shut the door, Lewis walked in and held her. "It's over." He felt her relax a little in his arms and hoped they would enjoy smoother days now.

She looked up at him. "I'm not sure. It feels wrong. I didn't get that from Mike. I just don't think he is the one."

"Gwen, don't look for reasons to be sad. Lizzy will have justice now. We should celebrate."

Gwen let it go. She knew Lewis wouldn't understand her gut feeling any better than Curtis. A nagging in her mind said something seemed too easy, and wrong about Mike. She would keep digging, but do it in a way that Lewis or Curtis didn't give her any grief. If her instincts proved right, when it came time to charge Mike, they would fail and need new people to look for. Maybe she could find answers before then.

Lewis followed her around for most of the day as she puzzled over things in her head. She used the nervous energy to unpack everything still in suitcases, and to make some changes to the kitchen.

Could the family history Mike worked on really link William and Mike? Due to his young age, Mike could not have committed both murders, but something in her gut said they were linked.

When the liaison called with news of her approval as a visitor for the junkie, Lenny, she decided she still wanted to go. She wanted to be close to the man and decide for herself if he killed William, or if they got that one wrong too.

Visitations took place on Mondays or Fridays so she arranged to go out Monday.

"Why are you still going there?" Lewis asked, after she hung up.

She turned to see him perched close by. "You eavesdropping on me?"

"I don't see what good that will do is all."

"Lewis I just need to. Can't you understand that?"

"No, but I will support you, my witch."

She jerked her head back and looked at him through pinched eyes. "That was awful agreeable for you."

"Yes well, you have enough ugliness to deal with. I won't be adding to it."

That made her wrinkle her features even more. "Stop drinking the Kool-Aid."

"You need to work on your facial expressions. Especially if you are going to be Miss Socialite. You can't run around wrinkling your nose at everyone."

She laughed. "I probably need to work on my habit of saying what need not be said immediately after meeting someone as well."

"Did you want to learn some new magic?"

"Lewis, you are scaring me now." She gave him a puzzled look. "Seriously."

He thought a lot about how to make the transition smoothly, but now he doubted his approach. He spent so long convincing her not to practice magic that no matter what he did, it wouldn't come off naturally. "Yes, seriously. It is why I am here."

Rather than let the opportunity pass, she decided to go upstairs with him and worry about his motivations later.

He taught her how to focus her attention and work with intent. It surprised him how easily her desires became reality. He didn't plan to teach her anything elemental without Sebastian there to help mask it, especially since Gwen altered the environment on whim. He could only speculate on what she could do with full intent and instruction.

The thought of her linked with Sebastian, even for a second, made him feel bitterness, but he pushed it aside. If Sebastian could help keep her safe and keep his secrets too, then he would have to give on that, temporarily. Even now he could feel the heat of the talisman as it fought off Fannie.

"Let's break," he said. "You need to eat. I need to think about what's next. There will be some things I will need Sebastian here for."

"Sebastian?"

"Just for added precaution."

She looked at him, opened her mouth and then closed it. "Okay, Lewis." She walked out and started something to eat, Lewis stayed close. "I need to call him. I forgot all about Mike. Sebastian will be happy to hear they made an arrest."

She called and left a message that she needed to talk to him in person.

"You know he never answers his calls during the day. I swear he is some sort of CIA agent or something," she said.

Or something, Lewis thought, but smiled at her and watched as she cooked. They went back upstairs to work on some protection circles.

Sebastian called, agreeing to come over, so they wrapped up their practice and cleared the room.

When she told Sebastian about Mike he reacted similar to how she did. He did not seem convinced Mike had it in him to be a killer. The news didn't give him the peace it should have because he also wanted the justice Lizzy deserved. Gwen assumed if Lewis met Mike he would agree with them. Something seemed wrong.

"I'm going to the prison Monday," Gwen said, as they all sat in the main room.

"That sounds unpleasant." Sebastian looked to Lewis.

"I agree, but she insists on following that path to its end."

"I think William holds the answers we need to piece it together, so I am going. I will get the answers the sheriff is too stubborn to get." Gwen stood up. "I'm getting coffee."

Both Lewis and Sebastian looked shocked by her tone and stance.

"She's feisty tonight," Lewis said, loud enough for her to hear as she walked out.

"So I see. You've been practicing."

"Did you feel it?" Lewis turned his head sharply toward him.

"No, relax. I feel it now. I would like to be alone to tell Gwen about me."

Lewis frowned and shook his head slowly. "Do you really think you should?"

"We talked about this already. I do."

Gwen walked back in and sipped her coffee. She sighed deeply as the first sip washed over her.

"Did you want to see what she's learned?" Lewis asked.

Gwen cut her eyes at them. First Lewis had been acting way too attentive to her, and now he acted chummy with Sebastian. Things grew stranger by the minute.

"Have you done anything elemental?" Sebastian asked.

"Not yet," Lewis said, and smiled at Gwen. "We could."

"We could?" she asked. "What, now?"

"Sure, with Sebastian here to shield things we could go outside and see what you have in those fingers of yours."

"You are full of surprises lately." She walked over and kissed Lewis on the forehead. "Fine, I'll call your bluff. Let's go."

Sebastian smiled to see the sort of interaction he expected between a witch and their familiar happen with them, finally.

They all went outside, none of them really knowing what to expect.

Sebastian made a circle for them to work in. He explained to Gwen how she could make one anywhere without powders as he did.

"So why ever use powders at all?" she asked.

"There are reasons for specific elements, salts and the like. In a pinch this, what I just did, will be enough to protect you from most things."

"But if we are about to do something, strong, shouldn't we use something else?"

"Usually, I will give the needed extra protection tonight."

Lewis shifted and sat perched on her shoulder. She could feel his magic join with hers, and hear his voice as a gentle whisper in her head.

"Start with water," Lewis said. "Feel it all around you, inside of you. Make yourself aware of its presence everywhere and call it to you."

Sebastian couldn't hear what they said, but he could feel they worked with something powerful. He did his best to make sure none of the magic leaked out.

She drew water from the air around them, the ground below them, as well as herself, which made keeping it concealed more difficult than he anticipated.

In front of her hands water formed into a rotating circle. It swirled and swayed as they all watched. "What now?" she asked.

"Now you can give it back, since you have no real need for it," Lewis said.

She allowed it to flow back from where it came from. "What would I have used it for?"

"Water gives life, you could use it for healing, growth, cleansing, as well as protection. In force or frozen it has destructive strength as well." Lewis held a look of pride at her success.

Sebastian walked over to her and took her hand. "That felt beautiful."

"You felt it?" She turned to see he also looked at her with pride.

His eyes held an adoring sparkle to them as well.

Lewis shifted and said, "I never imagined you'd actually call up so much on the first try."

"Hey, I made it snow already," she said.

"That she did, and storm. I wouldn't underestimate her," Sebastian said.

"Can you, either of you do things like that?" she asked.

"Very subtly. Enhance a blowing wind, perhaps, make rain from an already cloudy day, nothing like what you can do. We certainly can't call the elements from nothing," Sebastian said.

"Let's not make her arrogant. We have enough of that from you," Lewis said. He cut his eyes at Sebastian while smiling.

"I'm not sure what pool you two have been drinking from, but I like the changes," Gwen said, and laughed. She waved her hands and a warm wind of peacefulness and happiness wrapped around them.

When the wind left, Lewis and Sebastian cleared the circle and they walked back inside, chatting for a little while longer before Sebastian said he needed to leave.

Gwen walked him to the door where he lingered as he watched her.

"Would you join me at my house tomorrow evening?" he asked.

She felt a rush of heat and imagined her cheeks were red. "Of course."

"Come hungry. I will feed you and then I would be honored if you would let me paint you."

She agreed and watched him walk away before she turned back to Lewis. For most of the night she forgot about killers and Mike. She decided to enjoy the rest of the weekend before she went back to that reality.

Chapter Thirteen

Gwen felt like a nervous teenager while she stood waiting for Yardley to answer the door.

This isn't a date, she chided herself. Was it? It was. He did ask her for dinner and a sitting. Maybe it wasn't. Did she want it to be a date? Were the feelings she had for him real feelings, or were they byproducts of magic and a shared stress? Was she reading too much into them meeting at his house versus meeting at hers as usual?

As her mind raced with questions she shifted her weight from one foot to the other. Now that she made herself so unsure about what the night was, she doubted her choice in clothes. She viewed it as a date or something special so she didn't wear her usual jeans and frumpy sweater. She wore thick leggings and a form fitting sweater dress. She even brushed on a little makeup and pulled her hair up. She wondered what he might think about her dressing up for dinner at his place. Could she blame it on the idea of being painted?

When the door opened, the time to change her mind about her clothes or being there slipped away.

Yardley gave her a warm smile. "Welcome Miss Hensley." He opened the door fully, took her coat, and hung it up. "Follow me, you are expected."

The palms of her hands sweated a little as they made their way through a few halls. She looked forward, too nervous to take in any of the paintings or carpets they passed. When the smell of something cooking started to fill the air, she assumed they neared either the dining room or kitchen.

Yardley paused and opened a door, "Sir, Miss Hensley has arrived."

She walked toward the opened door. The magical vibrations of Sebastian filled the air as they got closer.

When she saw him stood in the kitchen, an apron hung over his suit without a drop of food on it, looking more like a decoration, she felt her heart flutter. A much more intimate feeling replaced the normal calm feeling she usually got from seeing him.

"Thank you," Sebastian said, excusing Yardley. "Come in, I need your opinion."

"You're cooking?" she asked, still trying to get her nerves to behave. The proximity to him was making her flush.

"Of course, I don't have a cook, for obvious reasons." He stirred the soup, smiled, put the spoon down, and walked over to her with a smooth grace. His eyes danced across her body and back up to her eyes.

She looked away as the weight of his gaze touched her. She knew if he saw her eyes he would easily read what she thought, and see how he affected her.

When he stepped to her, he leaned slightly and kissed her on the top of the head. He breathed in the smell of roses and smiled. Tonight her scent mingled with thick desire and uncertainty. The predatory side of him drew to that strongly. He fought that, allowing the side of him that wanted to protect and pamper her to quiet his own desires.

After taking a few steps back he looked at her again. The dress she wore clung to curves that already caught his attention, even when she concealed them with jeans. Protect and pamper gave way to an image of pinning her against the counter and kissing her.

Those good intentions didn't last long, he thought. He drew in a sharp breath and closed his eyes. "You look particularly breathtaking tonight." Sebastian pulled his attention from her and turned to the soup. "Taste this, please. I don't cook often as I don't have need." He held out the spoon and stepped closer to her.

Gwen sipped a little of the soup and closed her eyes. "It is delicious. I love it." Saying those words with him standing so close seemed to make the space between them close in even more.

"Delicious," he said, his voice low and smooth as it seemed to dance across her skin.

It felt to her like a tether formed between them and pulled them together. She looked up at him, and let herself get lost in his eyes. She sensed he felt the same tug and struggled with words as she looked for an appropriate response.

Their faces stayed dangerously close. Before she realized it, she reached up with a finger and touched his jaw. Time suspended as the heat surged between them. It transferred from her one finger to his entire body. In that moment, she only thought of the way he felt. No magic, no voodoo, no death. She pulled her hand away. "Sebastian, I…"

He placed a finger on her lips.

She resisted the urge to kiss it.

The air grew thick with passion and the smell of potato soup.

He whispered her name, his breath on her lips.

She felt herself reaching out for him, her hands at his waist and then hesitated.

Some soup spilled on the burner and made a slight hissing sound.

"The soup," she managed to say.

The spell between them broke.

He let out a breath along with a sigh of disappointment that the moment ended so soon.

"Yes," he said, and stepped back. Tonight things were different, right from the start. He wondered if with all they still faced, he should even contemplate crossing lines they couldn't uncross. He didn't want his emotions to allow him to underestimate Fannie.

He poured out a bowl of soup and she followed him to a large dining room. He sat the bowl down at the head of the table and pulled her chair out. Once she settled in he sat next to her.

She felt a little odd eating while he watched but soon relaxed under his gaze. "I've never sat for a painting before. Will we be able to talk, and move around?"

"Of course. I have been memorizing your features since the first night I saw your beautiful face."

"I, that's good, I'm not very practiced at sitting still."

He laughed.

"Can I be serious?" she asked.

"If you must." He mocked a frown.

"Thank you for Thursday. Thank you for everything."

"Of course." His eyes twinkled as he studied her face.

She looked away from his gaze, toward her soup. "Is that why you look at me like that, with such attention? You are painting my features in your mind?"

"No."

She didn't need to ask any follow up questions, his tone and eyes told her everything she needed to know. She grew hyper aware they were alone, almost alone, at his house.

He embodied everything she craved in a man. She felt her stomach fluttering and sipped her water.

Relax, she told herself. It's Sebastian, the same comforting Sebastian that helped you cope with almost every night for the last week. It's also the same Sebastian you wanted to make out with in the kitchen.

He could feel her tension filling the air and tried for a warm smile, while switching to idle chatter about her room and how she settled in.

When she finished her soup, they walked together to the room they spent time in the other night.

Once she sat down he stood by an easel at the side of the lounger.

She relaxed as he told her to and tried not to think about how closely he looked at her.

"What are you knitting now?" He tried to shift things to a lighter frame for her. He didn't realize just how much them being alone and relatively stress free would ratchet up the intense desire between them.

"Squares for the blanket. Oh, I forgot to even mention it. Kathy and Mel wanted me to ask. Well, I want to ask too." She paused and her cheeks grew warm.

He laughed. "What are you asking, that you have failed to ask?"

"Do you want to go with me to the festival in a few weeks?"

"Are you asking me out, on a date?" he asked, in a playful tone she hadn't heard him use before.

"Yes, yes I am."

"I would go with you anywhere. Even the festival." He winked at her. His hand moved gracefully over the canvas as he sketched her.

"I thought you painted?"

"I do, I will. I'd like several sketches to work from."

She sat up and looked at him, her nose winkled. "What's wrong with the festival? It sounds quaint."

"It is that. I do try not to spend a good deal of time in town," he said, and paused. His eyes looked at her as he tried to gauge if they reached the moment to tell her why. It certainly needed to be addressed very soon. Before they could make any magical bond. Certainly before they made any other bonds. The thought of how close they came to crossing lines in the kitchen made up his mind. "I won't be able to join you for the daytime events." Once he said it he wished he could take it back. It needed said, needed addressed, but he wished it didn't.

Her eyes now studied him. She noticed he never came over in the day, even on the weekend. She felt his demeanor change, the uncertainty coming from him grew stronger, different. She knew they reached an important moment. The time to talk about the thing he hinted at before. His dark past, the thing she still didn't want to hear.

She stood up and walked over to him. On the canvas, he had made one large sketch of her lounged back and several of different angles of just her face. She looked from the canvas to him.

His eyes held a look of fear.

It was going to be bad, she thought. She reached up, and placed both hands on his face, one on each side. Her eyes searched his expression.

He felt her magic pulse out as a gentle vibration while she explored what he radiated.

She would sense it; he knew she would. He braced himself for the recoil when she did. He expected that, knew it would happen. He closed his eyes, not waiting to see the disgust in hers when she felt it.

She closed her eyes and stepped closer, the space between them filled with magic. She could feel the familiar vibration of his magic. She could feel his magnetism and the way it tugged her. She forced herself to ignore those things and tried to feel him on a deeper level.

She felt sadness, she remembered how that felt. Something colder, darker even than his engulfing sadness lingered under the surface. His heartbeat sounded steady and his breathing remained relaxed as she listened to every sound he made.

She breathed deeply. Sandalwood, animal, man, musk. She felt drawn to him again. Her hand traced his jaw. She stood on her toes and gently kissed his face. The way his skin felt against her lips sent waves of desire racing across her entire body.

Something else nudged at her senses. She ran her nose across his skin, and nuzzled. Her lips barely made contact. Under the surface something cold touched her aura. Deep, penetrating cold reached out from beneath his soothing warm buzz.

She stepped back when it clicked.

Death. Cold, death.

Her eyes shot opened and she sucked in a sharp breath.

The sound forced his eyes opened in time to see the look of horror on her face.

"You're dead? How are you dead, and warm and alive? What are you?"

She stepped back. She needed away, further away. She stumbled a little over her own feet as she walked backward, her eyes still locked on him.

Sebastian reeled from her look, and tone. Lewis knew her well, he horrified her. He could not deny the monster inside of him, regardless of the gray areas. There was no pretty way to spin it. Nothing he could say to make it anything else.

"I am both dead and alive."

"No," she said. She shook her head and took another step back toward the door. "I've seen the undead in New Orleans, they are not like you. They are not warm. They don't look like men. What are you?"

"I am what happens when a magical creature is turned by the undead."

"Sebastian, no," she said, her voice rang with sadness, fear, and disappointment.

The air in the room seemed too thick to breathe as he fought the urge to go to her and hold her. He couldn't give her the comfort she needed. "I'm sorry," was all he could say.

She continued to shake her head no, still not able to reconcile what she felt, what he said, and the man in front of her. Sebastian did not resemble the hideous, pasty, pale, monsters with black eyes, and cold, dead flesh. She thought about how easily he made himself appear older. Maybe he just glamoured a pretty face over his true vile form.

She shivered as she thought about how close they stood just moments ago. She could still feel his arms around her and the way his face felt against her lips.

He watched as her thoughts played out on her face. He could feel her disgust fill the air. He should have listened to Lewis. Sweet Gwen would not suffer a monster like him.

"Do you, must you feed?" she asked.

He turned his head and his mouth opened.

She knew the answer even before he managed to get yes to croak out. Her eyes filled with tears and her hand raised to her mouth. "I need to go, I need to go," she said through her hand.

His eyes closed and she turned.

She took the last few steps to the door. She ran into Yardley and paused, her eyes scanned him. He didn't pulse magic, didn't feel dead, but he looked at her knowingly.

"I need my coat, please, thank you." Her hands trembled.

"Miss." He walked her to the door and placed the coat on her arm. "He…" Yardley started to say, but she shook her head no.

"Thank you," she managed as she walked outside and raced to her truck. Once inside, she stared at his door through the windshield.

How could she not have known? How could Lewis have known and not told her?

Lewis, she thought. She started the truck and drove to her house. Inside she raced toward his presence.

"Did you have a good night?" Lewis asked. His smile faded when he saw her and felt her less than happy vibrations. "What did he do?"

"You. You knew he was a monster. A killer? How could you not have warned me? Lewis, what the hell, he's a, he's…" She started to cry and let Lewis take her in his arms.

"I'm sorry. I thought…"

"Thought what? That we would have parties with the townsfolk so he could drink them?"

Lewis held her tight against him. "He wouldn't…" he started but stopped. Did he really want to defend Sebastian? He did warn him not to tell her. Sebastian should have listened; he should have known his charming smile wouldn't be enough to erase that little tidbit.

He failed to mention to Sebastian that Gwen saw a vampire feeding before, and that it traumatized her. As he held her he wondered if he deliberately held that back?

No, he thought, *it just came to mind now*. Sebastian kept the secret for Lewis. He also gave him the charm to keep Fannie from seeing them. Plus, he offered his help to train Gwen.

"I don't think he would hurt anyone from town," he finally said.

"No? You think it's okay then? That he kills people, because we don't know them?" she asked, and pulled back.

"No, I did not say it was okay. I don't know what he has to do. I don't know what happens when a being like us gets, well, we don't die. So what he is should never be."

"But it is," she said, and started to cry again. "I can feel his, he is dead. I can feel it."

"Did he tell you what that means, for him?"

She pulled all the way out of his arms. "I didn't ask. Jesus, I don't want to play twenty questions with the monster. I thought we were having dinner. I thought I liked him. I have crap taste in men."

Lewis didn't know what to say. He didn't know if he should feel happy or not about the shift in her view of Sebastian. Part of him felt elated and yet he knew Sebastian would play a vital part in the answer to their problems.

Once the initial shock wore off, Gwen let Lewis rub her back while she watched the fire and thought about what happened. Things transformed so quickly. Hours ago she stood in his kitchen, seconds from kissing him. She wanted to, she wanted to explore the something they both felt between them.

Her mind flashed to the long-ago night in New Orleans when she found a monster, vampire, undead, whatever they called themselves, feeding on a screaming man.

She thought at first that she walked into a mugging and stepped forward with her pepper spray. When the thing turned around and looked at her with its bloody fanged mouth, beady black eyes, and oatmeal gray skin, she dropped her spray, summoned Lewis and ran as fast as she could.

It was the first and last vampire she had seen.

Until Sebastian.

Her eyes closed and an image of his handsome face appeared. She pictured the smile he always wore for her. She could see his deep blue eyes and their alive twinkle.

The image changed and she could see his smile fanged, dripping in blood.

She shuddered and leaned closer to Lewis.

As she drifted, he felt her dreams turn bad and shifted their direction to happier things before he got up and left.

He found Sebastian at the lake and they stood together in silence a moment.

"It would appear you were right about your witch," Sebastian said.

"Sadly."

"Is it?"

"For her it is. Give her time and space. It's what I found works best when I have disappointed her."

Sebastian sighed. "I do think this might be more complicated than disappointment."

"What are you? I know you are a vampire, but what does that even mean for us?"

"That is a good question, isn't it? A soulless undead creature with an undying soul. A magical creature with no true body, trapped in a body that will live forever."

"But you bear all the curses of the undead while still being alive and still having your magical gifts intact."

"Yes, that is as best as the enigma can be summed up. It is a punishment from the council. I suppose since my soul is eternal the virus couldn't kill it, and it couldn't destroy my form because it is held together by magic."

"But you feed. You told Gwen that?"

"I do, and she asked."

"Maybe I should mentor you on women. Honesty is not always the best policy."

Sebastian laughed. "Is that how you fill your dance card? With lies and whatever they want to hear?"

Lewis laughed as well. "It may be why my dance card is empty. You care for my witch more than you should. I don't like that, but I understand why."

Sebastian drew in a breath and sighed. "How is she?"

"Better than you perhaps."

"I need to get inside. I will still help however I can. I would hope you do not go back to Fannie, and let me know what you need or if you have any concerns training Gwen.

Lewis agreed and watched Sebastian walk away. He still wouldn't count him among his friends, but he did understand what he felt. He knew how it hurt to lose Gwen's affection.

He suffered it daily.

Chapter Fourteen

Gwen attempted to make her way through Sunday without thinking about Sebastian. She started by cleaning mindlessly. Even though it was a huge drafty house, she couldn't find enough dust or cobwebs to help her move past what she felt when she touched him. Her thoughts drifted from his sexy face and voice, to fangs and blood. She gave up on cleaning after she realized it didn't help.

She tracked down Lewis, who seemed happy to try and distract her. They practiced some new ways for her to see into the past, worked with stones, and even went outside to learn new ways to call up her elemental power. It didn't help.

As a last resort, she asked Lewis to show her what all still needed caulking or repaired on the house. She thought maybe harder manual labor would stop the images of Sebastian as a monster from settling into her mind.

Lewis did his best to pull her back when her thoughts veered off. He could see that no matter what they did, she could not stop thinking about it, him, the monster next door.

After fighting off dark thoughts all day, she took comfort that with Monday came deeper things to think about. Regardless of the state of her personal life she needed to focus on justice for Lizzy, and William if it turned out as she suspected.

The drive to the prison felt longer than it should have as she fought back thoughts of Sebastian, the monster inside of him, what it meant, and why she still felt so drawn to him. When she finally arrived, her eyes drew to the high fence lined with barbed wire while she pulled into the drive leading up to the prison. Her mind wandered to the kinds of people it kept inside. People who killed innocent police officers.

Stopping at what she assumed would be the first of several check points, she showed the man who stood in a small booth all her paperwork. He looked it over with the same unemotional face she disliked on Curtis. After a few minutes, he instructed her on where to park.

She made her way through a few more stops. They searched her at all of them, she left belongings behind at a few of them. When she made it to the little room where the meeting took place, she felt relieved.

The room reminded her of a school cafeteria, with white laminate flooring and white industrial looking walls that held no art. The hard, plastic chairs shared the same school look.

She stood back and looked at the clear window with the gray metal circle in it. She wondered if Lewis and Curtis were right and she didn't belong there. The wall separating them stood there because the prison housed convicted killers, just like the one who she intended to sit across from.

What did she hope to gain? They charged Mike and no one else saw a connection between William and Lizzy's deaths. She knew she wanted a family so badly she would grasp at anything to get to know them better.

She watched the second hand jerk forward on the clock on the wall and wrung her hands together. How would she react seeing the face of the man who killed her grandfather? She wondered why the man even agreed to see her; the liaison explained to her he could have refused.

Even though she watched the clock, she didn't pay attention to the time. She didn't know how long she waited before a tall thin man, who looked pale and hard aged, walked over and took a seat behind the glass. Her heart raced and her throat went dry.

He looked like a gentle old man. His solid gray hair matched his thick bushy eyebrows. Deep wrinkles lined his face. He watched her walk over with yellowed, bloodshot green eyes, and chewed on the side of his mouth.

She wondered if he could see her hands shake, or tell that she could drop any second from her anxiety. She sat down across from him and summoned a little magic to pull herself together. "Thank you for seeing me." She folded her hands in her lap and looked him in the eyes.

He had a softness about him, and as she probed him with her senses she felt a kind soul. If she could feel that from him maybe she couldn't trust her judgment of Mike too.

Sebastian told her that instincts would be her best guide on people. He was probably the best example of why she couldn't trust her instincts.

He nodded, and she thought she saw a small smile start to form. He looked over his shoulder to make sure no one listened.

She assumed someone always did.

"I'm really sorry what happened to your grandpa Miss," he said.

His eyes told her with their softness he meant what he said.

Again, she let herself reach out with a touch of magic to try to get a read on him. She picked up sadness and a little fear, which she thought seemed strange. Maybe someone there harassed him. She imagined prison as a pretty scary place on the other side of the window.

She puzzled over his wording and the way he disconnected himself from the crime. She knew he did recant his confession.

"I, was hoping…" She took a deep breath. What did she want to ask? "Did you know him?"

The man nodded his head yes.

She swallowed. Everyone made it sound like a random accident. That sounded wrong to her from the start. It seemed likely in a small town everyone would know a local junkie. Especially the police.

"He was good to me," he added, and frowned.

"How so?"

"Always had blankets and hot food. I never meant… I never would…" He paused as he looked around again and then focused his attention back to her. "I'm sorry about what happened to him."

"He was kind to you? It was an accident?"

The man pursed his lips. "I'm really sorry."

She felt more fear radiating from him and noticed he started to fidget. "Did you know Lizzy?"

He nodded yes. "She's kind too, like him."

"She's passed," Gwen said, and watched his eyes sadden.

He cut his eyes to the side and then frowned.

"Were you alone that night?"

His eyes got big as saucers. "I'm sorry what happened to your lovely family, Miss."

"Someone else had the gun?"

At that suggestion he started to shift in his seat. He leaned in to the little metal speaker opening. "Them questions gonna get you or me hurt, Miss," he spoke barely above a whisper.

Gwen sat up shocked and took in a breath. "By who?"

"Can't say Miss, don't ask anymore. Forgive me my part if you can."

"Part, wait," she said, as he started to stand. She thought quickly. Mike was too young to have been there in an active role. Who else could be the connection? "Trisha?"

He just shook his head no and started to walk away.

"Who can I ask?" she asked loudly.

He took a few steps back. "The shelter," he said, and then walked away.

She paced the few minutes it took for the guard to open the door and walk her out. As they walked and she made her way through the various points, her mind raced over who could have been there that night, and also still be around. Pretty much everyone. No one left town.

The sweet ladies she met didn't seem like the type to shoot William and somehow frame or get that Junkie to take the fall. She needed to find out more about him. Maybe she missed a connection, some friends, school mates? Anything. A shelter. She could dig around and try to find some sort of local shelter.

She couldn't see a link to Mike and both murders due to his age. She didn't even consider Trisha because she would have admitted it just to get her son released. No doubt about that.

While Gwen visited inside the prison the weather outside turned bad, again. More snow. She looked at the clock when she got in the truck. It gave her some comfort that enough time remained to get home before the sun went down. She did not want to drive in the snow after dark. The prison sat isolated from towns in the middle of nowhere as she assumed most prisons did, since no one wanted to see that in their backyard. Since the roads probably remained unsalted, before she started the truck she made a small request to whomever might care, that not too much snow already did or would fall before she got back to the main, more used roads.

It took her longer than usual to get back to town. She pulled into Mel's to grab something to eat. Just enough people filled the place to ease her lonely feeling. She didn't want to eat alone. At least she thought she didn't want to eat alone until Curtis sat down at the table across from her.

Mel walked over and they both ordered the shepherd's pie special of the day. As they waited for their food he looked at her with his blank eyes.

"Did you enjoy your visit?" he asked, and then sipped his coffee.

Gwen tilted her head. "I... How did you know where I have been?"

"I thought we agreed your nerves weren't up to such things. I was just wondering how you are holding up."

Sensing compassion in his words, she sighed and decided to ask him some of her hundred questions. "It was okay, I guess. He seemed normal. I mean, even timid."

"Psychopaths can seem as normal as you and I."

She heard that somewhere before. "Do you think he could have had help?"

"Help? It only takes one crazy to pull a trigger, Miss."

"Gwen, Curtis, it's just Gwen."

"What I think, Gwen, is that you lost your family and want a reason. Sometimes the only reason is that life is awful and people do things that don't make sense."

Mel sat their plates down and patted Gwen on the back while she looked at Curtis with a huge smile. "Holler if you need anything else, darling."

Gwen looked from him to her. Mel and Curtis? A smile formed at the thought of the odd couple they would make.

"I guess. Of course, you are right. You would know more about people like that than I would. It just seems. Well Mike and him, they just both seem so normal. Harmless even." She thought about her judgment and if it could even be trusted anymore. She felt like killers were normal, monsters were desirable, and lawmen, like Curtis, were untrustworthy.

Instincts indeed, she thought.

She watched his face soften as he ate and she also sunk into the delicious warming pie. "Is there a shelter of some sort here?"

"No, not in town."

"Was there?"

His eyes narrowed. "No, not a proper shelter, why?"

She wondered if she should even tell him why, when she considered how he felt about her worrying her pretty little head over things. "Oh, I was wondering since..." she started and paused.

"He, Lenny, lived in the church, Miss Gwen, if you must know. Your grandfather, William, was a donor and often worked there making repairs."

"Was Father George there then?"

He nodded, the cold look returned to his eyes again.

Gwen decided not to press him anymore, she could ask Father George anything else she needed to know. "I'm looking forward to the festival," she said, hoping to switch to something that would take the cold look out of his eyes.

He looked to the right, his eyes following someone and then back to his plate. "That's good. Should be fun." He took another bite as his eyes drifted over her shoulder.

"Should be, I hear they have blue and pink cows." She tested to see how much he paid attention to what she said.

"Yes, lovely," he said, and then looked back to see her smiling at him. He furrowed his brows. "Yes?"

She turned her head to see in the direction he looked.

Mel stood talking with a customer.

When she looked back she thought she saw a hint of a blush on his cheeks. She didn't bother trying to engage him anymore as they ate. She watched the way his eyes seemed to follow everyone in the room as they moved.

Gwen imagined it would be hard to live with a police officer if they always did that. She almost giggled as she imagined doing simple things like brushing your teeth with cold eyes watching you, judging how you push the paste up in the tube, or watching to make sure you put the cap back on.

After they ate he walked out with her and stood at her truck. His arm leaned on her opened window. "I know it's hard not to have anyone waiting at home, no one to call family." He gave her his card again. "I'm always up."

"Curtis, do you really think Mike killed Lizzy?"

"I really do, and I wish you would leave it at that. Let me do my job and lock him away for good. For her and you."

As she watched him walk away she wondered what sort of man hid under his cold exterior. Most of the time he seemed emotionless and disconnected as she assumed his job demanded, but a few times he seemed almost like he tried to reach out for anyone who might notice.

She started her truck and headed toward the church. The late service would have just ended and she imagined Father George took time to chat with stragglers before he shut things down.

As she drove her mind drifted to Sebastian. She wondered again how she could have missed that about him, and if she really had any instincts for people at all. Not that he was a person. Not in any sense of the word. A shiver ran over her as she thought about the last night they spent together. The way he felt when they stood in his kitchen. She could almost smell his scent, and feel his pull.

"Way to torture yourself, Gwen," she muttered to herself. Maybe she fell for her own familiar. Maybe she started to fall for a retired wolf familiar, but she would never fall for him now that she knew he was the undead.

How could Lizzy know and let him in her home? Around her daughter? Her pregnant daughter? He blessed her room. How can a cursed creature bless anything? What did it mean that she found comfort in the arms of such a creature? Maybe she should have the Father pray for her soul. Should she get him to bless her? Give her a cross? Some holy water? Would she need garlic? She didn't sense him following her, and deep down she didn't think he would hurt her, not physically.

Chapter Fifteen

Gwen listened to the sound of crunching snow under her feet as she walked across the parking lot at the church. She liked the natural sound, much the way she liked to walk in leaves in the winter down south.

She thought the church looked big for such a small town, especially since she saw several more. By her math, the town had one church for every ten people.

The lights glowed warmly through the stained-glass windows of the brick building. She noticed one of the doors sat slightly ajar as she made her way up the four steps. Her hands held the rail in case there was any ice on the steps.

She pulled the door shut behind her and walked deeper into the warmth of the room. The size of the room with its high ceiling and tall windows running down both sides made her feel minute. She walked between the two aisles of pews on either side, noticing a random hymn book or bible laying out.

The soft carpet made her steps silent. As she neared the front she saw the confessional and looked closely at the details of statues at the front of the room.

"Can I help you?" a man said, startling her.

She turned, expecting to see Father George, but instead saw a disheveled man with a rag in his hand. She took a step back and tried for a smile as she looked at him.

The tall, lanky man looked unfed and smelled unbathed. His dark blonde hair pointed in a hundred directions as if he just rolled out of bed. He watched her with tired looking brown eyes and gave her a gaped smile filled with crooked teeth that leaned into the gaps.

"I'm here to see Father George." She tried not to make any sudden moves as her mind went back to the way she found the door cracked open. She turned to plan her easiest escape when she saw Father George walking up.

"Gwen, child, how are you?" the Father said.

She felt herself washed with relief at feeling that he didn't seem to think the dirty man posed any danger. "I'm good, thank you."

"Finish up Jim," the Father said.

The man walked away, carelessly wiping his rag on random surfaces and putting away bibles.

Gwen felt a little flush of embarrassment at how quickly she judged the man to be some sort of robber, or worse. Maybe she didn't have the nerves to think about murderers as Curtis suggested.

"Did you need to confess, or pray?" he asked.

"Oh no, nothing like that. I was hoping we might talk. Or set a time to talk later if you are busy."

"I'm never too busy to talk. I missed seeing you in service," he said.

She looked down and back up. "I'm sorry. I..."

He laughed. "Don't you go making excuses, God knows your heart. What burdens your mind?"

They walked together to an office. He left the door opened and offered her a seat.

She sat down and he asked her again to tell him about her troubles.

"My family. I mean Lizzy and William, they volunteered here?"

"Yes, they both did. Kind souls." He watched her more closely.

"What did William do?"

"Are you feeling alone? Did you want to pray for comfort?"

She shook her head. "I'm just trying to piece things together, I talked with... Well I mean to say, I went to see Lenny, to try and find some peace and he mentioned here, the shelter."

The Father frowned and leaned forward. "I've been to see him as well. Many times. His heart is heavy with guilt."

"Did you know that he knew William? Before he, the, accident, shooting?"

He nodded. "Yes, very well. It shocked us, especially us at the shelter. William had sort of taken a shine to helping Lenny."

"Helping him how? Why?"

"Lenny had drug problems as you might imagine from what you have heard I am sure. Many of the men at the shelter did. We only kept about five men at any time. It was just beds in the basement really. It's a soup kitchen now. After William, the city decided not to allow anyone to stay here like that. I didn't fight it. Lizzy was beside herself with grief and I thought it best as well."

She rubbed her hands together. "What did William do with Lenny?"

"Some nights he would fetch him for dinner at Mel's, even take him in the patrol car too. We thought he had cleaned up."

"So, that night, it was a relapse?"

"From what I gather. I leave those dealings to lawyers and the like. I only worry for his soul."

"Why do you think William picked him to focus on like that?"

"Oh, that was easy to figure out. They were both orphans. From the same orphanage in fact. I shouldn't say much though. Lizzy and William kept that closely guarded."

Gwen sat back in her chair. "Do you imagine that might be why Lizzy didn't want Mike asking family questions?"

He shook his head. "I wouldn't know anything about that. I did hear Mike is being charged."

She pursed her lips together. "Do you know the orphanage?"

"Sure, sure, let me write that down. Of course, you know now it is just a church. They don't take children anymore, too many regulations." He wrote down a name and shuffled a few things, finding an old-style Rolodex under a stack of papers, and then he scribbled down a number for her. "It's a fair way off, take you the better part of the day as it is east of Wichita."

Gwen didn't know the area or how long it would take to get there. She knew she would find out. "Is there anyone else who was at the shelter that is still in town?"

"No, most moved to other shelters in the bigger cities."

"What about volunteers?"

"I think every able-bodied soul in town helped in any way they could."

Gwen nodded. "Of course, was there anyone else involved like William?"

"All William's men did maintenance things around here."

They talked a little more. Before she left, she wondered again if she needed a blessed something, but pushed aside her fears of Sebastian. She knew her fears about him revolved around how much she wanted to run back to his arms.

On the way home she puzzled over the new information. William grew up an orphan, like she did after Winnie died. It made her clingier to people she considered friends. Did it make him vulnerable to Lenny who used him to get on his feet again? That made it seem even more tragic. Could Lenny have stumbled into it? Wrong time, wrong place? Could the person who did kill him know about them being together and use it as a cover? Would the orphanage hold anything useful? She sucked a breath in when she thought about the family who left him there.

She could have family after all.

When she got home she couldn't decide what she wanted to do first. Call the church, or pack.

"Where are you going?" Lewis watched her throw things haphazardly in a suitcase.

She explained to him about her visit at the prison and her talk with the Father.

"I still don't see how this will help anything." As soon as he said it, he realized if she chased down leads on that side of the family, she wouldn't have time to chase down answers to Lizzy's past and Fannie.

"I need to do this. I could have family left. Maybe William had brothers or sisters."

"I will go with you. Whatever you need."

She stopped what she was doing and looked at him with serious eyes. "Can I make people do things?"

"No, even if you could, no."

"Can you? I mean if they won't give me the information I need, is there anything we can do?" She narrowed her eyes at him.

"Not like that, no. We don't play games with people's freewill, ever. We can be sneaky, distract them, raid files, and break laws, but we will not play with their minds."

She agreed. She did not want to sacrifice their morals. She kept packing, entered the address in her GPS, and they headed out. As they passed the drive to Sebastian's house Lewis sensed her tense up and saw her face reflect the sadness she felt.

"Did you want to talk about him?" Lewis asked, still not one-hundred percent sure how he felt about that. While he enjoyed not having him around, he didn't like to see her upset. He also didn't like that it complicated the help Sebastian offered them both.

She looked at the road ahead. "Maybe, it's a long drive, but I don't know what there is to be said. He kills people."

"Yes, maybe he found another way. He doesn't suffer the monstrous curse the way other vampires do."

"He said he fed, Lewis, that means he kills people. I'm not sure how a pretty face and warm blood would make that any better."

Lewis drew in a breath and exhaled loudly. Sebastian needed to have some good answers for her, or he didn't see a path back to even a superficial friendship.

The road flew by and minutes morphed into hours. When they neared the area, he talked her into getting a few hours of rest, even though the drive already took the better part of the night. They rented a room at the first place that didn't look like they would get mugged.

As soon as they walked inside, she started the heater and lay down. "Do you think he killed his last witch? Drank her blood?"

Lewis stroked her hair. "I wouldn't know. I know she died. I know what he is. But I also know whatever happened haunts him, so it could well be the case. You would have to ask him."

"I'll pass." She knew her words held no truth. She needed to know. Did he kill his own witch? Could the dark sadness that she felt in him be guilt or remorse? Did soulless monsters like Sebastian feel? With her eyes closed, she pondered how she felt about the monster who she could smell if she thought about it, and who she longed to feel close again.

Lewis went outside and perched where he could watch the door. He thought about how things ended up, glad she latched onto finding out if William had any family. It would more than likely occupy a good deal of time and energy. He needed time. He considered if he could do it without Sebastian. If not, he would have to help her see another side of the beast, a side he couldn't see himself.

There was something between Gwen and Sebastian, something he felt every time they shared the same space. Did he really want to watch that unfold? No. He knew he didn't. Gwen loved as fiercely as a familiar did. If Sebastian ever did win her love, he knew it would be forever. Forever and heartbreaking to witness. She deserved that kind of love, but not from a monster.

Inside the room, Gwen slept deeply.

Gwen stretched out on the lounger in a clingy red dress with a deep v-neckline. The fire raged behind Sebastian as he painted her. She watched his hand make quick flashes across the canvas.

Desire rose everywhere he caressed her with the intensity of his gaze.

She laid her head back and moaned softly, enjoying the sensations he sent out. She felt him getting closer. His heat and his scent filled her space. She opened her eyes to see him stood just beside her. His look passed desire as it filled with need.

She reached out, touched his fingers and sent a wave of pleasure racing from his fingers across his body. He growled. The low animal sound sent a quake of need racing across her.

He knelt on the lounger over her and nuzzled her ear, breathing in the scent of roses from her hair. The feeling of his breaths on her neck sent her need to touch and taste him to a level she could not deny.

Her hands ran through his hair and tugged at him as she pulled his face to meet hers. His lips hovered inches from her lips. She swallowed, her mouth hot and dry from desire. She heard herself make a slight moan, and the word please escaped her lips. She needed to feel his lips on hers, wanted it more than she ever wanted anything.

When his lips pressed to hers, they parted slightly. He nibbled gently and explored with the tip of his tongue. His hand slid up the side of her neck. It rested gently behind her head as he pulled her into a deep kiss that reached her soul.

When he pulled back, she stared breathlessly into his eyes. The desire mingled with a questioning look. A question. He asked her something. She focused on his voice and watched his mouth.

"Can you love me?" he asked. His smile showed fangs. His eyes turned from blue to black.

Her desire left. The room suddenly felt cold. His hands felt cold and heavy, dead. His black empty eyes looked at her with a different kind of hunger.

"Love me," the monster demanded.

She backed off the lounger and scrambled to her feet. "No, no, Sebastian."

Blood pooled from his mouth, dripping onto his white shirt, soaking it a deep burgundy.

She screamed.

L ewis walked in, having sensed her distress from outside.

Sweat covered her and her head tossed from side to side. She muttered, 'no, Sebastian, no.'

He frowned and woke her by gently rubbing her face.

She sat up, leaned into his arms, and cried.

Chapter Sixteen

Gwen had no real idea what to expect as she walked up the narrow cement sidewalk to what looked more like an office building rather than a church. The whole place looked very institutional. Several buildings ran off the back of the main one in the other direction. She didn't see remnants of playgrounds or anything that looked even remotely inviting. It reminded her more of a school than a religious center.

Lewis walked beside her. His eyes searched the grounds while he took in the complex as well. It also seemed sterile to him, but he based that on the vibrations of the place, rather than the superficial appearance. An efficient coldness emanated from the ground itself.

Gwen called just before they left the hotel and arranged to meet with one of the sisters in ten minutes to talk about the old orphanage records. When she explained her research of her family related to a personal tragedy, the woman quickly agreed to help. While she didn't like playing the sympathy card, she would do it to get the information.

One of the two doors at the front hung opened. Gwen stepped inside and said hello loudly in effort not to startle anyone. A clean lemon scent hung in the air. The room looked like a normal reception area with two desks.

A plain but pretty, middle-aged woman who sat at the closest desk looked up and smiled at them.

"Gwen?" she asked. When Gwen nodded, she added, "I'm sister Jane, we spoke on the phone."

"Thank you so much for seeing me." Gwen shook the hand the woman offered when she stood, and introduced Lewis.

They followed her down a long white hall, which had blank walls except for a single simple wooden cross. The white laminate tile floors added to the sterile impression Gwen felt when they walked up.

When they entered in another room, the woman flipped on the lights.

Gwen looked around to see several filing cabinets along one wall, and a simple table with a chair on the other.

"I went by the age you gave me for your grandfather, and looked in a fifteen-year time frame. We had a lot of boys. I narrowed it down to those of Caucasian descent. I would have narrowed it down more but I didn't have time." The sister pulled out the chair, and put her hand on a stack of folders. "You are welcome to browse and take notes, but I must ask that all the originals stay here." Her words and face both held a sweet but firm demeanor.

Gwen thanked her, and the sister left her and Lewis alone in the room with the door opened, to start sorting the pile, looking for clues. A lot of the files named the adoptive parents but none listed Hensley. Gwen set those aside.

Lewis wrote down the names in case everything else ended up a dead end.

She realized Hensley could be just a name William took later on.

"How many are you down to now?" Lewis asked. He gently rubbed her shoulders as he sensed her get a little frustrated.

"I've narrowed it to six that look good. Three stayed in the Kansas area, which may or may not mean anything. Since I can't find anything anywhere about the Hensley name I may really need to look at them all. I don't know," she said and sighed.

"I've written them all down. Why don't you take pictures of them with your phone and we can look at each one in more detail at home." Lewis knew the longer she dug into who adopted William, the longer she would stay away from tracking things from Lizzy to Fannie.

She agreed and they took pictures of potentially helpful pages from each file. Most of the files didn't have a whole lot, with the exception of a set of brothers who came to the orphanage after a bloody tragedy.

"Lewis, look at this." She reached out and handed him the newspaper clipping on two young boys.

They stood with a police officer, covered in blood. The headline read, 'tragedy in suburbia' with the byline 'two local boys escape father's rampage by hiding under their dead mother for hours.'

Lewis frowned and handed it back to her.

She looked at it a moment longer before taking a picture.

"Something about this catches my attention," she said.

"Of course it does. It's awful."

"No, my gut says to start here," she said, still looking at the boys in the picture. They both wore such empty, sad looks on their faces.

Lewis shook his head. "I certainly hope not."

After looking through the clippings about the boys a little more, she moved on to the last few files. Once done, she made sure to put everything back neatly like when they started.

They walked out and found the sister at her desk.

"Can I ask you about one more time frame?" Gwen hoped her friendly smile would persuade her.

The nun gave her a puzzled look and said nothing as she waited for Gwen to continue.

"It seems the man that killed my grandfather also was here, and that was why they became so close."

The lady looked at her, considering what she asked. "Do you know his name? Best I can do is tell you if we had him. I can't share personal information that isn't related to your family."

Gwen didn't want to point out she just gave her a stack of files and all but one would end up being a stranger, so instead she smiled and agreed.

Lenny didn't have a secret past or closed adoption. She confirmed that Father George remembered correctly and Lenny grew up there.

On the drive home they talked a little about possible boys from the files. They both knew that it would all come down to more research and time.

Before they got home, Gwen stopped and picked up a pizza. She really wanted to be able to sit down and get straight to looking up things.

They arrived at her cold, dark house and Lewis set to making a fire while Gwen started coffee to go with her pizza.

She sat eating a piece while her laptop started and then she uploaded all the pictures from her phone. "So, who does your gut say to start with?" she asked Lewis, who sat perched behind her.

He found he needed a little extra magic to keep Fannie at bay since he'd held his man form so long. He suggested a little boy named Patrick, even though he felt she might have been drawn to those other boys for a reason. He didn't want her digging into something awful just yet, regardless of who they turned out to be.

She started with Patrick; a little boy adopted by an unidentified couple from Georgia. The file gave the boy's birth name and that ended up a dead end. It also gave the parents' first names. After deep digging she found no links to him or his birth parents. There had been no re-connection.

"How am I even going to start?" she asked out loud, frustrated.

"Detective? You have the resources to hire a private investigator. They would have access to places on the internet and things like that, we wouldn't."

"Lewis," she said, and reached out petting him. "You, I adore." Her smile faded.

"What, my witch? That was the shortest-lived celebration I have ever seen."

"I never gave Sebastian the blank check to transfer funds. I don't want to see him again. Not right now. Maybe not ever."

"Ever? Shouldn't you at least let him explain to you what he is?"

She shook her head. "He kills people. That is all I need to know."

"And you need him to have a check now so that you can access your funds?"

"I guess I could take one tomorrow, to Yardley. He seemed harmless." She sighed. If she called Sebastian, he would have the resources from the fund he set up for her.

"You could call. If you don't want to see him, I am sure he will respect that." Lewis couldn't believe he heard himself suggest that. A small part of him still wanted her to decide Sebastian was okay. The part Fannie tugged. He needed to answer her call and needed Sebastian to be there with Gwen, just in case. Of course, he needed to see Sebastian again himself because the pull kept getting stronger. Soon she might just summon him away. "I can take it, if you really don't want to talk to him."

"You would do that? You don't even like him."

"No, but I love you, and if you need me to talk with him for you, I will."

"No, Lewis, we are not five. I will call and arrange to handle it thorough Yardley."

Once she decided to call, Lewis gave her privacy. He flew outside to try to ground himself a little better. How strong the pull felt worried him and he wondered what Fannie wanted so urgently.

Gwen didn't know what she expected to feel, but when she heard that smooth Mediterranean hello, mingled with sadness, she almost hung up. Her own hello sounded far away and she heard herself talking as if she felt much more in control than she actually did.

She told him about the orphanage and her plan to hire a detective to chase down the leads. Then she explained that she forgot to give him the check and needed some of the disposable funds to get started.

"I can have that ready for you by the time you get here if you would like," he said, even though he already knew she would not come over. He heard that much in the unspoken words and tone of her voice. It was clear she still struggled with what he was.

"I will be by first thing in the morning if that is okay. I can grab it on my way to meet with an investigator."

"Of course. Can I do anything else for you?" he asked.

She thought she heard a crack in his voice and felt herself fight the urge to comfort him. Comfort him from what? Her own disgust at what he was? How do you comfort a creature like that? Ever since she arrived in town, he provided her with a soft landing from every hardship thrown at her, even from Lewis.

She felt awful that rather than pay him back the kindness, she caused him more sadness. She argued with her own mind between wanting to make this better and wanting to pretend she never laid eyes on his cursed face.

"Gwen?"

"I'm sorry, Sebastian, I can't do this right now," she said. "I will be by in the morning. Thank you." Her hand trembled as she hung up the phone.

The house felt like the walls were going to come in around her and she walked outside, where she saw Lewis on the porch railing.

"Is all well, my witch?" he asked, even though he could see the answer on her face.

"No, I don't even know what I am feeling. Confused."

"Can I help?"

"Why did you change your opinion of him so quickly?" Her voice sounded firm and pulled together, much to her surprise.

The question threw him off and made him glad he already held his raven form. He could go the Sebastian honesty route, tell her about Fannie and the charm Sebastian made, and get similar results, but he didn't want to go down that path. "Things were not as black and white as I first assumed."

"You think I…" She paused. "I don't even know what I want to know. I'm going for a walk."

"Walk? It's freezing out here."

107

"I need to think. I'll summon a fire if it gets cold."

"Gwen, really, that's reckless."

"It's practice."

"Oh, practice for what? For the coming ice age? Besides that, you never learned fire yet."

"Don't be a smart ass," she said, and walked away.

Lewis gave her the space she needed. He needed some himself. Later he would go talk to Sebastian and let him know he still struggled. Maybe he could rework a few things into the charm for added protection.

Gwen walked into the cold night. She listened to the sound of the snow under her feet, felt the air sting her face, and smelled the minty cold scent carried on the frozen wind. She didn't pay attention where her steps took her. She ended up on a small, uneven stone path. The overgrown roots pushed the stones at awkward angles.

The cold air sunk through her coat, into her clothes, and reached her skin. She could feel cold from the inside out. Her soul felt alone and as dark as the night sky. Even the small quarter moon seemed to refuse to shine on her.

At the end of the path she stopped at a small well. It rose about calf high and she carefully sat on the rim. She ran her fingers along the edge. She wondered if Lizzy ever went there, or who sat there before her? Had they made wishes? Were they answered?

It seemed like every answer she uncovered led to five more questions. The spinning in her mind got faster, even as she tried to put her feet down. She looked down the well and saw blackness. She wondered how deep it sank, and if any water remained at the bottom. She wondered about those things because they were easier than wondering about Lizzy, William, Fannie, Lewis, and Sebastian.

Sebastian, it always came back to that. He stayed at the center of everything. He gave her most of the answers she gained about Lizzy and probably held more answers, answers she may not want. Answers to deeper questions about life, death, and sadness. Why did Lizzy trust him close to her family that she loved so dearly?

The better question, the question still dancing in the back of her mind, was why did she still want to see him again? She did want to see him again. Wanted to see his eyes, feel his warmth and get lost in his strong, comforting arms. What did that mean? A witch who craved the touch of a monster. Could something like him even love anymore? What was it in his eyes when he looked at her?

The coldness started to make her stiff and shivery, so she used the things Lewis taught her to manipulate some downed branches into a small pile on the stones beside her. She enjoyed the way the magic felt as it raced through her. It surprised her how easily she pulled fire from nothing. The branches exploded into bright white flames that warmed the area.

S ebastian and Lewis stood just outside of Sebastian's house. The explosion of magic stopped their talk about the best way to proceed with Fannie.

"What is she doing now?" Lewis said, frustrated. "She's in the woods alone. God knows what she'll attract. Help me get to her."

"It's magnificent." Sebastian shifted and followed her scent, with Lewis flying overhead. He found her trail easily. Her magical vibration tugged him toward her. Just at the edge of an opening he saw the fire. He knew the spot, the old wishing well. He felt her and knew she felt him too.

Lewis circled overhead, not wanting to interrupt unless they needed him.

Gwen looked to the woods and saw the wolf watching her. The wolf bore beautiful markings in its deep colors. The unmistakable blue eyes seemed so full of life. She felt drawn to him, she wanted to walk over and stroke his fur. The need to connect with him frightened her.

In the back of her mind she sensed Lewis. Were they still working together for her?

Her eyes glanced up to see him as a black spot in the sky.

She imagined calling up the fire prompted them to both come and protect her from any danger. Didn't Lewis think Sebastian posed a threat? Did she? No. She didn't feel that from him. She never had.

He sat as still as the air that seemed to stop while it waited with him for her to decide how this ended.

Her eyes locked on his and she made a few steps toward him.

He stayed perfectly still as he watched her movements.

She stopped after just a few steps. She tried to imagine what it meant that the beautiful man, beast, and monster were the same creature. She imagined he felt her hesitation, just as she felt his sadness deepening with each passing second. Had he thought she would easily accept his dual nature?

Her mouth opened and she watched the cloud of air that carried her words. "We need to talk."

Her words danced like music in the air as he shifted to a man and stood watching her.

She turned and walked back to the fire. She sat on the edge of the well again. She felt him behind her. "Was this a wishing well?"

"It is." He fought the need to hold her and take away her unease.

"I wouldn't even know what to wish for anymore." She turned to him with tears in her eyes.

"I do." He stepped a little closer.

"No, don't. I need to know more about you. It can't be like it was. I can't even be here like this with you right now. It feels, different." She stood and walked to the fire.

"I'm sorry, Gwen."

"Sorry for what?"

"That I made you feel anything unpleasant."

The hurt on his face sent her mind to that confused place where she wanted to run away from him and to his arms all at the same time.

"What can I do?" he asked.

"We need to talk about what you are. What you really are. But not now. Sebastian, I can't yet. I still feel too raw looking at you."

"When you are ready. I should have stayed at home." He turned to leave.

She wanted to run after him more than she imagined she would. Instead, she called to Lewis and they cleared the area of her magic, before walking home.

She dreamed of Sebastian again.

Chapter Seventeen

Gwen held her breath as she waited for Yardley to return. He left her in the study again, where she would be warm.

She didn't sit in the chair, she remembered what happened last time and could already smell and feel Sebastian in the air. She didn't want the rush of his scent that she knew would come from the fabric where he must have spent so much time.

Every few seconds that passed she considered leaving a note, leaving a message, telling him she missed him and that they needed to have that talk, but each time she pushed it away, remembering the image of the vampire feeding in New Orleans.

She was relieved and grateful her resistance held out when Yardley came in with papers, a checkbook, and a debit card.

"It's not as you might think," he said, his voice sounding somber.

"Thank you for the help with this," she said, ignoring the conversation he wanted to have. For all she knew he was some sort of slave to Sebastian's blood. She didn't know how things like that worked but in movies they, vampires, could make people do things, and always had a day servant who was somehow enslaved to them. "I should go. I have an appointment to keep. Tell him. Tell him thank you."

"Yes Miss," he said, and then turned, leading her out.

The sadness she felt when the door closed surprised her, and again she considered calling and leaving him a message. She fought that urge all the way to Mel's diner.

Mel had a happy greeting for her and was fast to have french toast and coffee ready, since the morning rush had ebbed.

Gwen almost frowned when she saw Curtis walk in, but managed to get her facial expression in control. She even managed a smile when he sat down across from her.

"How are you, Miss Hensley?" he asked, and nodded to Mel who hurried over to double check he wanted his usual.

"Good. How about you?" Gwen asked, before taking another bite. She was mulling over if she wanted to even mention her appointment.

"Been a quiet day so far." His eyes scanned the room, stopping on the few faces of people eating with them. "Thank you love," he said, when Mel sat his plate and coffee down.

She smiled at him and walked away to tend to other customers.

Gwen tried several times to make idle chatter but got the impression she bored him, and began to wonder why he always sat with her if he didn't want to talk to her.

She finished her food and coffee and left a tip under her cup. "I should go, I have an appointment," she said, and felt her breath suck in. She really needed more practice on her thought to speech filter.

"Oh, getting your nails done," he said, his tone flat as if he assumed that was the extent of appointments she could possibly have.

She caught herself before she wrinkled her nose. "I have family business to tend to." She gathered her purse. "Thank you for joining me for breakfast." She wasn't sure which of them found it harder to be polite, him because he was just naturally rude, or her because she found him naturally rude.

"Family business?" He gave her his full attention.

"Oh, I'm just working on a family tree is all." It wasn't entirely a lie. She was tracking down William and his birth parents, that was like making a family tree.

His look said he wasn't buying it. He ran his tongue over his teeth and made a sucking sound that merited a look of disapproval, so she gave him one. She could feel his eyes on her as she paid and left.

The detective she found was a few towns over, but not too terribly far. Since she wasn't sure how long the ride would take, she allowed a little extra time and arrived about fifteen minutes early. The office was in a three-story brick building that looked no different to any other building on the street. There were no signs for the detective on the outside, just a small sign that said Playton Business Offices. Had she not made an appointment or had the address, she wouldn't have been able to find it at all. She assumed walk-in business wasn't something he relied on.

She walked inside and found the bottom floor was a large opened room with a listing of suite numbers posted between the elevators. She scanned the listings, finding detective Pratch was on the top floor. The elevator was small, dingy, poorly lit, and groaned as it traveled up. Gwen was glad it didn't have far to go as her claustrophobia started to get the better of her. She tried not to leap off when the doors opened, though she imagined she did step off with a bit more speed than usual.

After finding the right suite, she walked in to the small office to find a receptionist gabbing on her phone. Apparently, the woman was having a thrilling conversation because she didn't even look up to acknowledge Gwen when she said hello.

Gwen looked down at her hair. It was a dingy shade of blonde that made it hard to tell where the blonde and grays differed. When the lady looked up, Gwen guessed her around fifty, but a hard fifty, with her share of wrinkles and an uneven skin tone that the heavy makeup she wore did not hide.

The lady put her hand over the phone and in a cracked voice said, "Can I help you?"

"I have an appointment with detective Pratch. I'm Gwen Hensley," Gwen said, and smiled.

"You're early, have a seat," she said, and went back to her conversation.

It was fifteen minutes before she hung up and buzzed the detective to let him know Gwen was there. If the chairs had a bit more cushion Gwen wouldn't have even noticed the time, but since they didn't, and she shifted in her seat every few minutes, she was very aware of how long she waited, and how fast the detective called her back when his unfriendly receptionist finally announced her.

Gwen followed the woman to his door, which was just to the right of the waiting area. When she walked in, she almost wanted to turn around and leave. His office was a mess, papers everywhere, smelled like smoke, and had overflowing ashtrays lying about on top of the papers. *Was it even legal to smoke in offices anymore?* Gwen wondered. It was too classical a representative of a burnt-out detective.

"Miss Hensley, please have a seat," he said, and offered his hand.

Gwen shook his hand and sat down. She explained to him what she needed done.

He furrowed his brows at her. "That's a lot of people to look into, ma'am."

"Yes, I realized that, but it is very important to me."

"You got no way to narrow it down more?"

"That was why I wanted to hire you," Gwen said, feeling like maybe she should just pick another place. "Look, I have lost my whole family and I need these answers. I need them quickly."

He gave her a sympathetic smile. "Of course, and I can get you those answers, quickly will cost more."

Gwen sighed. "If you impress me with how quickly, that is fine."

She got the impression from his office, demeanor, and receptionist, that he would use any means needed to get answers if the price was right. Maybe she was in the right place after all. Once they agreed on a price, she left him a retainer, all the pictures from her phone, and started home feeling better. The bonus she offered was on a sliding scale that meant he would get a much higher rate if he had something quality to tell her sooner rather than later.

She looked at her phone every few minutes all the way home. Sebastian would still be sleeping, dead, whatever it was vampires were during the day, and she knew calling would be pointless, but she wanted to.

Rather than going home, she decided to have another visit with Father George before time to go to the knitting group. She wanted to ask him a bit more about the orphanage. The church was locked, but Father George walked over from a small house to the right of the main building.

"Oh, I'm so sorry to disturb you," she said, wondering if he was making dinner or some other personal thing that she interrupted.

"No, no, I am always here whenever you have need. What can I do for you?"

"I was just wondering if we could talk more."

"You are troubled still?" he said, and gently took her hands.

"I am still trying to understand what happened to my family. I went to the orphanage."

"Did they not have what you are looking for?"

"No, they had a lot of information to sort out."

"What else can I answer for you?" he asked, as they walked inside the church and sat in his office.

"Do you recall that night?"

He frowned at her. "I do."

"Can you tell me what you know?"

"It was a summer night. I know that William had come by to see Lenny. They were supposed to go to Mel's and Lenny wasn't here." He shuffled some things around on his desk. "It had been an odd night; a lot of nuisance calls I recall because we were trying to get the shutter's closed for a storm that was due to roll in the next night and William's men kept getting called away."

"Wasn't he clean at this point? Lenny, I mean."

"As far as we knew."

"What happened?"

"William was called to the old campgrounds just outside of the city proper. Someone had seen what they thought were kids and suspected maybe pot or necking type things. Since everyone was already on other calls he headed off to send the kids home." He paused and looked at her with sad eyes. "I never saw him again."

"Where are the campgrounds? Are they still used?"

He told her that they were derelict and gave her simple instructions to get there. They talked a little more and he gave her the standard invite to service when she left.

There was still a little time before the yarn meeting so she went to Mel's to grab a bite beforehand.

"You ever leave here?" she asked Curtis, as she slid down across from him for a change.

"Evening, Miss Gwen," he said, and then sipped his coffee.

Mel came over and took her order with her usual cheer, and eyes that lingered on Curtis.

Gwen enjoyed his quiet demeanor while she ate.

"You off to do crafts with the gals tonight?" he asked.

"Yes, I am. Is there anything new with Mike? I'm not even sure I should go now that I think about it." She looked down at her food and shuffled the last few bites around on her plate.

She didn't want to make Trisha uncomfortable or sad, and she was the newcomer.

"Nothing new yet. He was denied bail."

"Wow, that is new. Why?"

"Why? It was a violent crime, Gwen."

Her mind went back to the image of Lizzy burning. "Yes. I, I guess I pushed that part out of my mind."

"As well you should."

They had a little more of an awkward conversation before Gwen left to go to the yarn shop. She was almost relieved to find that Trisha wasn't there. It wasn't that she thought Mike had done it, she was almost convinced he hadn't, but she was afraid Trisha would be upset with her somehow.

When they all sat down, Kathy started sewing on the last squares that had been brought and they talked about the next project. They were going to be making baby blankets and chemo caps for the local hospital.

"Did you get Sebastian to agree to coming to the festival this year?" Kathy asked.

Gwen shuffled the patterns nervously. "I didn't pin him down yet," she said. Her mind raced back to that night, he said yes, said he would go anywhere with her.

Pat and Pam giggled and rambled about him knitting again while Gwen started a practice swatch for one of the patterns. They all avoided mentioning Mike or Trisha. Instead, Gwen listened as they talked about what they were hoping to find at the bazaar and auction. Linda apparently was most looking forward to seeing what new things were going to be fried to eat this year.

Gwen took enough supplies to make a few hats and a few of the patterns, she also grabbed some delicate undyed yarns so she could work on a new magic something. She wasn't sure what she wanted to make yet but she was getting the urge to weave some magic.

As soon as she walked in the house, Lewis greeted her, asking about the detective. She told him about the meeting and about what she learned from Father George.

When he stepped in her space she could smell Sebastian.

"Was he here?"

Lewis gave her a puzzled look. "No, why?"

"You were with him. I smell him. I can feel him."

"Really? I'm surprised your senses are so sharp."

She narrowed her eyes. "Why? I am supposed to be some super witch. I can feel his magic. What have you been doing?"

"We were just practicing a few things for me to teach you," he lied. It came out smooth and sure.

She didn't question the truth.

They actually reworked the charm, made it stronger. Hopefully keeping him from being summoned away.

"You really still trust him?"

"Yes. Gwen, I knew what he was all along, remember?"

"I'm going to the campsite tomorrow, during the day. I want to walk around and see if I pinpoint where it happened. You need to come with me." She cut her eyes at him.

"Why?"

"Why what? I want to pinpoint it because I want to try and see what happened. I need you because it is far in the past. I need your magic aid.

You are mine remember? If you can work magic with monsters, you can work magic with me."

"Easy. You are not mad at me, my witch. I will go with you, of course."

Her face softened and she frowned. "I'm sorry. I'm edgy. I still don't know how I feel."

"I think you do," he said, the words threatened to choke him.

He knew how she felt. She wasn't mad at him. She wasn't mad at Sebastian. She wasn't mad at all. She was brokenhearted.

Chapter Eighteen

Lewis smiled at seeing how Gwen dressed to go to the campgrounds. She had her hair down and the black was a sharp contrast to the bright pink and white knit hat she wore. There was a hopeful look in her eyes and even though she may see something disturbing, the air felt light and happy. He hadn't seen her look that close to happy and carefree in a long while. He also noticed she was only wearing jeans and a sweater before she pulled on her coat, and he frowned.

"It's a cold day," he said.

She gave him a fake sigh and then smiled. "I have on long-johns too. I also put on boots and socks, even though they may need to come off."

"Suit yourself. It is cold."

"So, you keep me warm."

He started to say that he wasn't Sebastian and didn't have the same gifts, but he didn't want to mention him and ruin her good mood, so he just smiled and they walked out. He could feel the air start to get thick with her nervous tension as they drove.

"Why the shift? Are you okay?" he asked.

"Yes, I guess the closer we get, the more the excitement seems to be changing to fear."

"Why?"

"What if I see him die?"

"Isn't that what you want to see?"

"Well yes, but I want to see who killed him. I don't want to watch or feel him die. That happened with Lizzy. I found out nothing other than that she suffered. I don't want to feel him suffer."

"We can go home. You can let Curtis solve the murders."

"Lewis, damn it. I told you he's not right about Mike. I really believe the two murders are connected. Lizzy and William both deserve justice."

He slid closer to her and put a hand on her leg. "I'm here. I'm here to do whatever you think best and help however I can."

She kept her eyes on the road. "You still think I'm wrong. You have no faith in my feelings. How can you in one breath say I am some natural force, and in another say I can't even tell a killer from librarian."

"Where is this coming from, Gwen? You aren't mad at me."

She let out a heavy breath. "No. I'm afraid of what I will see. I guess I am also afraid you and Curtis are right and the only reason they died is because people are awful."

"Don't let what happened with Sebastian taint your view of your instincts, my witch."

"Ouch, is it that obvious?" She glanced from the road to him.

"To me. I love you. I know you."

Gwen looked back to the road and spotted what looked like a man-made clearing in the woods, she pulled the truck off and into it. She guessed by the clearing, the still standing bathroom, and the broken-down sign that had no legible words left, that they were at the right place. She turned off the engine and looked at Lewis again. This time her look held determination and trepidation, both equal in her expression, and he felt the same radiating from her thoughts.

"I love you too. Thank you," she said, squeezed his hand, and then opened her door.

Since she was going to be using her magic to pinpoint the crime scene, he shifted to give her extra power to draw from. She allowed her mind to drift until her thoughts cleared, which took a fair bit longer than usual since they seemed to float to Sebastian when she wasn't thinking of anything else.

Once his face stopped appearing, she started walking in slow methodical steps, making sure she covered every inch of ground. Her eyes focused on the dirt and the tips of her shoes so that she wouldn't be distracted by anything else. The snow had mostly melted, leaving a damp earthy smell that was mingled with the smell of the icy air.

On her second set of laps she noticed a spot that felt a little different. It was very subtle and that was probably why she missed it the first time. She assumed the faintness of the impression left was because the feelings she was looking for were very old, and their imprint on the area had dulled.

She paused, standing at the spot, concentrating harder. There was fear, anger, betrayal, and pain. "I think I found it," she said, opening her eyes.

Lewis flew over and stood in the mud at her feet.

Gwen sat on the ground, ignoring the dampness that quickly soaked through both layers of her clothes. She smiled at Lewis, took in a breath, and closed her eyes. The damp, cold soil was harder than she imagined as she dug her fingers in. It was littered with roots, debris, and sticks, giving her a bit of a challenge as she tried to bury her hands.

Lewis felt her calling on the earth to give in to her and used a little of his own magic to shield that from emanating out of the area.

Once her hands were buried and her mind blank, she felt herself slowly drifting back. Every time she did this it was different, but she never actually felt herself travel back before. There was a moment she had a bit of nausea that felt to her like motion sickness.

The movement stopped and she knew she was at the time and place she needed to be. Her eyes slowly opened and tried to focus on the dark woods in front of her. She took a few steps and found herself looking out at the clearing. She could see herself sitting on the ground as a ghostly shadow. The air was warm and on the breeze carried the scent of leaves and earth.

Her eyes focused on movement to the right where she saw a much younger Lenny, pacing nervously by a fire. She didn't move closer, just stood watching. Lenny looked to her, his eyes pleading, his mouth started to open, but then his head jerked sharply to the road.

Had he seen her, she wondered?

A patrol car pulled up and Gwen tried to control the urge to run and warn William. She knew she needed to stay still and watch or she would risk pulling herself back to the present.

The door opened and she was mesmerized as William got out. The memory was so real she could hear the squeak of his leather gun belt as he stood up and moved. The smell of his cologne filled the air as he walked closer. He was tall, and looked to have muscles under his uniform. She couldn't make out his eye color, but she could see he was smiling with his thin lips, and his short black hair was neatly trimmed. There was a shadow on his cheeks, indicating he hadn't shaved in a day or so. He was handsome. Again, she fought the urge to run and warn him or hold him.

"Lenny, what are you doing out here?" William asked, his voice deep and filled with authority, yet also friendly.

"I'm sorry Will," the young Lenny said. He looked back to her and down to the ground, appearing like a scared kid, not a killer.

"Naw, don't be sorry. It's been a busy night. I'm glad for the distraction. You know you scared old lady Francis by being out here. She figured crazed teenagers were about to start rampaging. How about we go and get something good to eat?"

"I'm really sorry," Lenny said, taking a step back.

"You okay?" William asked, his head cocked as he studied Lenny.

Lenny shook his head and Gwen felt herself stepping out from the woods. She heard the leaves under her feet crunch. William spun his head and locked eyes with her.

Had he seen her? Was this like before, like when she interacted with the memory of Lizzy?

She heard the squeak of leather again, this time it was coming from her and then there was a snapping of a button. Her arm raised, and she was now looking at William down the barrel of a gun.

Dear god, I am the killer.

She struggled to stay in the past as her mind processed what that meant. She wanted to close her eyes. Did she dare stay to see if William said a name? She realized that she wasn't going to be able to see who it was. Could she watch him die, watch through the eyes of his killer?

"What are you doing here?" William said.

Gwen could tell from the tone and the way his features wrinkled, he wasn't happy to see whoever she was watching through. He looked more aggravated than afraid and he didn't reach for his own gun.

"That's it? All you have to say to me is what are you doing here?"

"I thought we agreed you were leaving town. Go home and pack. Don't make it harder than it has to be."

She felt her finger starting to pull the trigger, and even though she knew it would not change things, she did fight it.

Lenny shifted his weight from one foot to the other in the background.

There was hesitation. She felt a rush of emotion. Whoever it was, wanted William to change their mind. "You are a cold man."

"No, I am a fair man. You leave here, leave me and Lizzy alone and I won't..."

"You would rather help that junkie than me? We are family."

The look in William's eyes grew hard. "You are dead to me."

Gwen felt her finger squeeze tighter and the trigger moved.

She heard the sound of the gun fire. It was so loud her head hurt and her ears started to ring.

William fell to the ground, his blue shirt already saturated in blood. Whoever shot him was a good aim. It was a chest shot. William said something inaudible and closed his eyes.

She felt herself stepping forward, her eyes focused on Lenny who was now shaking and crying.

"Pull it together shithead. You get your story right and I will see to it you don't face too much jail time."

Lenny nodded and she felt herself kneel beside William. "Don't you worry. I'll take care of your family."

As she watched his chest stop moving, she felt the emotions of the person she was watching through. There was mostly emptiness, but there was also a little relief, as if a chore had been done. She was shocked that there were no deeper feelings. No shame, regret, or fear. She felt her own emotions starting to boil up, sadness, despair, and then she started to cry.

Seconds later she sat in the present, cold, wet, and crying. She could feel Lewis put some distance between them and realized why, when she heard footsteps approaching.

She looked up to see Curtis walking over, his patrol car parked just beside her truck.

"Miss Gwen, everything alright here?" he asked.

"Sheriff, I was just, I was..." she wiped her tears and started to stand, taking the hand he offered for help.

He looked at her and his forehead creased. "You're wet," he said, and took off his coat, wrapping it around her. "You may not take my advice on other matters, but it's not wise to sit outside in the cold and wet this time of year."

She sniffled and walked with him back toward her truck. "I wanted to see where it happened."

"Understandable."

"I think Lenny had help, Curtis. If I can find out who or why, can you help me look into it?"

Curtis snorted and opened the door on her truck. "I worked that case already ma'am. Are you going to tell me I got that one wrong too?"

"I didn't mean it like that. I'm sorry. I guess this place had me thinking irrationally," she said, realizing she probably had been offending him with her insinuations that he was not doing his job right. "I'm really sorry."

He narrowed his eyes. "You've seen Lenny. Now you've seen this place. Save yourself the legwork and just ask me the next time you have questions, okay?"

She agreed and he seemed happy with that. She gave him back his coat and watched as he walked away, getting back into his car. Once he was gone, Lewis flew over and shifted, getting in the truck.

"I don't think he likes me," Gwen said.

"I got the feeling he did. He's been pretty patient with you I'd say."

She gave him an exasperated look. "Okay, whatever."

Once they were on the road, Lewis asked her what she saw and she told him everything in detail.

"I think the hardest part was doing it. I felt the trigger pull. I felt the hatred and then the emptiness. It was a strange feeling. The man who shot him almost seemed to be hoping William would do or say something to stop him. He cared about William. Or so it seemed. He was hurt, angry, betrayed, and then once it was done there was nothing. He said they were family. Do you think it could have been a crazy love triangle? Maybe the man came back later and killed Lizzy because she never did love him?"

"That is a whole lot of speculation. Hurt and betrayal could be over anything. Maybe a promotion, high school bully, and yes love. If they were family, then it could really be anything. Families bring out the worst in each other."

"I guess. I don't know what to do now. I don't want to watch it again, not like that, it was awful."

"Maybe the detective will have something helpful," Lewis said, not really sure that would be the case.

"It just makes me so angry to know that someone killed William, and has been free this whole time, while that man Lenny is in jail. He's not a bad person. I felt his soul."

"There has to be a reason he was willing to take the fall. I wouldn't write him off as being totally innocent yet."

"True, but Jesus, the person who did it probably killed Lizzy, and they are still free. They could still be in town. Lewis, they could be watching me now," she said, her voice sounding more strained as she realized she could really be in danger.

She pulled into the drive and they went inside. After she changed out of her wet clothes, she made something to eat and sat by the fire, thinking about what she had seen. She told Lewis again, every detail she could remember, trying to make sure she hadn't missed a clue.

Chapter Nineteen

Gwen puzzled a bit more over what she saw, then called the prison and tried to get scheduled for a visit for Friday, the next day, to see Lenny again. The liaison told her that was too soon since all visits needed approved, and that they could schedule her for Monday. Gwen was frustrated, it would be approved, they both knew that, since she was on his list now, but the red tape still caused a delay. He knew who killed William, she knew that much for sure.

"If there really is another person, one who actually pulled the trigger, maybe you shouldn't go back to the prison. Maybe you should let the detective find things out for you," Lewis said, not liking the dangerous turn things had taken. He also worried that he still felt Fannie pulling at him. The thought of Gwen chasing killers around while he could still be called away, wasn't a good one.

"Lewis, he knows. He was there, he spoke with them. He knows. I know he will tell me if I can make him believe that I won't tell anyone who told me."

"You said he was already edgy. Why don't you wait, see what the detective finds out and give that information to Curtis?"

She sighed. "I'm going to at least try to talk to him. There is no guarantee that detective will find anything. Lenny can give me a name for sure."

They talked a little more and then she ate and paced the house, thinking about what she had seen. She couldn't shake the feeling of her finger pulling the trigger. The look on his face when William realized he was shot and the blood that soaked his shirt almost instantly was all heartbreaking. She even found the empty feeling the killer had to be painful. Every little bit of her life seemed to have that feeling. If she could just figure it out and get the justice her family deserved, maybe that would change.

When she went for another walk after the sun went down, Lewis considered going to see Fannie, to see what sort of reassurances she needed, just to ease her off before things got too sticky there. He lingered at the house, finishing up his latest list of repairs, in case Gwen needed him though.

Gwen found that walking her property was soothing, even in the frigid weather. It gave her a feeling that she was connecting somehow to Lizzy, going places she had gone. The sound of sticks under her feet and animals rustling started to wash away the emptiness that threatened to swallow her.

She allowed her mind to drift to William. She could see him get out of his car and walk over to Lenny. He was warm and genuinely friendly. She puzzled over the emotions of the man in the woods. He felt betrayed. Gwen couldn't imagine what could have made him feel that way, considering the feelings she had about William. It had to be something personal, like a love triangle or family issue.

The crunching under her feet stopped and the winds picked up, letting her know she wasn't protected by the trees anymore. She looked up, and saw the lake. Her lake. The lake where William built a gazebo for Lizzy, where they had been married. She walked over to the gazebo and ran her hands along the wood, trying to see if there was anything left behind, any emotions, or sensations. Happiness was there. Peace was there.

After a minute stood looking over the water, she realized she either needed to move or make a fire. It was too cold to just stand there.

As she walked toward the fire pit, she felt Sebastian and started to look at his side of the lake. He had said he came out there to paint at night.

She stopped walking, wondering if she should start a fire and risk bothering his peaceful night, or just go home and find another way to relax herself.

It was too dark to make out much, but she could feel him, and there were shadows that looked man-ish across the lake.

The chill made up her mind for her as she decided even if it drew him over that would be okay. They would need to talk at some point. There was no way she was just going to forget about him. He invaded her thoughts daily, hourly.

She waved a hand and felt heat surge from her fingertips. A bright white flashed and the wood that was in the pit burst into flames. She felt warmer instantly and stood rubbing her hands together, wondering again about William, and what could have been between him and this person that would warrant his death and Lizzy's.

After she thought about it from every angle, with nothing triggering any revelations, she decided to walk toward his presence. The cool air wrapped her in doubt as she took the first few steps. Was now the best time for this? Was there any good time to ask a killer about how he kills? Why was her whole life revolving around death and killing? Sebastian had been the still waters in all the madness, now he was part of the madness. Could he ever be the still waters again?

She could feel that she was getting closer. His presence replaced the cold air with a warm sensation. Even when she had been so cold to him he still protected her. She looked up to see him standing several feet away behind an easel.

He wasn't painting; he was watching her. His eyes locked on her, almost beckoning her to take a few more steps.

She did. The closer she got the more he hugged her in warmth.

She paused just the other side of his easel, trying to figure out what exactly she was feeling. *Honesty*, she thought. That was what she could always count on from him. He deserved the same.

"I'm still confused about how I feel, but I've missed you," she said, and saw his expression soften.

He watched her standing in front of him, radiating with a mix of astounding power and tragic vulnerability. "Would you like to come inside, talk, and warm up?"

She hesitated a second and then waved her hand toward where she had come from, extinguishing the fire.

He smiled at the sensation she sent out and then walked toward his house with her at his side.

She didn't reach out for him and he let her have the space she needed while still wrapping her in his magic blanket.

They were greeted at the back door by Yardley, who Sebastian instructed to start coffee for Gwen. As they started down the halls she felt herself tensing up. She wasn't even sure why. She didn't really think he would hurt her.

Sebastian felt her apprehension and thought about the best way to allay that. "Tell me where you want to talk? We can go to your house with Lewis, if you like."

Did she want that? No, she didn't need chaperoned. Was that what she was afraid of? Not that he would hurt her, but that they would pick up where they left off. "No, here is fine," she said, amazing herself with how firm, and assured she sounded. She knew he could probably sense that she wasn't, just like she could sense he was nervous about how it would go.

She recognized the room they went to. The easel was gone, but she could still feel the passion that had been here, as well as the fear. She wondered why he chose there. "It feels like what happened here is still here," she said as she walked over to the lounger, trying to decide if she wanted to sit or stand for now.

"Yes, I've been in here a lot, thinking and feeling. It lingers. I wanted to feel it."

She walked over to the fire and watched the flames, not wanting to look in his eyes. They always had the same effect on her and tonight things needed to be serious and not passionate. "I need to ask you some hard things. Things I don't want to know, but that I think I might need to know."

"I understand."

She didn't look at him, but she felt him standing close. "I need to know about you feeding."

"I imagined that would be the case. I want you to know I never set out to hurt you, Gwen. If I had imagined what I felt for you would run so deep and be returned, I would have told you sooner."

She swallowed. What was he saying? She didn't want to think about that. Not now. Not until she had her answers. She didn't say anything, just waited for him to continue.

"I do have to feed. I told you that. It isn't often. Not like humans turned by vampires, who feed every night or week. I can go months, close to a year before there is a need."

She rubbed her fingers together, put her hands in her pockets, and took a few deep breaths. "How do you decide who gets to live, and who has to die so that you can feed your curse?" Her voice sounded strained.

"I try to do so with compassion. I don't pick someone who is happy, healthy, or has something to live for. I pick addicts, those desperate for release, the ill."

She turned to him, her eyes hard. "That is not for you to decide. What if they were a day away from cleaning up, getting well, finding a reason to live? How do you live with that?"

She watched as he closed his eyes and ran his fingers through his hair. It was one of the few times she saw him physically show that he was anything less than pulled together.

"It isn't easy. It isn't pretty. I know it isn't my place to judge the value of one life over another. I do the best I can to make sure they are at the end of their path."

"How?"

"I can read thoughts like any other vampire can."

"Before you steal their life, you violate their minds? Have you done that to me?"

"No, Gwen, I wouldn't. I would never do that to you."

"Why? I am just a blood bag."

"You can't really think I see you as that. I don't see people as food, or simply as a resource."

She let her gaze drift back to the fire. "So, after you violate their mind, what do you do?"

"Do you really want to know that?"

"Yes."

After a few deep breaths, he continued. "I create a gentle reality for them, and once I know they are relaxed, I take them as painlessly as possible."

"Do they know? Do they struggle?"

He sighed. "Yes, at times. Not all of them."

"They don't all want to die?"

"I imagine most, in the last seconds, have doubts and fears."

"I don't understand how you can live with what you are. What you do. It seems against everything you portray yourself as."

"It is." His voice was barely above a whisper.

"Does what you are have anything to do with your witch? The one you lost?" She regretted asking when she felt the air in the room thin.

Sebastian looked at the fire, struggling to breathe, blood tears started to roll down his cheeks.

"I'm sorry," she said, and reached for his face to wipe them away.

He stopped her, holding her hand. "You must never touch my blood."

She looked to her hand in his and then pulled it away. "I'm sorry. We can talk about that later. I should leave you to finish your painting now."

"If you must. I have nothing more pressing than making things right with you."

"You say that like it can be right. The best we can hope for is to be friends again. I can't love you like that, not anymore. You kill people. You kill people and your heart belongs in the past with your witch." As her words floated in the air she realized that might be as big a problem as him killing. She could see herself in his arms even knowing he was a monster, but she couldn't give her heart to him when he loved someone else.

"It's not as you think. Gwen, I didn't love her like that. I've never loved like that. As a familiar I could not feel human love. What I felt, what I feel with you is different."

"Words. How can you love? You are a familiar, you are also a monster."

"If it is just words, then I hope we can string them into a sentence that will never end."

"No. Those are just more words. I need to think about what you've said. You kill people. I just can't look away and pretend you don't."

"Take as much time as you need. Gwen, I do love you. I will be here however I can, in whatever role you wish. Even if that role is to leave you the hell alone. Your happiness is what matters to me."

Her eyes met his and they locked together. She felt that same tension that was always there. She wanted to wrap her arms around his waist and let his embrace shield her from every awful thing, but he was part of the awful things. When she felt the heat between them start to intensify, she looked away.

"I saw William die," she said flatly.

"Oh, sweetheart," he said, and took a step, but stopped himself. "I'm sorry you had to see that."

She told him about what she saw, the appointment with Lenny Monday, and the detective.

"You've been busy. I hope you are taking care of yourself. Did you need me to take any grief from you?"

"No, I'm fine. I've had to stay busy. It's the only way I don't think about you all day."

He loved her frankness since the first time they spoke. "I'm sorry I've troubled your mind."

"We seem to have both added to each other's burden. I hope we can at least fix that much."

"I know we can, mi belleza," he said, and reached for her face.

She reached up and took his hand. "No, not yet."

"Let me see you safely home at least." He gave her as best a smile as he could. The talk hadn't gone as good as he had hoped, but she had listened and that was better than things had been.

He suggested they take his car, but she wanted to walk. He enjoyed the walk because she kept her hand laced in his, her fingers gently caressing his.

Deep down he felt that things were going to be as they should be, in time. Time was something he had.

While they walked, they talked about all she found out, and puzzled over people who it could have been.

It didn't escape him that her poking around put her in more danger. There was still Fannie to consider as well. The bond he discussed with Lewis was still the best option, but since they had just started out on shaky ground again, he didn't think tonight would be a good night to suggest it. Tonight he would keep her warm, hold her hand and be the friend she desperately needed.

Lewis greeted them when they walked in. Again, he was torn between a need for Sebastian, and a distaste for him and Gwen as a thing.

They sat together for a while, making idle chatter before Gwen decided she needed to go to bed.

After a long silence, Lewis shifted and perched behind Sebastian. "Is all well now?"

"Not yet," Sebastian said. "I take comfort that it will be."

If Lewis were in his man form, he knew he would have rolled his eyes. Instead, he just assumed Sebastian could feel what he thought about that. "Fannie is still tugging at me. I think I need to go see what she needs. I can placate her for a little longer probably."

"That is not a good idea."

"No, it isn't best, but we can't have Gwen chasing murderers and fighting voodoo as well. How about we work together to make this as easy on her as possible?"

"I can't make the charm any stronger. I may have trained under her, but she certainly didn't teach me all she knows and she is undoubtedly stronger than I am as a voodoo practitioner."

"Which is why I need to go see her."

"She will strengthen whatever she has done. She won't want you to be able to resist. What if she does something I can't counter with a charm?"

"Can you just stay here tomorrow night with Gwen so I can go?"

"Now, amid all that is going on? She is closing in on a killer. A killer who is probably aware of her already."

"Which is exactly why I need to go before I am summoned away. If you hadn't told her what you are, you could have made your charm, blood voodoo, whatever it is, and Gwen would be able to count on you."

"I won't lie to her."

"I will. You just be here for her. I shouldn't be gone too long."

Sebastian shook his head and stood up to leave.

"Will you be here tomorrow?" Lewis asked.

"For her. I would still strongly advise you not to go. I may not be able to help you undo it if you do."

"There are no options left. Your charm isn't going to last."

Sebastian shook his head, again. "Did you think of what lie you wanted to tell Gwen regarding why she needs to connect with me?"

"I'll talk to her tomorrow before you get here."

"Yes," he said, and turned leaving.

Lewis watched him walk out. He was still grateful for his help, but that didn't change how he ultimately felt. If there were a way to do this without him, he would have made sure Gwen never got over what she was feeling. Maybe when it was done and Fannie was no longer an issue, he could rekindle her doubts in Sebastian.

Chapter Twenty

"I'm not sure even picking people who are ill or ready to die makes it okay. There are people who come back from the ledge you know," Gwen said. She sipped her coffee and watched Lewis preening in the glass room.

"It may not make it okay, but he has made the best of what he has been dealt. You can't imagine he asked to be a monster."

"I didn't ask him how it happened. I don't think he would have chosen it either though. Still."

"Still he kills I get that. Gwen, I need you to understand a few things though."

"That sounds too serious. Let me pour more coffee." While she was making her fresh cup, her phone rang and her meeting with Lenny for Monday was confirmed. She was glad but considering the time, she felt like they could have let her visit that day, rather than making her wait.

"What is it I need to understand?" she asked as Lewis appeared in the room.

"We need Sebastian. We have lost time on your training, and things, well, they could get hairy. I just don't want to fail you."

"Why exactly did 'we' lose so much time, Lewis?"

"Good reasons, but they don't change facts."

"Are you ever going to tell me?"

"When you need to know. I think you have dealt with enough. Hell, you are still trying to come to terms with his secrets."

"No, Lewis, he didn't keep secrets."

"Fine, Sebastian is great, so why are you arguing with me about him helping us?"

She sipped her coffee and made a sandwich. "I'm sorry. I have been short with you. I think it is because of everything on my mind. William, the killer, him, you, it's all so much. I'm trying to smile and stay my chipper self, but it's coming from all sides. You and Sebastian were my stability and it seems like you both shifted to, well, something else." She paused and took a bite of her sandwich. "You and I were feeling better, and now you want to lay something else on me. I'm just not sure how much more I can take with any grace."

Lewis shifted and walked to her, holding her in his arms. "Never, ever, doubt me being here for you. I love you and I will always do what is best for you."

"You think he is best? The monster next door?"

He swallowed hard. It felt like the hardest lie he ever told. "I think right now he is what we need, yes."

"Fine, I will work with him. I will do my best to mend the friendship."

Her agreement, while it was a relief, still felt to him like a punch in the gut. "I need him to be more."

She pulled away from his embrace. "What? What are you asking me to do? I told him I can't love him. I can't."

Hearing that made Lewis feel better. "Good. You shouldn't. I mean, well, that is between you two. I need you to make a bond with him."

"I gather you mean more than friendship, but less than… What do you mean?"

"Magically."

"That's not even possible. One witch, one familiar."

"Yes, usually. We can work some magic. He can. I think you will need his boost to face what is coming."

"Why, what's coming?"

"Bad things. Strong things. He agrees."

"You've talked about this? About me, when I wasn't around?"

"We talked about it before, before he told you about what he was."

"I see," she said, and ate some more, sipped some coffee and then started out of the room.

"No, it's not like that. We both worry for your safety and he can help."

"What exactly do you want me to do with him?"

"I have no idea how it is done, that he knows. I know you will not be linked in any permanent way, and yet when and if you need him you can be linked. His magic will give you a huge enhancement. Like what you feel with me, only much stronger."

"You've always been enough."

Her words made him want to hold her again. He wished they were true, wished he could be enough. "You always practiced very light magic."

"You know I am just trying to get to a point I can stand to be in the same space as him, and now you want me to share a link with him?"

"It will be a charm. You can put it on only if and when you need him."

"I don't know, Lewis. Maybe if I knew why it was important. He knows why, correct?"

Lewis knew this answer was vital to her not knowing. If she pointblank asked Sebastian, he would tell her. "Not exactly. He has guesses, but that is all."

"I have to go to town. Can we do this later?"

"What are you going for? Do you need me?"

"No, I am getting something from the grocery and leaving some hats with Kathy. I need to grab more yarn and patterns for the baby blankets."

"I need to make a re-connection. I can go now and that way I should be back before the night is over. Sebastian can stay with you tonight."

She frowned and cut her eyes at him. "You are leaving? I'm close to finding out who killed William and Lizzy and you are leaving? What if they are, I don't know, watching and know when I am alone?"

"That is why you should tell Curtis what you know, and also why I think Sebastian should stay with you tonight."

She shook her head, frustrated. "I don't need a sitter. Plus, if I find things out, why should I trust Curtis to do the rest? He didn't exactly solve the murders right the first time, did he?"

Lewis knew from her tone to let that go.

She agreed to at least consider having Sebastian over and to talk with him about the link, before she left for town.

As soon as she was gone, Lewis put the charm Sebastian made him in a safe place and left to see Fannie. He knew that Sebastian was probably right and she was only using him to make Gwen vulnerable, it made sense, but he still needed to buy a little more time so that Gwen wasn't facing too much when things did finally blow up.

Gwen made several stops in town. Each place took a little longer than she imagined because she seemed to run into someone she knew at every stop. She had expected to see Kathy at the yarn shop. They talked a little about Mike and Trisha, apparently, Trisha wasn't doing well as Gwen imagined would be the case.

Kathy seemed to think a visit would make her feel better, so Gwen stopped in on her way to the grocery with a bag full of yarn and some fancy new needles.

Trisha was happy to see her and invited her in for coffee. Trisha cried at seeing the gifts, and again told her that she knew Mike would not have done it.

"I know that. I have been following my own leads for whatever it's worth. I intend to find out who killed Lizzy. How is he doing?"

Trisha squeezed her hand and then sipped her coffee. "He's not well. He's never been anywhere like that jail. He's just not jail material, Gwen. I'm afraid it will change him."

"No, he's a good man and will be a good man when he gets out."

"I appreciate that. You should see the looks I get in the shops now. People just assume he did it. I'm sorry. I know it is hard for you too."

"It's hard for us all. We missed you Wednesday. I don't think the ladies will be judgmental."

"No, I didn't want to make it awkward."

Gwen smiled at her. "I considered not going too. I will get to the bottom of this. For Lizzy and Mike."

They switched to lighter things although both of them didn't stop thinking about Mike, or Lizzy.

When she left, Gwen realized it was going to be late when she got home, so she decided to stop at the diner after the grocery store to avoid one more task that night.

At the grocery she had a nice chat in the line with Pat. Gwen hadn't been sure if it was Pat or Pam until she laughed because Pat always made a little snort sound when she laughed. She again asked her about bringing Sebastian to the festival and Gwen said she would ask him. She guessed she would. What harm could there be in some carnival foods and a hoe-down if they were going to be linked anyway?

Gwen's mind was still bouncing between Mike, Lenny, and Sebastian when she walked in the diner.

"Hello, Mel," she said, and smiled as she walked over to the bar area.

"Hey, Sweetie, what can I get you?"

"I'll have whatever is on special and a coffee," Gwen said, and watched as Mel handed a slip to the cook, who Gwen had come to know was Mel's nephew.

"You getting excited for the festival?" Mel asked.

"I am. I hear you are working on something special to eat."

"Linda talking to you about fried things? Don't you mind her, the fried things are just for fun, but I am working on a special meat pie. Something hand held, so you can walk around and play the games while you eat." She smiled with pride and winked.

"That sounds awesome. I can't wait to try it, and the fried treats."

Mel kept up chatter while Gwen ate and it was dark when they finished visiting.

Once she was in the car she called Sebastian, and asked if he wanted to come over and talk about what Lewis mentioned. As she assumed would be the case, he knew about it already, and Lewis already asked him to babysit her.

"I'm sorry he made you feel like I needed to be tended to," she said as they walked inside.

Sebastian walked the groceries into the kitchen. "It's probably best you don't be alone until Curtis gets the right person locked up."

"Maybe he is the one who needs his hand held so he can do his job right. What cop screws up twice? I mean it is his job to catch killers."

Sebastian watched her putting things away and could see as well as hear her frustration. "There seems to be something else bothering you."

"Yes, there is. It bothers me that you and Lewis talk about me and both know things that could affect me, and yet you both conspire to keep that from me. It goes beyond bothering me. It makes me feel like, like I am all alone."

Sebastian took in a sharp breath. "What happened with Lewis?"

"That doesn't matter, what matters is you are both keeping secrets. Now he wants me to make some bond with you, that I didn't even think was possible, and I am supposed to do this because you both decided it was needed. I think I should get to know why. I may not find it to be needed. I shouldn't be asked to do something so out of the ordinary on his word alone." She paused and he was about to address a few points but she continued. "He's my familiar, shouldn't he have to tell me things? What if we do this, make this bond, does that mean the same rules apply to us?" She stopped, stunned by her own question. "Not that there is an 'us.' I just want answers, not more questions."

"Are you done?" he asked when she finally paused.

She nodded and opened one of the candy bars she bought at the store.

"Let's talk about this one thing at a time. I don't conspire with anyone on anything. I certainly don't conspire against you."

She sucked the chocolate slowly, savoring the way it melted in her mouth. It was as smooth as his voice. "But you talked about me, and what is best for me when I wasn't even there."

"Yes, you didn't want to see me, and Lewis wanted my advice. It is just that simple. I did not seek him out to keep tabs on you."

"Why won't he just tell me? Did he make you promise not to tell me?"

"He's afraid, Gwen. I made no such promises, but I would prefer for the sake of peace that he told you his secrets."

"What exactly is it we need to do?" she asked, and then looked into his eyes. "First, do you think it is needed or did he tell you it was?"

"I suggested it."

Her eyes grew wide. "You did?"

"Yes, all I wanted was to make sure you stay safe."

"Okay, let's go by the fire, and you can explain to me what exactly I am considering," she said, and started out of the kitchen. "Even if you won't tell me why."

She sat on the couch.

He sat in the chair beside her, still not sure how much space she wanted between them. "Not won't. If you really want me to, I will. I will not ever lie to you."

She thought about it a moment, considering what it might do to what she knew was still a fragile friendship between Lewis and Sebastian. "Maybe, if he won't soon. Tell me about the link."

"There are two ways we could do this. As you know, I can't be given a witch like Lewis was given you, and even if I could, you are his witch." He paused, she nodded, watching him closely as he talked. "Both ways use dark magic. Magic I would have hoped you never needed to mess with."

"Wait, I need to work dark magic? Isn't that against those rules Lewis is always harping about?"

"Yes, and yes. There will be a cost. I am sure Lewis explained to you that a broken rule isn't a game ending thing, but it has a price."

"Right, like if he and I were lovers we would lose our mental connection."

"Yes, like that."

She frowned. "What is the cost?"

"I don't know. Everything is weighted by the fates and by our intentions. We do this with good intentions. I don't think there will be a severe cost. I wouldn't suggest it if I did."

"Okay, go on."

"The first way is voodoo and I am not sure about that because I am not as strong with voodoo as your adversary."

"This is about Fannie? You think I am not strong enough for her? What changed?"

Sebastian looked at her, watching her eyes as she looked at him searching his. "Lewis changed. His ability to aid you changed."

She licked her lips. This was the secret. Something Lewis was afraid to tell her. Something had changed him. Was it fair to let Sebastian tell her if it were something personal to Lewis? No, she decided. "Okay, what is the other way."

"My blood has very unique bonding properties, and additionally I am well versed in blood magic."

"Okay stop. First you said I should never touch your blood, and what the hell is blood magic?"

Sebastian crossed his right leg over his knee.

Her eyes were drawn to the movement. All his movements were always so graceful.

"I won't have you handle my blood. I will do that. Blood magic is just that. It is magic that is powered by the supernatural properties in blood. Sometimes human, sometimes not."

"Dare I even ask how you learned that?"

"Only if you want to know." His eyes were sharp and his expression said that he would tell, but that he would rather not have to.

"What would we need to do?" she asked and thought she saw a little relief in his eyes.

"You will need to take part in a ritual with me where we both agree to the binding of our blood. By the nature of what we are doing it will require blood from us both. With that bound blood we will make a charm of some sort for each other. When you want to be linked to me you wear the charm. We both need the charm on. It wouldn't be a case of me putting on a charm and having access to your thoughts."

She chuckled. "You already do, as what you are, don't you?"

"I could, but not like a link. This will be deeper. My blood will make this link something we both have never experienced."

She watched him, feeling like time stopped for her to stare at him. His lashes gracefully danced as he blinked. His jaw tensed as he swallowed.

He felt the intensity of her stare. He knew she was considering what to do and he knew that considering what happened between them she might object. The bond would be very intimate, vulnerable for them both. As he watched the shadows from the fire dance across her face, he knew he would always be willing to put himself in her hands, but he also knew that his hands were not as gentle and she couldn't be expected to show the same trust.

"Deeper how?" she finally asked, letting him know she was at least still considering it.

"Deeper in that you will be able to see my thoughts, and memories as I can yours. Deeper in that you can call me to your dreams, or I can walk into your dreams at will. It will allow the ability to touch with thoughts on your end and enhance it on mine. You will be able to summon me, and while I can't summon you, I would be able to beckon you, which would be irresistible. Most importantly, you can use my magic as you do with Lewis. That is why we would do this. The rest is a byproduct."

"A byproduct? That is a pretty intense side effect. You are in my dreams already," she said and then looked away blushing.

"I wouldn't use any of them. I promise you. This would be a bond for you to use when and if you needed."

She knew he was telling the truth. He always did and she felt certain if he lied she would be able to read it easily. "I won't need dead animals for the charm, will I?"

He smiled. "No. I was thinking since you knit magic that might be best. You could knit me something and I could make a charm of some sort."

"Well if I am going to work our blood into yarn, why don't you knit me something too?"

"I don't knit."

"I can teach you. I'd like to teach you something. You've taught me so much, and I imagine you will teach me more."

"I hope so. I would love for you to teach me."

"Good, let me think about it and talk to Lewis. I'll call you. Probably this weekend. Is there a rush? Do I need to be scared now?"

"Sweetheart, there is a killer on the loose and Lewis is away. That worries me now."

She agreed. She didn't like to be alone considering what she had seen at the campgrounds.

He observed the fear in her eyes. "Did you want to come to my place? I have to go in the morning as you know and Yardley can watch over you until you wake up."

She wanted to ask about Yardley but decided she had enough to take in for one night. She agreed that she didn't want to be alone at night in the empty house and they drove her truck to his place.

They spent the rest of the night in his library, talking mostly about what would be done in the blood ritual and how to knit magic.

She drifted off well before time for him to go.

He moved her to a guest room and gave Yardley instructions not to disturb her, but to make sure he answered the door to absolutely no one until she was awake.

It was the first night in many he felt peaceful as he bolted his door.

Chapter Twenty-One

Gwen rolled over and tugged the blankets up to her chin. The bed felt soft, the blankets plush, and the pillow cradled her head. The smell of exotic spices reminded her of Sebastian. She caught a glimpse of his blue eyes, lashes dancing when he blinked before her eyes opened. She looked around, seeing she was in a strange bedroom, on a strange bed.

Memories of being in his library came to her and she assumed he moved her when she fell asleep. She blushed a little, seeing that she was sleeping in her shirt and long johns, her pants were folded on the dresser. After a moment of thinking about it, she hoped it was Sebastian and not Yardley who had tucked her in.

She got up and dressed, before making the bed. It was a huge four-post bed made up with fluffy soft sheets and a thick comforter, all in rich red, all calling her to lay back down and forget about her troubles. There was a wooden dresser and a small night table beside the bed. She used the huge mirror that hung over the dresser to make sure she didn't look too disheveled.

Still half asleep, she opened the door and started down the hall.

"Hello?" she called out as she searched for, found, and started down the stairs.

Every hallway, every inch of his house gave off the same luxury and grace he did.

At the foot of the stairs Yardley greeted her. "Ma'am, I have coffee and some pastries if you are hungry."

"Coffee would be lovely, thank you." She followed him to the kitchen.

"Would you like to eat in the dining room?"

"No," she said, and sat on a stool in the kitchen. "This will do."

As she drank her coffee and ate a raspberry danish he had given her anyway, she watched Yardley, wondering what the connection could be or if he were really just hired help. She assumed there must be more because she got the impression he knew what Sebastian was.

After she ate, he asked if she needed anything else and then escorted her out, having her coat and purse waiting by the door. When she walked out he smiled at her and said, "I hope to see you again soon, Miss Hensley."

When Gwen got home she was a little sad to feel that Lewis wasn't there. Her mind drifted to the night before and she wondered where he was. Could it be he was lying about making a re-connection and he was actually doing whatever voodoo stuff it was that had Sebastian so worried?

After she changed, she walked to the glass room and thought about what she wanted to do. Did she want to make a bond like that with Sebastian? What did she want with him? He still drew her to him like they were connected at the soul already.

She had never seen a fang when he smiled, but in her mind she could see it, see them, as a snarl and dripping in blood. Would she ever not imagine him as a monster? If they were only bonded by a knitted something she could take it off, she could never put it on to begin with, not unless there was a real need.

She needed to ask him what the actual blood bond would do. Would they still have some sort of forever bond just from doing that? They must. At least in some way.

Restless, she walked upstairs and took one of Lizzy's journals. With everything else going on she had forgotten all about them. Most nights she fell asleep too tired to read anyway.

She sat at the window seat, letting the sun warm her as she read. The story picked up with her mother leaving. After she left, Lizzy clung to some unnamed lover to keep from spiraling into sadness. From the references to others Gwen figured it wasn't her familiar or Sebastian. Gwen flipped through the juicy details, not wanting to pry like that.

After Winnie had her accident, Lizzy and Sebastian again disagreed on what to do about Gwen. He had wanted to go get her, and Lizzy thought this Fannie woman would find her too easily there. They all stayed in touch with the foster home who had taken in Gwen. Gwen tried not to judge Lizzy for abandoning her. It was clear from her words that she felt a true fear for her safety and really believed what she did was needed. She mentioned it daily, mourned for William and Winnie, and struggled to carry on herself.

Watching Will's brother everyday makes my heart sad. I wish he would have left town as they agreed on before Lenny took my Will away.

Gwen felt her head spin. They were family, she knew that from what she saw at the campgrounds. William had a brother? In town? One he and Lizzy wanted to go away, why? Was whatever they wanted him gone for bad enough to kill over? Did Lizzy not know it wasn't Lenny? Gwen closed the book. Maybe she figured it out and that is why he killed her too.

She stood and started down the stairs, book in hand. Someone would know if William had a brother. Father George and the yarn ladies had said he had no family. Who would know? Someone close to him, maybe one of his men, Curtis? He might know. Lenny would know for sure, he could give her a name. She wished it were Monday. Getting through today and Sunday was going to be torture.

She called and listened to Sebastian's recording. There was something soothing about hearing his voice. She left a message about what she had found out and then walked downstairs to make something to eat.

After she ate, Gwen looked at the un-dyed yarns she had, and decided to prepare them both. If she were going to make this bond she would need them ready to dye as soon as possible. She was hanging the freshly washed yarn to dry when she felt Lewis come in.

She was so relieved to not be alone she forgot all about how mad she was at him for talking about her to Sebastian, or for keeping secrets, or for leaving. She went to his arms as soon as he shifted. "I've missed you."

He folded her in his arms, breathing in her pure clean scent, letting it wash away the darkness of where he had been and what he had seen. "I'm sorry I was gone so long, my love."

She told him about what she read, about the talk with Sebastian, and after she finished the yarn, they went to the main room.

"So, you think it is those boys? The ones who were in the article?" he asked.

"Well they were the only brothers. Maybe I should call Monday and make sure that Pratch looks at them next."

"What about the other, with Sebastian, have you decided?"

"Is it pressing, Lewis? Really pressing? I mean I made some yarn in case it is, to make the charms with, but if it isn't, I'd like more time to decide how I feel about him."

Lewis looked to the right. How was he really going to push her into this? He didn't want her bonded to him. He wanted to take her and run away, but he knew they wouldn't be safe. Fannie had made sure he was under her evil thumb. Gwen would need Sebastian. "Yes, it is. It could be."

"Will you tell me why?"

"Please, Gwen, can't you trust that the less you know for now the better."

"It's about that voodoo lady, Fannie? Has she hurt you?"

Lewis pulled her to him so she wouldn't be able to see his face. "It is about her and it's complicated."

"Will you be okay? I mean if I have Sebastian to protect me, who protects you?"

"You do."

"I will. Lewis, I promise whatever happened, if I can help you I will. Let me help you. Tell me what I need to know so that I can."

"I will. Not now."

"But you will?"

"I will."

"Fine, I will make the bond with him."

He didn't know if he should celebrate or cry. Instead, he hugged her tight. "I love you, Gwen."

"Forever, Lewis, I love you."

He held her a while longer before she looked up at him. "Did he tell you it would need blood magic?"

Lewis wrinkled his nose and frowned. "Yes."

"I hope it isn't too gruesome. I don't have a stomach for stuff like that."

"I will stay with you, as close as I can."

The rest of the day was uneventful. They talked about the boys, about the journals, about the detective, and who it could be. Even though it was a small town they hadn't met everyone, so it was possible it was some older man they just hadn't happened across. There were hundreds of people it could be.

Sebastian called after the sun went down, and Gwen filled him in on everything. They decided that things could be done that night, agreeing to work the magic at his house so there would be no risk of calling something dark to her house, and so her place wouldn't have anything dark lingering after they were done.

Lewis and Gwen drove over.

Yardley was expecting them and Sebastian was quick to greet them in the main room.

"I need to have a brief talk with Gwen first," he said, and Lewis waited out in the hallway as they walked into another room.

Gwen looked at him, watching as he chose his words. "I know we already talked about there being a price, but I just need you to be sure. This, what we do here tonight will forever shift your path."

"You said the cost would be small."

"It will, but make no mistake it changes your path. This is dark magic; it links you to a monster."

"To you. Sebastian, we have been linked since the day I arrived. I felt it and you felt it. I get the impression from what I have read in the journals, we may have been linked even before I was born. Who are we to say that this isn't part of my path, you are part of my path."

As he stepped closer she didn't back away. His arms wrapped around her and he leaned down, kissing the top of her head. "I will always endeavor to make your path as beautiful and gentle as you are."

She enjoyed his embrace a moment before they walked back to Lewis. Together, they all went to his altar room. Gwen instantly got the impression it was a much darker place than Lizzy's was. She could feel something left over from the last time he worked magic with Lewis. The room was a good size, though still just a room, not a whole floor like at her house. There was a small altar table and a few shelves with various things on them against the walls.

She didn't realize how hard she had been holding on to Lewis until her hand started to ache.

He reached up and stroked her back gently.

When Sebastian closed the door, she felt her heartbeat ramp up.

He looked at her, his eyes were sweet and filled with worry. "Are you certain you want to do this? We could figure out something else."

"No. I'm fine," she said.

Sebastian nodded and started to gather some things from the shelves, placing them on the ground in the center of the room. "It will probably be best for you if you wait outside the circle," he said to Lewis.

Gwen slowly released his hand and gave him a quick hug before she walked over to where Sebastian stood. She watched nervously as he closed them in a circle. She had no idea what he used, but it didn't look like any of the powders he used when teaching her to make circles. It wasn't so much a powdery substance as it was flakes, and they were a deep gray.

She looked down at her feet, there were a lot of herbs and liquids set out. There was also a decent size cast iron pot, but her eyes were drawn to something more menacing. The small dagger with red and black jewels running along the handle made her shudder. She stared down at it, watching her reflection in the blade.

When Sebastian finished with the preparations, he helped Gwen to kneel and joined her on the ground.

She listened as he chanted in a hard tone. It was in a language she had never heard, it was not his smooth rolling Spanish, but something more utilitarian sounding.

When he looked to her, his eyes were still gentle but his words were firm. "I need you to repeat exactly what I say and then take this." He handed her the dagger. "After you say the words, close your hand around the blade and slide the knife out. Please, do it gently. It is very sharp."

She nodded, her throat was too dry to even let her croak out a yes.

He reached out and touched her jaw with his thumb. His eyes said 'I love you' without him needing to say a word.

She took the blade from his hand and drew in a few calming breaths.

Sebastian said a few words, and then gave her the response she needed to say, repeating it to her slowly so she could get the enunciation correct. He watched and listened. When she completed the words, he nodded in approval.

Gwen closed her eyes, wrapped her hand on the blade, and slid it down. She didn't open her eyes; afraid she might pass out at the sight. She felt his hand take hers and dared a look, seeing he had guided her hand so that the drips of blood would fall into the pot on the ground.

Sebastian watched the blood dripping, again wondering if this was the right step for her to take. When he had enough to work with, he turned her hand and opened her palm. He ran his finger along the cut, whispering a few words and the cut sealed, stopping the bleeding.

"Repeat this question to me," he said, and then very slowly said a few words.

Gwen repeated the words and listened as he responded the same as she had. Her eyes were drawn to his hands as he cut into his palm and let his blood drip into the pot with hers. She was shocked at how much thicker and darker his blood was.

His cut stopped bleeding on its own and she watched as he crushed some herbs and blended a few liquids. He said some more words and added a final liquid that hissed and caused the pot to burst into flames.

As she watched the fire burning, she considered what they had just done. It crossed her mind that the way they exchanged questions and answers was similar to a wedding vow and she wondered what sort of ritual it was exactly. As the fire died down, she thought it was a bit too late for more questions.

He turned to her and gave a weary smile. "It's done. I will pour this into something so you can make the dye. That will be the part you have to do. We both have to have a hand in this." He stood and said a few words and opened the circle. "You want to clear the darkness from her?" he asked Lewis as he left the circle to get a vial for the mixture.

Lewis had watched the whole blood marriage in horror, trying not to flash back to the things he had done with Fannie. Cleansing Gwen of Sebastian's tainted magic was something he would gladly do.

Gwen watched Sebastian as Lewis cleansed her. She could feel something was different, even though she still needed to weave the shawl. That tension and pulling to him that she always felt was even stronger. There was a deeper feeling that she was his and he was hers. They belonged to each other.

When he handed her the vial, he still had a look of worry for her.

"I'm fine," she said softly.

They all walked back to his front room.

"I wish I could stay with you. I'm sorry," Sebastian said, as they lingered at the door. He knew things were still not right between them and as much as he hated it, he needed to give her the space to figure it out on her own.

"I'll work on the yarn tomorrow. I need to get a few things from town first. If you want, I can teach you how to knit tomorrow night. The yarn may not be dry, but regardless, I can teach you tomorrow since you need to learn on some scrap stuff," Gwen said, and paused, considering a hug but didn't. She knew she was rambling. Her nerves were shot and she needed sleep. "It should be dry enough to work with Monday."

"I'll watch over her," Lewis said, and pulled her under his arm, putting an end to any thoughts either of them were having. He could feel her vulnerability and see that things between her and Sebastian were turning back to where they had been quickly.

When they got home, Lewis laid with her until she drifted off, thinking about how things had ended up. It seemed to him an awful tragedy that he should end up with Fannie and Sebastian got his witch. Fannie had been awful interested in what Sebastian was doing, and that made him wonder if there wasn't a way to flip this on end. Could he offer Sebastian to her in place of Gwen?

Chapter Twenty-Two

After making some coffee to go and giving Lewis a brief hello, Gwen made her way to town to get the few things she would need to start the yarn. Her thinking was she needed to get started before she changed her mind.

She made two stops, one at the florist and one at the grocery. She decided on red, because if she did it right, it would be a deep red that would suit both a man and woman, and somehow seemed fitting considering what the garments were.

When she pulled in the diner she saw the patrol car there and assumed it was Curtis. For a brief moment she considered pulling out, but quickly pushed the urge away. He may be gruff and he may have no knack for his job, but he didn't deserve to be snubbed. She figured he was genuinely trying and that he was there so often because of something between him and Mel, which still made her smile.

"Hey sweetie, you want toast or danish today?" Mel asked, already having her two favorites memorized.

"Hmm, how about a danish and coffee," Gwen said, and took a seat at the counter. She didn't see Curtis, but there was a deputy at a table in the corner, who was probably driving the car.

Maybe Curtis took a day off after all, she thought.

As she was finishing her coffee a big question came into her mind. *Mike.*

Why was Mike set up? If Curtis had evidence and Mike didn't do it, there was a reason. Could he have known something? Found something in his family history search.

Gwen drained her cup and headed to her truck after the usual good-byes with Mel.

She dialed Trisha and waited nervously for an answer. They talked briefly and Trisha said she wasn't doing anything so they met at the yarn shop for coffee and a chat.

Kathy was happy to see them and even happier to see them hugging. After they were settled in with coffee, they each pulled out a blanket for the hospital and started knitting while they talked.

"Does Mike talk to you about his work?" Gwen asked.

"Of course, he tells me everything."

"I think something in my family history is the reason William and Lizzy died. Do you know if he found something? Maybe there was something so dark, that was enough for the person who killed Lizzy to want to frame Mike in particular."

Trisha's needles stopped clicking and she looked up at Gwen. "You think the real killer framed my baby on purpose to stop him finding out something? You really think he didn't do it?"

"Yes, and of course, I told you that from the start. I don't think Mike is a killer, I never did. I have been working steadily to find out the truth like I said."

"I thought you were just saying that to make nice. Do you..." she started to say and paused, sipping her coffee. "Do you want to come look at his work?"

"I would, but you should ask him first. Can you call him or ask him when you go see him? I don't want to rummage through his stuff without him knowing first."

Trisha reached out and squeezed her hand. "You are sweet, Gwen. I will call him. They let me talk to him any time since it's me and everyone there knows me."

Gwen looked down at her knitting, a little shocked Trisha pulled out a phone and called right there. She explained to him what Gwen said, and from what she couldn't help but hear, it sounded like he was agreeable. When Trisha hung up, she smiled and started to shove her things in her project bag.

"He said sure. You want to follow me home?"

149

Gwen agreed and they both said goodbye to Kathy, Gwen grabbing a little of some of the new yarn that had come in. It was so soft and such a pretty shade of green, she couldn't resist.

At Trisha's, she was shown to a small office with a simple desk and side table.

"He says what you need is in the stack on the table to the right," Trisha said, standing behind Gwen in the doorway.

"Did he think there might be something that would help?"

"Yes."

Gwen looked at the stacks and then sat down in his simple, slightly uncomfortable chair, looking at the papers. As soon as she was able to determine it wasn't related to Lizzy or William, she sat it aside in a quickly growing pile. When she neared the bottom she found something that made her breath catch.

"Trisha, come here, look at this," Gwen said, and handed her a paper.

Trisha read the paper. It was a petition for a name change. William Hensley was the new name. "Wow, so Hensley was just a name he picked? Wasn't he adopted? Maybe it was his birth name and he changed it back?" Trisha asked as a stream.

Gwen took a picture of the page with her phone. "This must be why they didn't help Mike with his work. If they wanted his past a secret. *Why* is the question of the day?"

Gwen looked at the rest of the papers, not finding anything else.

"What do you make of it?" Trisha asked, as they sat in the living room.

"This name, the one he wanted to leave behind must hold some dark answers about things that are worth killing for. I have an investigator already looking into his adoption. I'll give him this Monday, and that should speed things up."

"Thank you, Gwen. It means a lot that you believe in my Mike."

"We'll get answers for everyone," Gwen said, and smiled weakly.

They chatted a bit more before Gwen decided from her rumbling tummy it was getting to be late. She needed to get home and get the yarn done before long, if it was going to be ready to work with.

Trisha looked more hopeful than she had in days and when Gwen left, she gave her a big hug and promised to call her Monday.

Gwen headed home to find Lewis working on some siding the wind had started to pull off. She let him know what she found out and that she was going inside to start the yarn.

"Did you need my help?" he asked over his shoulder.

"Nah, it's simple to dye in spells."

"You can still change your mind," he said, turning to her.

"I know. It'll be a temporary thing."

There was something in her voice that he read as doubt, but he left it and watched as she walked away to get started. Each piece of wood he pulled off and each nail he pounded in, took the brunt of his frustration.

When he came back in, Gwen was hanging the dyed yarn on racks to dry in the main room so they could get the benefit of the fire.

He walked over and checked to make sure she hadn't been tainted in anyway by working with his blood. He didn't sense anything, but offered a cleansing anyway.

Gwen sat down and relaxed back on the couch, letting Lewis run his magic over her, just in case. When he was done, she noticed he was hovering, looking sad.

"Did you want to learn too? I didn't ever offer because knitting, well, it isn't usually a guy thing. Though I guess it might be a bird thing."

He laughed. "You ramble nonsense when you are nervous. I don't need to learn to knit. Do you want to do anything to ease your mind?"

"No. It just feels like things are on hold for the weekend. I want to see Lenny; he knows what I need to know. I can't call the detective to tell him to focus on the brothers or find out what he knows. It'll be at least Monday until I can follow up on what I found at Mike's. Everything is paused."

He agreed it was a frustrating time. He had things he would rather be doing than nailing on old siding or watching her bond with Sebastian.

She was relaxed, her head in Lewis's lap, drifting in and out as she watched the flames dancing in the fireplace, when Sebastian called to make sure they were still having a knitting lesson. Even though she had offered to teach Lewis and he refused, she still felt a little bad about Lewis not being a part of it.

After exchanging greetings Lewis left, saying he had things to do. He ignored the look Sebastian gave him and the sigh Gwen let out. If they thought he was going to sit around and bake cookies while they had a knitting date, they were mistaken.

"Everything as it should be?" Sebastian asked.

"I think this makes him feel inadequate or something along those lines. It can't be easy to admit the one thing you have trained for is too much to handle alone."

Sebastian pursed his lips together. It wasn't fair she should feel bad for Lewis. If she knew why he was inadequate, it would be a wholly different set of emotions she had.

He walked over to the mostly dry yarn. "This is beautiful. Burgundy is my favorite color."

"I was thinking I might make you a scarf. It would contrast beautifully with the grays and blacks you wear," she said, watching him move as he walked over and sat on the chair beside the couch.

"What do you need me to make you?"

"You could make a hat; they are easy beginner projects."

"Perhaps, but what would you make yourself, if you were working with that yarn?"

She looked at him, his face held a defiant I can do anything look.

"Okay, I would make a shawl. Something with interesting lines. Maybe even a half circle"

"Perfect. Teach me how to do that. I like the idea of my shawl wrapping around you."

She swallowed and smiled. It was a lovely thought, but not really something to take on as a first project. "That I am afraid would take some time."

"I have time."

"Do we have time? I thought this was pressing."

"I am a quick study, love."

"Fine, how about we make a start with some practice yarn and see just how quick a study you are?" she asked, and cocked an eyebrow, looking at him in a way that indicated she didn't think he was up to the task.

"A challenge? You are a constant source of joy."

She cut her eyes at him. "Things are, they are still..." she started, but wasn't even sure what things were.

He put up both hands. "They are as you wish. Let me see the study yarn."

She got some bigger yarn and huge needles to teach him on and explained that the yarn and needles they would be using would be much smaller and more delicate.

"Should we start with something smaller then and save time?" he asked.

"You're not accustomed to being the student, are you?"

He smiled and leaned back in his chair.

"There is a reason we are starting off this way. You need to get used to the motions before you also have to worry about the yarn slipping off," she said.

After he agreed she was the teacher, she showed him how to cast on, which he practiced for a little while before she showed him how to knit and purl. She watched, trying not to laugh as the last few stitches he made fell off the end of his needles. She wouldn't normally laugh at him struggling, but since he thought he would be such a natural, she found it amusing.

He looked up and smiled at her, taking her breath away as he always did when his eyes locked on her. "I'm much better at hands on learning," he said, and walked over to the couch where she was sitting. He sat down beside her and gently turned her so her back was facing him.

She felt herself holding her breath as his arms reached around her, slowly working down her arms to her hands. It took a lot of effort to steady her hands and not drop the needles as his fingers laced over hers.

"Show me how to knit," he said, his words caressing her soul as they danced across her ear.

He was so close she could feel his breath on her skin and the heat of his body against hers.

She closed her eyes. Knitting was not sexy, knitting was relaxing. When she opened her eyes, she pushed away the thoughts of how he felt pressed against her, and focused on her knitting. Her hands slowly started to work stitches. As they moved and the needles clicked she relaxed in his arms.

"Show me purl now," he said, crashing all the calm she had achieved, and again she was aware of him behind her, aware of his hands on hers.

Again as she knitted, he slowly disappeared as her mind gave over to the relaxing rhythm.

Sebastian became lost in the rhythm of her hands and steady clicking sound of the needles. The scent of roses begged him to bury his head in her shoulder and nuzzle her ear. Her relaxed breathing was soothing, peaceful. She was the only thing that had given him peace since he was turned.

As he sat behind her, her relaxing against him, he realized this was what he craved, her touch, her scent, her presence. He craved her. The room seemed to still. The clicking stopped and she sighed, her head leaning back on his shoulder. Her scent begged him to kiss her skin. He slowly leaned down, his lips hovering just above the skin on her neck.

Gwen felt his breath on her neck, and the tingles it sent racing across her skin made her let out a sigh. As she felt herself slipping back against him, she fought against her own desire and pulled herself away slightly. "Practice those stitches," she said finally, and sat up, taking her peace with her.

He walked back to the chair and closed his eyes, allowing his hands to mimic her motions.

After some time passed she checked to see he had made lovely progress. She showed him some increases and decreases that he would need to make any lace or lines in a shawl. He was a quick study as he said he would be.

"Did you want to learn to read a pattern, maybe something basic to start with?" she asked

"How are you? Getting tired?"

She stood up and stretched. "A little, but pattern reading is pretty basic."

He agreed and she went over one of the hat patterns she had from Kathy with him.

"I've already made this if you want to take notes on it or something."

"No, tell me what you want in a shawl, sweetheart."

"Sebastian, seriously, just make something basic. I will have your scarf done in a few days. Do you like cables?"

"Cables?"

Gwen smiled and walked to the room she had made into her craft room. When she came back, she had a book that showed various cabled scarves.

He looked at several and showed her which styles caught his eyes. She was surprised that they were what she would have picked for him.

"Now, your shawl. Do you have a book with what you would make for yourself with this yarn if you had the time?"

She talked with him briefly about design elements and then he followed her to the craft room to see some designs she had been contemplating making.

He looked around the room and smiled at seeing this intimate side of her. It was so far removed from witches, vampires, and killers. He hoped that soon she could sit in there without such cares and rock in her recliner while she knitted.

"What?" she asked, seeing the smile on his face.

"Every little thing," he said.

"Not now. Now we have to think about William and Lizzy, and even Mike. They are all counting on me."

"I worry you are backing a killer into a corner. What if you do it during the day when I can't be here?"

"I'm a witch. More powerful than you, so you say."

"Potentially, we stopped lessons when, well, we need to teach you more things so you can control it should you need to use it."

She looked down. "Soon. We have other things to do."

"You can't hunt killers at night. Let me teach you again." He reached out, taking her hand. "Please, let me help you be what you should be."

She left her hand in his, enjoying the way it felt. Gentle, yet strong. Everything about him was dual natured. "Let's get this bond sorted. When our nights are not spent knitting, we can practice."

"We should work on both. There would be no damsel in distress if you could master the elements."

"I wouldn't need you then."

He huffed in false protest. "No, you wouldn't need me. Not for most things. But the increase in power you get from me will take your magnificence and amplify it. Besides, I am hoping you will want me, regardless of need."

She returned his smile and pulled her hand back. "Let's talk more about the magic tomorrow. I'm tired and tomorrow is going to be a busy day."

He agreed and she walked him to the door. There was an awkward pause.

"Did you want me to stay? Where is Lewis?" he asked.

Gwen reached out her magic, caressing the area and making Sebastian smile. "I don't feel him. That's strange."

"I can stay or you can stay at my place again," he offered.

"No, Lewis often runs off. He'll be back. I can't hide in a hole every time I have to be alone."

"No, I agree but right now. At least until things are sorted with either the killer or your magic, I wish you would indulge my protectiveness."

"No, you go. I'm tired, I'll go right to bed."

He turned to walk away but paused again. "Why don't I at least stay until I must go?"

"Fine," she relented, more because she was way too tired to stand there in the cold doorway arguing the point.

While she slept, he looked through patterns and practiced techniques, trying to decide what he wanted to make for her.

Chapter Twenty-Three

Lewis landed on the balcony railing on the second story of the small two-story house. The clapboard siding was light green with dark brown trim. There was nothing exceptional to distinguish it from any of the other houses on the street. The smell of licorice and burning incense floated out of the opened door.

"'Tis some visitor tapping at my chamber door," a silky voice said from inside the room. The statement was followed by a sweet yet sinister laugh.

Lewis shifted and walked into the room. He looked at the beautiful woman stretched out on the bed. She was tall, and sleek with light definition in her muscles. Her long, slim legs caught his eyes and he lingered where they met at her hips. The soft light from a lamp beside her bed danced across her chocolate skin as he trailed his gaze up.

She looked at him with amusement behind her dark brown eyes. "I didn't beckon," she said, sitting up and looking at him as he walked over to her.

"No, I'm here for my want this time."

"Oh," she whispered, and stood, walking over to him. "I imagined you'd tire of that little girl soon, lover."

Lewis pushed the image of Gwen that flashed in his mind away. Everything he had done so far had been for Gwen. Even being with Fannie had been for Gwen at the start.

When her long fingers trailed up his neck, into his hair, and she pulled him into a kiss, Gwen vanished from his mind.

He could not love like Gwen needed, but he did enjoy the sensations of flesh against his magical form, and he wanted Fannie who required no love in return.

Her hands explored him, her lips trailing behind, leaving him craving more.

He easily lifted her off the floor, depositing her back on the bed. He paused a moment longer, looking at her as she lay there, her eyes taunting him, before he crawled on top of her.

Hours later, laying intertwined in her legs, in sheets drenched in sweat, Lewis let a moment of nothingness wrap around him like a blanket. For that moment, he didn't worry about anything. He didn't feel anything other than her skin against him.

When worries started to trail back into his thoughts, she took him to that place again, and again, until he lay there exhausted.

"I should go," he said finally, when he had the energy to sit up.

"Should you? Did you bring me something of hers?"

"Yes, I should, and no, I didn't."

"I told you I want to sever her hold on you. I need something personal."

"I… I can't do that. I can be here with you. I can give you something of his. I won't betray her like that. I know you wouldn't use it just to sever our bond."

"Oh, how do you 'know' this. Is that what Sebastian tells you? You know he can't be trusted."

"She won't come after you," Lewis said in a flat tone.

"Bring me something of hers," she said, her voice hissing.

"No, I will not. I will never hurt Gwen."

Fannie licked her lips, her hand trailing up his thigh. "You need more persuasion?" she asked, and he felt a sharp pain in his head.

"Cruel doesn't get you far with me. You should have learned that by now."

"No? Come here," she said firmly, and walked into another room, a room he was familiar with.

He walked in behind her and she handed him a mirror. "Make a link with your child witch," she demanded.

"Why?"

"You have a nasty case of the stubborns tonight. I have a cure you may recall."

Lewis winced, remembering the pain she had caused him on one of the many times he tried to refuse her. "Why?"

"I want to see what her and Sebastian get up to in your absence before I decide what to do with you."

"What to do with me?"

"I might have a little cage ready for my favorite pet." Her eyes danced across his handsome face and she stepped closer, kissing his jaw, working to his lips where she bit him, drawing blood. "Link with her now. I won't ask nicely again."

Lewis held the mirror and gently let his mind connect to Gwen. He tried to be as subtle as possible, not wanting her or Sebastian to sense it. The image in the mirror made him want to drop it.

Gwen leaned back in Sebastian's arms, her head on his chest, his face buried in her hair. Had they really fought? Had they been lovers? Was all his help just to get closer to Gwen? Why had she lied to him about Sebastian? She had been with other men, dated, she always told him. Now he knew the soul crushing feeling Gwen must have had when she realized he was keeping things from her. It wasn't just that she was in 'his' arms of all people, but that she had lied about it.

He handed the mirror back to Fannie, who easily felt he was in a vulnerable place.

She reached over, stroking his shoulders, kissing the back of his neck. "You belong to me," she whispered in his ear. "Bring me something of theirs. I will free you from her, and punish him."

Lewis tried to get the image to go away, but when he closed his eyes it seemed even more clear. He could feel Fannie wrap her arms around his waist, feel her pressed into his back. Was this what he wanted? To betray his own witch. Could he leave her alone like that? She wasn't alone, she was with him.

The bond, he thought, enraged.

"They are connecting," he offered as an angry grumble.

"As we did?" she asked, circling him and watching his face for truth.

"Similar, but not as deep."

Her lips curled in a sneer. "You do as I say and we both get our revenge."

"I still can't hurt her," Lewis said, defeated, when he realized he still loved Gwen. It didn't matter that she had moved on with Sebastian. He still loved her even if it wasn't the kind of love she felt. That made him feel a strange mix of hurt and angry.

With her hand on his throat, Fannie backed him up against the wall. "I can be your lover and you can have all the pleasure you ever imagined, or you can defy me and find out what eternal suffering feels like, pet."

Lewis reached up, pulling her hand away. "Bitter will give you wrinkles."

She raked a finger across his bare chest, drawing his magic essence. She sucked gently on her finger, chanting a few words before he fell to the floor.

Fannie used a small dagger to cut his arm and then she let his essence drip on her mirror. She swirled her finger in it and watched as the image reappeared. She laughed as Gwen banished Sebastian to the chair, thinking the timing of the first image was perfect. The baby witch hadn't betrayed Lewis but he need not know that.

She spied on them a bit longer, growing bored with the sweet scene, wondering where the dark Sebastian she mentored had vanished too. The thought of that baby witch tapping into his power and knowledge made her cringe.

No matter what Fannie had done with Lewis to aid her against Gwen the vision of her death still haunted her. If she broke the bond between Lewis and his witch for good and the visions still showed her death at the hands of Gwen, Sebastian would have to be the answer. Maybe he was the answer all along and she had been wasting her time with the bird. She thought back to the day she took Winnie and felt regret. Had she had the visions sooner, she could have destroyed Gwen while she was a harmless child, without all the games.

She looked down at him on the floor. At least he was a pleasant mistake if so, she thought and laughed. She kicked him awake.

Lewis sat up and looked around, remembering where he was.

"Bring me what I asked for," she said and walked out.

He stood up and rubbed his hands over his face. It was always like this with her. At her place, with her smell, and sweat still on his skin he thought he would do what she wanted and come to her bed again, the only place things were quiet.

However, as soon as he got home and looked at Gwen, heard her voice, smelled her sweet scent, the innocence tugged at his heart and he couldn't. Then there was Sebastian who whispered of things being okay. Sebastian who had failed to mention when he wasn't there, that he and Gwen took comfort in each other's arms.

Lewis walked back to her bedroom and regarded her. She looked at him with beautiful but cold eyes. Her sharp features made her look regal and dangerous. He could love her if she wasn't such an evil soul. Love wasn't what it was about though. It was about silencing the misery that his life had become, and that she did, evil or no.

He walked over and kissed her deeply before shifting and flying away.

At the house he paused, wondering if he even wanted to go in or if he just wanted to wait until sunup so the creature inside would be forced to go away. He could sense Gwen was sleeping and knew that Sebastian would have one of his glorious lectures ready.

The door opened, making up his mind.

"What are you doing creeping around in the dark, while she sleeps?" Lewis asked as Sebastian stepped outside.

"I thought you weren't going to see her again."

"I changed my mind. It happens."

"What changed? We..."

"We? No, we are done. You stay out of things."

"Now we are back at that? Look the link is made, it's going to be okay. Soon you will be totally free of her."

"Maybe I don't want to be free of her."

Sebastian looked at him with hard eyes and walked closer. "You reek of her. You reek of her bed."

"Sex, that is what I reek of. Her bed, don't play pretentious games with me." Lewis stepped into his space.

"Why are you so angry? Do you need a new charm? A cleansing? I can't help you if you don't tell me what's happened."

"What happened was simple. I didn't want to sit around and watch you two 'knit' so I went off for a little fun."

Sebastian narrowed his eyes. Something changed. Something changed dangerously. His instincts were telling him that Gwen might have more to worry about with Fannie and Lewis than he first imagined. It was too late tonight, but elemental lessons were in order. Quickly.

"I won't make your personal pleasures my business, but Gwen needs to be your priority. Let me know how I can help. I need to go home." Sebastian wanted to say more but he knew that agitating Lewis right now, when he couldn't stay to make sure Gwen was safe, wasn't best.

They walked in and Sebastian took the yarn she had dyed, all of it, based on his gut feeling about Lewis. He knew it was vital to Gwen's safety right now.

Lewis had clearly been affected by Fannie.

When he got home, Sebastian put the yarn in his room, feeling it would be safer bolted in with him. Before settling in he gave instructions to Yardley. "Don't answer to anyone today. Lewis, Miss Hensley's guide is not to be let in under any circumstances. Should she need assistance, do what you can to keep her safe until I wake."

"Sir, of course, Sir. Is there anything I need to do tomorrow?"

"No, just be aware. Things are about to become very dangerous. I rely on you."

"Yes, Sir."

After Sebastian bolted himself in, Yardley walked the house, securing doors and windows. It wasn't the first time he and Sebastian had faced dangers together. He very seldom saw Sebastian look so worried, but he assumed that was more about Miss Hensley than for the two of them.

Once alone, Lewis paced a little. He tried to sort out what he was feeling and what his next step was. He could leave them all. Leave Gwen with Sebastian, he would watch over her. Leave Fannie, take the charm Sebastian gave him to keep her at bay, go to some beautiful island, have sex with locals, and drink in magical vibrations until he didn't feel a thing.

What would happen if he left Gwen? Would he be called back to the other realm where magic lived as the collective? Would they turn him to a fallen, and strip his magic? Would he be banished like Sebastian? Locked in this awful world where humans used magical creatures to their own ends? He almost felt sorry for the bastard being stuck there forever.

He felt Fannie slip into his mind, felt her cold hands wrap around his thoughts. "Bring me what I want, pet."

He walked to where he had the charm hidden and put it on, feeling it heat up instantly as she tried to reach into his mind again.

Once he was sure it was holding her off, he walked in to watch Gwen sleeping.

So sweet, so innocent. Almost innocent. He thought of her in Sebastian's arms, relaxed against his chest. Why him? If it weren't for him trying to do right by her, she would be in his own arms. She had wanted to be. He had wanted her to be, but he knew it wasn't allowed. It would have put her in such danger, danger she was facing now. What did it matter now if Fannie had already tainted the bond he had with Gwen? They could be lovers, couldn't they?

He walked over to the bed and sat beside her, running a hand over her forehead. He leaned down and breathed her in again, enjoying her sweet scents. He kissed her once on each eye.

"I do love you, my witch."

She stretched and stirred a little.

He slid into the bed, cuddling behind her, holding her close to him, enjoying the way her warmth felt.

Chapter Twenty-Four

Gwen woke and hit the ground running. She paced, her phone pressed between her shoulder and ear, talking to the detective while her coffee was still brewing.

"I have two clues that might help you narrow things down," she said, after they exchanged hellos.

He made a grunting sound and she heard him exhale, imagining him blowing out a cloud of smoke into his unorganized office. "Miss Hensley, you may want to leave this to me from here on out. I've found a few disturbing things that I am trying to piece together. Once I have something solid I will call you. Probably by Wednesday I should think."

"Well don't you even want to know what I found?" she asked, put off that he would just let that slip.

"Go on," he said, now sounding a little frustrated.

"I have a record of William requesting and being granted a name change. I can send you the picture of the document. I also have reason to think he had a brother, or family at the least. It might be best to start with the boys that were brothers."

"Send me the picture. What was the surname?"

"Livingston." She listened as he drew another drag on his cigarette.

"You will want to make sure you keep the brother card close to the vest."

"What, why?"

"Don't tell anyone close to the victims about it and I will be in touch very soon."

"Wait, you tell me."

"Those boys were involved in another murder."

Gwen felt the room spin. "Who, which one?"

"I'm getting those records. Juvenile files are sealed and harder to get into. I have my ways, it ain't gonna be cheap Miss, but your answers should be here this week."

She asked a few more questions and she hung up, feeling worse for having found out that bit of information. While she got dressed, Lewis stood in the door watching her.

"That's creepy you know," she said, sensing him staring.

"You didn't used to mind."

"Lewis, behave yourself. I have to get ready to go see Lenny. Today is important. Today I could find out who the killer is. We both need to be sharp."

He shrugged his shoulders and walked in. "This killer is just a person. Once you have a name, give it to Curtis, problem solved."

She furrowed her brows, cinching them as she looked at him. "Why are you being so flippant? You know how important this is to me."

"Me, flippant? Nah, I'll be here doing handyman things, waiting for your next orders."

"Orders? What the hell, Lewis? What is it now?"

He stepped into her space and she got a strange vibration from him that caused her to take a few steps back. "Stop it. That feels awful."

"Sometimes things do feel awful." He stepped closer, backing her to the wall.

She pulsed some magic at him, not knowing what else to do as she got uncomfortable with his nearness. Her instincts told her to get away and leave him a lot of space.

"Now, that feels nice," he said, and reached a hand for her face.

She batted his hand away. "Stop, now, I'm serious."

He watched her face, saw the fear in her eyes and smiled a little before frowning and stepping back. He wasn't sure where that had come from exactly, but it was a nice change from skating through the day frustrated. "Eh suit yourself. I'll be around if you want to play."

"Play?" she said, to his back as he walked out.

As she finished getting ready, she thought about what had just happened. She had been through a lot with Lewis, but fear was never something they had between them.

She sighed, wondering what was next. Was there ever going to be a normal, happy day where something crazy didn't happen?

She was in the kitchen making her to go coffee when the doorbell rang. She grabbed her cup and purse and headed to answer it on her way out.

When the door flung open, she was startled to see Curtis standing there on her porch, looking official.

"Miss Gwen, we need to talk."

"I'm sorry, can it wait? I have an appointment."

"No ma'am. It is about your appointment."

"I'll be late," she protested, trying to edge by him, but finding he took up too much of the porch to skate around. "I'll call you after. We can meet at Mel's," she said and looked at him impatiently, waiting for him to move.

He narrowed his eyes at her. "Miss Hensley, Lenny is dead."

Gwen reached out, taking the arm he offered. "Dead?" she asked, and stepped backward. "Dead?"

"Let's go inside," he said, and walked inside with her on his arm. He closed the door and helped her to the couch. Her hands were shaking and she had a hard time focusing on him.

"Dead? What happened?" she asked, and sipped her coffee, hoping it would warm the chill she felt race over her.

"That's what you need to tell me."

"Me? How the hell would I know?"

"That's not language for ladies."

"No, what makes you think I would know anything?"

"You were the last visitor he had. You were due to see him again. Seems your visits prompted him killing himself. You want to tell me what you were talking about?"

The questions flew over her comprehension as she still tried to figure out what he was saying. "Oh, Curtis, dead? He killed himself?"

"Yes. What was it you were going to see him about today?"

"I have reason to believe he saw who killed William." Her eyes drifted around the room as she thought back to talking with Lenny. He had seemed afraid. Maybe someone in the prison was harassing him, unrelated to her visits.

"He killed William."

"No, I am getting close to answers."

"Answers," Curtis said, and moved a little in his seat, his gun belt making a squeaking leather sound that took her back to her memories of when she watched that night.

"Yes, he wasn't alone. He didn't pull the trigger." Her voice shook a little as she remembered watching William die.

"He told you that? You know a killer can't be believed." Curtis spoke in a reassured tone that pulled her back from her thoughts.

"Let me make you coffee. There is more to this, maybe you can help."

Curtis followed her, watching as she made coffee. He took both cups since she was unsteady and they walked back to the main room.

"Tell me what you think you know Gwen." His tone was hard but not harsh.

She took a sip of her coffee. "William had family. Mike was looking into it and I think that he found something. Something he told Lizzy and she died for it. She died and the killer framed Mike. They are the same person. The same person killed William and Lizzy. His brother, I think."

Curtis sat up rigid in his seat. "This you heard from a condemned man? Did Mike tell this to Trisha?"

"No, there were papers at his house. Mike's house."

"Didn't I tell you to come to me with things? It's my job to follow the leads if you have real evidence. What were you doing in Mike's house?"

"I am friends with his mother, we were having coffee. Besides, I wanted to have something for you other than speculation."

"Right, and this is speculation. Wild speculation at that. What do you know about this mysterious brother?" While he waited for her to answer he sipped his coffee, his eyes still observing her in his suspicious police way.

"Well I know they were both involved in some juvenile case."

His eyes got wide. "Miss Gwen, you do understand that juvenile records are private."

"I, well, it is just speculation."

"Fine, give me all you have and I will look into this brother and the juvenile case. Okay? You better stay home. Knit things and do your nails."

"Curtis that's…"

"That's how ladies don't get themselves killed."

"What?" she asked, stunned at his boldness.

"If you think you are onto something, really tracking a killer, what do you suppose will happen? Let us assume you are right in all your wild ideas. If so, then this killer has killed just to keep a secret, a secret you are going to uncover. You have a gun? You trained to catch killers? You have any way to defend yourself?" His questions, his tone, and the way he looked at her made it all seem scary. Lewis and Sebastian had both insin-uated she was putting herself in danger, but Curtis said it in a way that made it feel more real.

"No, I don't. You will look into it. Really?"

"Yes, really. You tell me everything and I will. This paper you saw at Trisha's, where is it?"

"Still in his, Mike's office."

"Okay, I'll start there and re-question Mike. Make me a promise Gwen."

She looked in his eyes that seemed to be pleading with her. It was the most emotion she had ever seen on his face. "What?"

"You stop looking into this. It's dangerous for you. Promise me?"

"I…" she started and paused.

"Gwen?"

"I can't, Curtis. I need to for Lizzy and William. They deserve that much."

"Very well. If you keep interfering with my investigation I will have you arrested for obstruction of justice."

"For asking questions?" she asked, her voice getting shrill.

"No, for your safety. Juvenile records are private. How ever you were planning on looking at them is illegal ma'am."

"Did Lenny have family?" she asked as her mind shifted gears.

"No, and don't you be mourning a killer. I'll be in touch. Make some pretty crafts, get a cat. Redecorate, or plant a garden. Do something that isn't related to killers. Leave that to me."

She walked him out and after she was alone, she sat in the glass room thinking. The morning had been awful, starting with Lewis and ending with Lenny. Now she would never know why he took the fall for someone else. She knew she would find out who, no matter what Curtis threatened her with. He would have to arrest her to stop her from getting answers.

"Lewis?" she called, walking the house. She could feel he was some-where close, but he was sending a faded vibration. "Lewis, are you okay?" When she didn't get an answer, she tried to connect with him. Nothing.

"Gwen, what is it?" he said, walking in from outside.

"We need to talk about this morning, and Curtis was just here."

"I'm frankly tired of talking. Why don't you chat with Sebastian? You two can mull over why things happen and talk until the words run out, I've got things to do."

She looked at his face. His eyes read cold, empty, and watched her as close as she watched him. "Things to do?"

"Yes, things to do."

"Okay, what the hell is going on? Lewis, please. I need you right now. Lenny, he's dead."

"You need me? What is going on? How about we stop with the never-ending questions from you. I have a few of my own. You tell me what is going on. You say you love me, but recoil from my touch. He's a damn monster and yet you crave his arms."

"This is about Sebastian?" she asked and his response was a shrug and raised eyebrows. "You are the one who told me I needed to get over things and make that magical bond with him. You can't imagine I wanted to work magic like that. I didn't even want to talk to him again."

"No?"

"No, you suggested it. You are also the one who said we could never be like that. Never. You said that. You pushed me away. You broke my heart when you did. Have you forgotten that?"

"You recovered nicely."

"Oh, Lewis. What did you want me to do? Pine over you forever? Didn't I cry enough tears to sate your ego? I loved you."

"Yes, well, I still love you."

"That's not fair. I love you, Lewis, but I put aside those other feelings because you told me I had to."

"Put them aside? Like that, turned them off?"

"Not like that. You saw how hard it was, how long it took."

He started toward her and again she felt an unpleasant mix of desire and anger from him. There was something threatening in his presence.

"You are afraid of me?" he asked, now looking hurt.

"You're scaring me, yes, Lewis."

He pressed his lips together tightly and fisted his hands at his side. "I scare you? I scare you?" As he asked, he stepped closer again. Like before she backed up, keeping her eyes on him. "Me? Me who doesn't eat people? I am the scary one?"

"You need to go, please, please go." Before when she sent him away, angry about his lies, her voice had been demanding and she felt he would leave. This time she sounded timid and was afraid he might not leave.

He continued forward, pinning her against the wall again. This time he leaned in to kiss her and she reached up to push him away, finding he was stronger than she had even imagined.

The sensation that was racing across her skin felt invasive, prickly and she panicked, pushing at him with her magic again, this time using more force. "Stop it, please!" She didn't even try to fight back her tears.

Lewis reached out and snatched her hair, wrapping his fingers around a few strands and tugging.

She cried out.

He narrowed his eyes, and they both felt like the next few seconds lingered for minutes as they looked into each other's gaze.

He turned without a word, walking out.

After he stormed off she slid down the wall and cried.

Once she was done with the initial shock and crying, she stood up. If it had been anyone but Lewis she would have tested out her magic to the fullest, but it was Lewis.

How could she even consider hurting him?

She walked out of the room, feeling that he was gone. There was nothing again. Not even the usual connection they had. Lately it seemed weaker, especially when he left.

As she tried to decide what to do with the rest of the day, it didn't escape her that he had taken her hair. Was he going to work magic against her? That must certainly be against the rules he lived by.

Why did her life have to always be in a state of falling apart? Yesterday she was on the cusp of solving the murders. Today Lenny was dead, and her best friend, her lifelong friend was, was what? A part of the threats now?

She spent the rest of the afternoon practicing calling the elements, but then it occurred to her she might draw something to her and Lewis wouldn't be there to help.

She was alone.

She cleared the circle and started dinner.

In a few hours, Sebastian would be up and then she at least wouldn't have to be alone.

While she cooked, she called and left him a message.

Sebastian was at Gwen's door shortly after sundown. After she told him what happened, he helped her gather a few things.

"I thought something was off with him last night. That is why I took all the yarn and locked it up. I need to make you a charm. If he has a token from you that is not best. Do you have anything of his?"

"Like what?"

"A feather? Something like that. It's not needed, but would make the protection charm stronger."

She looked around. It wasn't like he stayed in a cage. "I don't think so."

"Okay, I may have something workable from when I helped him. You've done magic? Today?" Sebastian asked as he walked the room, making sure nothing had been attracted by it.

"Yes, why?"

"You were alone? It's still strong here. Tonight I will teach you how to clean that."

After he cleared the magic residue from her house, they got in her car and drove to his house.

Before they even stopped to sit, he took her to the altar room.

The whole time he was gathering things, she couldn't stop thinking about Lewis. "You think he is with her, Fannie? He is abandoning me?"

"Listen, what he is doing can't be the concern right now. He will come to his senses and when he does, we will help him as best we can."

"Sebastian, is he working with the woman who killed my mother?"

"I am erring on the side of caution and assuming the worse."

Sebastian made a circle and Gwen watched as he worked voodoo.

Despite trying not to think about Lewis, it was all she thought of. Why had he left her? Had she been a demanding witch? He had lived for her it seemed and she had lived as she pleased. That wasn't fair. Maybe she deserved this for being so selfish.

"Sweetheart, never take this off," he said, putting the necklace with the charm over her head. "Sleep in it as well. Never take it off."

"Okay, sure," she said, and looked at the charm. It wasn't anything special, it looked to her like a misshapen gold coin, with some wax melted to it. "Did I do something wrong? As a witch, I mean?" Tears started to form in her eyes. "He seemed so hurt and angry. Did I do that?"

Sebastian put one hand on each of her shoulders, looking her in the eyes. "We make mistakes, just like humans. We learn and grow. Things happen that change us. He is young by our standards. This could be growing pains."

"No, you didn't see the way he looked at me, or feel his hate, this must be my fault."

"We don't know what this is. What we know is you are days from getting justice for Lizzy and you are very close to facing a long-time family foe. You are also years behind in your magical training. Let us focus on that for now. I need to teach you."

"I've lost my best friend," she muttered, and turned, walking out.

Sebastian wished more than anything he could fix this for her, but he knew he couldn't. Lewis was pulling away and making bad choices from the day he met him. He was thankful they had already taken the biggest steps in her training and in their bond. They were pressed for time.

Chapter Twenty-Five

Gwen woke still feeling like her world was spinning out of control. The luxury of the bed was not a comfort that morning. It was a reminder that she was at Sebastian's house because of Lewis and what had happened to Lenny. Because she couldn't trust her best friend and the safest place for her to be was the home of a monster.

They spent most of the last night practicing with the elements, and then before bed they both worked on knitting some.

Sebastian had been patient with her as she was easily distracted with thoughts of Lewis, which interfered with their practicing. Despite all the interruptions with her concentration, they did have a productive night, and she felt like she learned a lot.

All the while she was getting dressed she kept thinking about Lewis. Until yesterday she never doubted his love for her. She loved him, he had to know that she loved him. He was there for the heartbreak she felt when he told her they couldn't be together in that way. He knew she loved him.

Fannie, she thought as she brushed her hair. The woman who had taken her mother had now, or was at least trying to take her Lewis. Why did she hate her family so much?

Gwen found Yardley at the foot of the stairs.

"Miss Gwen, coffee and breakfast are ready for you."

Gwen followed him to the kitchen, where he poured her a cup of coffee and offered her a few breakfast choices. She opted for a danish. "Do you drink coffee?" she asked as she sat on the stool.

"I do."

"Will you join me?" she asked, not wanting to be alone.

He walked over and poured himself a cup before sitting on one of the stools beside her.

"Have you been with Sebastian long?" she asked, testing the waters. "Yes."

She sipped her coffee and ate a few bites of danish while she made up her mind on asking any deeper questions. "I should leave you to whatever you need to do."

"I am to help you today, Miss."

"To help me? In what way?"

"How ever you need."

"What are you to Sebastian?" She watched him frown. One day she would learn to better filter her mouth. Maybe. "I'm sorry. I should go."

"Finish your coffee, Gwen. You are safe here. If you want to go after, by all means. If you want to stay, you will find that you can knit your magic, or work with whatever forces you want quite safely."

His eyes said, 'I know what you are,' and his smile said, 'there is more to what I am than meets the eye.'

She did feel safe and that was something she didn't feel at home. She reached up and rubbed the charm Sebastian made her. Did she really need protection from Lewis? She finished her coffee and decided it was vital that she feel safe on her own.

After talking it over with him, Yardley walked with her out back and watched from a distance as she practiced what Sebastian had taught her.

She cleared the area after each attempt and by lunch, she was feeling much better about her ability to call up the elements in a useful way.

"I should go home and make something to eat," she said as they walked in, and he locked the door behind her. "I need to check in on a few things as well." She really wanted to call and see if the detective learned anything, but he said he would call her. Her mind raced over a few things. Everything was paused again and Lewis was gone. Gone and she wasn't sure that was a bad thing.

She finally decided to head home, make pizza, and read the journals. Before she went upstairs, she walked around and made sure that everything was locked up. She took the key with her and locked herself in the altar room.

While she thought she would read in the window, what actually happened was that she stared out the window thinking about Lewis. Every bird that flew by caught her eyes and she started to feel empty inside. She left the journal on the window seat and made her way down to the altar room.

If she was a powerful witch for real, there must be something she could do about any of the hundred things wrong with her life. She paced the room, looking at the shelves. If she knew what to do, she was pretty sure Lizzy had the needed supplies.

Her fingers mindlessly rubbed the charm around her neck. Lewis. What did she want to do about him? Nothing. He was angry at being subservient to her and that was fair. She would let him be. Maybe if she had treated him more like a friend instead of someone there to do what was needed, he wouldn't have been so angry. No magic was needed; she would have to make it up to him if he let her once his anger passed.

Lenny was gone. He had the answers she needed but she couldn't talk with the dead. Could she? What was needed for that? Either dark magic or for the dead to be stuck there for some reason. If Lenny were stuck there how would she know? Where would he be stuck and how could she call to him?

More questions and if Lewis was there he would know. Rather than cry about that, she walked over to the bookshelves and started flipping through books and papers. Maybe there was a spell to call on ghosts, assuming Lenny was a ghost. He could well have passed peacefully.

He killed himself. *That's not very peaceful*, she thought.

Hours later, she had found a few ways to call on ghosts who had successfully passed; most of them required a token from the deceased. She had nothing of his, so she was going to have to work on her memory of his face.

She checked that the door was locked, gathered a few things, and made a circle. Before she started, she read the instructions a few more times. Her palms sweated as she wondered what would happen if she screwed up. Should she wait for Sebastian? Another few minutes passed as she read it again, and made up her mind. It seemed simple enough.

She said the few opening lines, as she placed the tokens at the directional points of her space. She read it again and then closed her eyes, pulling up an image of Lenny in her mind while requesting he join her.

She opened her eyes and looked around the room. She didn't sense anything different. She closed her eyes and repeated the process. Maybe he isn't at peace, and not in a place to be summoned, she thought after another minute passed.

She sat there a bit longer before she opened the circle and cleared the area.

"Gwen," the air seemed to whisper.

She felt a chill race up her back and she spun around to see nothing.

"Lenny?" she asked nervously.

"I didn't kill myself. Help me."

"Help you? Help me, who killed William, and you?"

The air heated up and she felt Lenny was being pulled away.

"Please tell me," she pleaded.

He was gone and there was a pounding at her door. She raced out of the room and downstairs. At least she knew she could call Lenny. She needed to ask Sebastian how she could keep him there to ask questions, and also how they could help him find peace. Or maybe she could find a spell for that in the altar room.

The house was cold and she wondered how long she had been up there, it was almost night, the last of the daylight was fading. As she swung the door opened, her eyes were drawn to a huge knife sticking out of the wood panel holding an envelope.

Did she dare touch it? She pulled the door closed and reached in her pocket for her phone, calling Curtis on the personal number he had given her. He told her to leave it, not touch it, and stay inside with the door locked until he got there.

She started coffee and paced the house, glad when she heard tires on gravel outside. She listened as he walked up the steps.

"Curtis?" she yelled.

"Stay inside, Gwen," he said in a firm tone.

Feeling better he was there, she went to the kitchen and made a sandwich while she waited for her coffee.

When she heard the door open, she walked quickly to the main room. He looked at her, worry etched on his face.

"I've got fresh coffee," she said, her voice shaking.

He walked in, holding a few plastic bags in his hands. "I warned you to leave things to me, Gwen."

"I have, really. I was home all day, knitting."

He laid one of the bags on the counter. Inside of it was a letter.

She looked at the scrawled handwriting. It was a threat, telling her to keep her nose out of the past or else. In the other bag she saw the large knife.

Her coffee spilled as her hands shook.

Curtis reached out and took her cup, setting it down. "You see why it's not a good idea to chase down bad guys?"

She nodded. "I was here alone. What if they had knocked? I could have let them inside. You have to find them."

She felt a familiar relief wash over her and saw Sebastian round the corner. "Curtis," he said as he walked in the room.

Gwen took a few shaken steps and allowed him to fold her in his arms. He had to fight the urge to kiss or stroke her hair while they had company.

Curtis eyed them suspiciously, and then sipped his coffee. "You may want to stay with her a while. She had a shock. I'll get on this, Miss Hensley. You rest and try to take it easy. Please, as we spoke about earlier, do something else, something safer."

"What happened?" Sebastian asked.

Curtis showed him the letter and knife.

Sebastian hated they were in plastic. He would have loved the chance to get a good sniff of them.

After Curtis left, Sebastian cleaned up the kitchen for her, and they went to his house.

Gwen told him about the day, about Lenny, and then the note, which he already knew about.

"Wait, you summoned a spirit?"

"Yeah, why?"

"Full of surprises. I wish you would let me show you things before you jump in with both feet. We will have to call him again and release him from your call. A passed soul resides in a different reality than we do. The longer he stays tied here, the more dangerous he becomes."

"I was going to ask you about that. Thank you."

"Anything at all from Lewis?" he asked and hated the sadness that instantly came to her eyes. She told him no and he let that drop. Rather than focus on that, he took her outside to work more on her magic. He wanted her to feel safe, wanted her to be safe, and there was only one way to do that.

"I think I should go to the yarn group. I don't want to let whoever it is pin me inside, in hiding," she said as they sat inside having a break.

He pursed his lips. "Can you miss this one? Your detective should have something this week, right?"

"Yeah, so he says."

"If it means a lot to you, I could linger close by."

"No, I have disrupted your nights enough. I'll go. I'll have my phone and call if anything odd happens."

After their break they settled in and knitted. Gwen was close to finishing his scarf and surprised to see he was making fast work of her shawl.

"That's looking lovely," she said.

He smiled. "Nothing will ever be lovely enough for you, but I do hope to make a valiant effort. I will work on it while you sleep and maybe tomorrow we can try these on. That would make your lone adventures seem safer to me."

"I'm a little nervous to be honest," she said, as she worked the next row, not looking at him.

"I understand. It's new and a little scary to me as well. I think you and I have enough respect for each other not to abuse the intimacies it will grant us."

"I know that. It's just with what happened to Lewis, maybe I don't need to be linked with anyone."

"Gwen," he said, and sat down the shawl, walking over to her. He ran his fingers through her hair and she leaned against his waist. "It's not your fault. I can't say exactly what happened, but you must know it wasn't you."

"You can't know that. I did demand a lot of him and all I offered in return was what? More demands."

"It's the nature of the relationship. When you raise a witch, it is like raising a child, they need you, they demand time and energy, and the reward is often just getting to see them succeed. It's worth it. He will grow into his role in time."

"It doesn't sound very rewarding."

"It is. There is nothing more wonderful than working magic with your witch, and watching as they blossom into something beautiful and powerful."

She looked up seeing pride, happiness, and sadness behind his eyes. "Do you think he will come back? Will he be the same again?"

"I can't say. I'm sorry. Know you will never be alone. I promise you that."

"But I am, Sebastian. I was alone today. I was alone when I clumsily called the ghost. I was alone when a killer stood at my door. Either of you would have sensed him, but I was alone. Lewis has left me and you can't be there all the time. Ever."

Sebastian hated that she was right. For all the precautions he helped her with, there was no way he could be there during the day. "No, I can't."

"Demanding witch, right?" she asked and laughed. "I think once the killer is caught I won't feel so scared to be alone."

"Once you feel comfortable with what you are, you won't be afraid to be alone."

"Maybe."

"No maybe, give me a little more time. You will amaze us both."

She leaned against him again and he stroked her hair.

He wished more than anything he could be everything she needed, but she was right. He never could. Ever.

Chapter Twenty-Six

Gwen finished the scarf for Sebastian and left it with Yardley, along with a note, before she left for the yarn shop. In his study, she saw the progress he made while she slept, and while he made an impressive and beautiful amount, it wasn't finished. She decided to go anyway. It was just to town and she would be with a group of people. Safe, normal people. Friends.

As she expected everyone was there, including Trisha. All of them were excited about the festival that was just a few days away. Most of the idle knitting chatter was about the various things they looked forward to the most at the festival. The more they talked, the more Gwen started to look forward to a weekend of normal activities to take her mind off the horrible things she had been surrounded by lately.

On the way home, she called Sebastian to let him know she was okay and to see if he wanted to watch over her while she tried some things he taught her.

He told her he was finished with her shawl and they agreed to meet at his house to try them on before they practiced her techniques. She was surprised he opened the door instead of Yardley. It was clear he was nervous about her being alone, and wanted to make sure the bond had worked.

"Hopefully after tonight you can have your nights back," she said, as they stood in his study.

"I wish I could make you understand that my nights are yours. There really is nothing I would rather be doing."

She gave him a weak smile, still feeling like she needed to work on being alone and not being so demanding of people who she loved. She was terrified to lose Sebastian and afraid to strangle his space like she had Lewis. She was determined to give him space to paint, or whatever else he wanted to do that had nothing to do with her or what she needed.

He held the scarf, which was masculine and refined just as he was. When he wrapped it around his neck she couldn't help but smile as his face lit up with excitement.

"It looks wonderful on you," she said as she adjusted it a little and ran her hands over it, smoothing it. She continued to smooth the scarf as she thought about what might happen when she put on the shawl, and wondered if she was ready for that type of connection with him.

"You're stalling, that unsure still? I expect you will feel a similar sensation as when you feel Lewis trying to connect with you. We can slowly walk through the rest together." He held out the done shawl and she beamed at him.

"It is stunning," she said.

He had managed all the design elements as if he had been knitting for years.

"Ready?" he asked, his voice gentle and his demeanor was patient as he had always been.

She nodded and he reached around her, placing the shawl around her shoulders. She felt a surge as her magic mingled with, and tapped into his. The rush made her cheeks blush. She held onto his hands as she adjusted to how his magic felt. "It's strong."

"Very, you have more than I imagined or sensed," he said smiling, the twinkle she missed seeing in his eyes had returned.

After she felt like she was ready, she asked, "What should we try first?"

"The most important thing right now is that you can get help in a hurry. I am going to go to the kitchen. I want you to talk to me after I leave."

"Okay," she said, and squeezed his hand before letting go. She watched as he crossed the room and paused at the door, turning, looking at her, and smiling with all his features.

After he walked out, she paced, letting herself feel him moving away. With his magic mingling with hers she found her senses were sharpened. She could hear his footfalls and smell the trail he left in the air as he walked away. When she felt him stop moving, she tried to reach out with her thoughts.

"I really sense you strongly now," she said.

"It is quite a mesmerizing sensation, isn't it?"

Even in her head his voice seemed so smooth. How was she going to function with him exuding sexy into her mind, she wondered?

"We'll figure that out together too," he said.

"Oh gawd." She put her hand on the chair. It was a very strong bond if her thoughts that she didn't project still found their way to his mind.

"Call me to your side," he said.

She only called to Lewis like that a few times in panic. She tried to imagine something that would cause her to panic in order to call to him with the right amount of intention. Her mind flicked to the knife in her door and she felt the cold, alone fear deep inside. She used that to call to him.

He felt her panic, felt her fear, loneliness, and desperation. He caught a flash of the knife in the door and the next sensation was a flash of movement. When the movement stopped, he was beside her, his arms around her. "I've got you."

She enjoyed the embrace a moment and then stepped away, looking at his face. He seemed very comfortable with the connection. "Is this how it always is with you? I mean in the past, with your other witches? I never felt so connected to Lewis. Not without a real effort."

"This is a different magic bond. I assume since we forced it we made it less pliable, perhaps? I've never felt anything like it either."

"I feel your emotions. I can hear even your most subtle thoughts. It's a little much," she said. "How are we not going to pry on each other's private thinking?"

"Practice. There are other things we can explore, but maybe we should first practice how to back away from thoughts and loosen this up a little."

She agreed and settled in by the fire in his study to practice talking without opening up so completely. The link was strong and they actually had to make a big effort not to share everything with each other.

"I'm not sure it is so much either of us prying as that there is an open flow now," he said, feeling frustrated that nothing they did seemed to ease the communication with any permanence. With effort they could close the flow, but as soon as they let their attention drift it started again.

"There are still things…" she started to say and paused. There were a lot of things she wasn't ready to know. She certainly didn't want to know what it was like to kill. "Things I don't want to understand, or feel."

"I would take the scarf off first. You will never have to experience anything like that because of me," he said out loud.

"Will my every thought always go straight to you now?"

"It seems, at least while we wear them. Maybe I should always have mine on and then you can just put yours on when and if need be."

"Maybe, but if I am alone and someone sneaks up on me, what good will it do me then?"

He sighed. He had never imagined the link would be so free flowing. None of his prior links had ever been. It wasn't his intent that they invade each other's minds like this.

"Maybe we are thinking about it wrong," she said after hearing his thought. Her hand reached out touching his face. "Maybe it only feels like an invasion because it is new. We've always been honest with each other. It's just a deepening of that."

"Breathtaking as usual," he said, and placed his hand on hers. He loved the way it felt when their skin touched. There was an instant peace that made him feel like everything would be as it should be.

"It's always that way for me too," she said. "Maybe we shouldn't do that tonight. This already feels too intimate."

He agreed and took his hand away from hers. They decided to spend a little more time getting used to the new communication.

"So, what else do you think we can do?" she asked as they walked around practicing comfortable dialogue.

"I would like to explore what this does for your elemental work."

"Yes, I do feel that the power inside and even outside of me feels much more..." She paused looking for the right word. "Available."

They walked outside and she did a few things, finding that a mere thought was all it took. Her intentions barely needed to be whims for there to be a response.

"This could be a little dangerous really," she said, half kidding.

"No love, even playing, your whims are gentle and sweet. However, should someone corner you, they are in trouble."

"Will you need to be there, with me? I mean if I am wearing this and you are far away, can I still call on your power?" she asked.

"Yes, this bond eliminates the need for proximity."

She took his hand in hers. "Thank you. I finally feel safe. It means a lot that I can feel safe even when I am alone."

They spent the rest of the night practicing, with and without the shawl because she still needed to be alone during the day. There was no way he could risk the connection while he slept. Even though she might still get benefits while he slept, if she panicked and summoned him, it would be very bad for him. They both understood the power boost was a nighttime only thing.

L ewis felt the connection between Sebastian and Gwen as soon as they made it. It wasn't that he heard their thoughts because he had disconnected himself from her when he left, but he felt the magic surge in the air. Sebastian was arrogant and probably took no precautions, he thought. Lewis would not be surprised if Fannie and god knows how many other creatures felt it too. That wasn't his problem, she had made her choice and he was done, he decided.

He hadn't gone back to Fannie, hadn't gone to reconnect either. He wasn't sure what he wanted to do yet. He flew, relaxed in the wind, contemplated what things meant to him, and where he wanted to go from there. He did love Gwen, and felt he would probably stick around until he was sure the killer was captured. Beyond that it wasn't clear. He liked that. No rules. No path. No fate. Just empty space to fill with whatever he wanted.

Chapter Twenty-Seven

Gwen spent Thursday at her house. She wanted to get used to being alone. She wanted to be self-reliant for a change.

Most of her day was spent in the altar room reading spells. Her and Sebastian had been so distracted with the shawl and scarf that they hadn't done anything with Lenny.

She was hoping to find some sort of way to make a stronger connection with him.

She felt a rush of hope when her phone rang and she saw it was Pratch. The hope was quickly replaced by disappointment while they talked.

"It seems someone else is working this angle on another case. The file has been pulled," he said regarding the juvenile records.

"Pulled, so it's just gone? You can't see it? Isn't there something digital in this day and age?"

"Think of all the records that would need to be made digital. It's temporarily gone until they are done with it."

"Do you know who? Who signed it out?"

"It was signed out by your sheriff. Maybe he is as close as I am to finding answers."

She took small comfort that at least Curtis had taken her seriously and was looking into things. Maybe she would run into him at the festival and ask about what he found in the file. "What did you find out on the name changing trail?"

"Still chasing that down for the brother. It wasn't the first change. From what I can tell, both brothers changed identities a few times. If you don't want to know what name the brother ended up using, I can stop now. I know your grandfather started as Gregory Weston and ended as William Hensley, everything in-between I have, though there doesn't seem to be any reason he kept altering his name, other than burying the past. I found no crimes under any name he used. His brother, who is five years younger started as Clinton Weston. He changed his name a lot as a young man, but with good reason. He had a slew of charges, some minor and some not so minor. A real psycho that one."

"Really?" was all she could manage to say as the information sunk in. "So, his brother, was he wanted? What sort of crimes are in his past? Are you close to his current name?"

"He is wanted for questioning in a few unsolved cases of murder, and missing persons. He has minor convictions for assault under every name he assumed. Has a really nasty temper."

"How on earth does he get granted name changes if he is wanted?"

"Miss Hensley, men like that don't get legal identity changes. Not like your Grandfather, that is why it is taking a little longer."

"Oh, I see."

"No, you don't. Some of the names he used were related to missing persons. Likely he killed them as well."

They talked a little more and he promised to call as soon as he had a name for her to give to Curtis. They agreed she was done asking questions herself. The hardest part for her to reconcile was that this man, this evil man who seemed to hurt or kill for fun was her great uncle. Her only family.

Any bit of bravery she had managed earlier was gone and she gathered her things before heading to spend the rest of the day with Yardley.

Just as it always was with Sebastian, Yardley made it seem like he had nothing better to do than spend his day keeping her company. He kept a distant eye on her as she worked magic in the backyard, giving her space, but never letting her feel alone or unsafe.

When Sebastian woke, he instantly felt her there and rushed to find out what had happened. Hearing the news from the detective was unsettling. If there was one thing he was certain of after so much time in this realm, it was that humans were by far the most dangerous of creatures that inhabited it, monsters included. Before they put the garments on, he watched as she showed him what she had been practicing, and how she did alone.

"That's very impressive. I think we might want to test this in practice since the threat is so real and so close."

"Meaning?"

"Meaning I want you to use these forces against a person, a moving, frightening person."

"No. I assume you mean you, and I am not going to do that."

"Using this aimed at still targets, or imagined threats is a wholly different thing than using this when you are afraid. Your concentration will be hard to control if you are fearful. I can make you afraid."

"No. Please, I am still working on getting beyond being afraid of you. We don't need any more of that between us."

That struck him close to the heart. It wasn't that long ago when he wasn't sure she would ever see him in any kind, light frame of mind. "Very well. Start at the beginning and do it again."

They worked late into the night and she found that he was a particularly hard taskmaster that night. Maybe the news about her uncle had struck him as deeply as it had her. This was clearly a sick man who had no issues with killing family. Not even his own brother.

"Once more," he said, while she cleared the last bit of magic she just worked.

"Really? I'm tired," she said. "Are we going to practice with the communication again?"

He looked at her weary eyes and frowned, realizing he had worked her pretty hard that night. "I'm sorry. Let's go inside."

As they sat on the lounger in front of the fire, relaxing, they put on their garments and allowed themselves more time to get used to how the connection felt.

They talked about everything from Lewis and the brother, to the festival and what things would be like after the drama was over.

"What happens to us when there is no danger?" she asked, leaning back against him and stretching her legs.

"I suppose we will figure that out if there ever is no danger."

"That's a mean thing to say. You know all I want is a normal day."

"You are a demanding witch, aren't you?"

They both laughed at that, and he stroked her hair, wishing it weren't so likely that she was wishing for a time that would never come. She felt his soothing presence so close when they both had on the garments and it wasn't long before she drifted off.

While she slept, he painted her and thought about what things might be like if the danger ever did pass. She was probably always going to be plagued by something, being as strong as she was, that just seemed like the logical reality.

As he painted her features, his mind drifted to the peace she gave him. Did he deserve that peace? He knew he didn't. There was no way he could ever change his past. He couldn't undo it. He couldn't forgive himself. He did not deserve peace. He craved it though. He craved her. Her smile warmed his soul. Her touch stopped the regret from eating away at him. Could he offer anything that would be as valuable? Sweet and gentle as she was, if he left her on her path she would find someone who was what she deserved.

The brush smoothed the paint into even strokes. He could be gentle. He could love her with a passion that ran deep and lasted forever. Pureness he could not do. He knew deep down the best he could do for her was guide her, build her up and then watch her fly. Perhaps on her own. Certainly not with him. He was a creature of practiced restraint. He could be a friend as he was with Lizzy.

Just be what she needed.

He put the brush down and carried her to the guest room, gently tucking her in. He leaned down, kissing her forehead, his lips lingered, pressed against her skin. "I love you, mi belleza. Sweetest dreams."

Her eyes fluttered a little and she rolled over. "I love you, my beast."

Her sleepy words touched him deeper than they should have and he turned and left. He made his way outside and stood just off the porch watching the trees, listening to various animals scurrying around.

"You are troubled sir," Yardley said, standing beside him.

"Sometimes the right thing is more troubling than one would think."

"That is most often the case, my friend."

"I hope I can be trusted to do the right thing when the time comes."

"I've no doubt you will, sir."

"Sadly, so do I," he said and fought back tears as he tried to let go of the idea of her in his arms.

Sebastian stood beside his old friend a little longer before Yardley walked back inside. Sebastian made his way to the lake to think a little more. He knew she would be safe with Yardley. He was faithful and may have appeared as just a servant, but he was no sheep and anyone who thought so would feel his teeth.

The fresh night air didn't ease the concerns he had. How had a person as bad as this brother managed to stay in town without him ever sensing them? It was possible the man was a total psychopath which would make him impossible to sense. He wouldn't have guilt or any of the things that would normally make a bad person easy to pick out.

The thought that Gwen could have been standing next to, shopping with, or even chatting with a dangerous psychopath made him angry. Where the hell was Lewis? She needed someone during the day. The thought of Lewis also made him angry.

He hoped whatever reason Lewis had taken her hair he had changed his mind. Most things that needed a token like that were not good. Not even remotely good. And if he gave it to Fannie. The thought hung unfinished on the night air.

Sebastian paced and tried to control his anger that he felt start to boil up. If Lewis wasn't called back and punished by the collective, Sebastian would do it himself. If he hurt her in any way, he would enjoy doing it himself. That thought startled him.

"Your monster is showing," he said to himself, watching as his words made a cloud in the cold air.

When he walked back inside, he let the sensation of her presence wash the anger away. He could still smell her in the hall. She left a trail of roses and peace everywhere she went.

"Not for you," he reminded himself and then bolted the door for the day.

Chapter Twenty-Eight

Gwen tugged the shawl around her shoulders, enjoying both the warmth and security it gave. There was added security in Sebastian's arm being around her as well. It seemed like every step they took was stopped by someone from town that knew either her or him.

After a few sideways looks, they made an effort not to be holding hands or have arms draping over each other. She imagined most of the looks came from the fact that he appeared so much older than her.

Eventually, the crowd felt like it was closing in on her and she started to wonder if every face was hiding a killer. Every set of eyes became scary as she thought about what menacing thoughts might be hiding behind them.

"Relax. I am right here. No one will even have a cross thought about you while you are at my side," he said, and she felt his presence hug her gently.

"Thank you." She wasn't sure why she was feeling so edgy tonight in particular, and just wrote it off to the fact that everyone was there. Everyone probably included the killer. She saw the imposing figure of Curtis walking toward them. Even out of uniform, he did command attention with his self-assured posture and gait.

"Evening, Miss Gwen, Sebastian," Curtis said, as he looked at them with judgmental eyes, as usual.

"Curtis, good to see you taking time to relax," Sebastian said.

Gwen smiled at him and listened as the men talked about idle matters. Her mind drifted to the way he always seemed to be lurking around every corner, judging her. He was like the father she never had, and she imagined how she felt about him was the equivalent to how a teenager might feel about their parents.

"Did you find anything interesting in the juvenile records? Or at Mike's?" Gwen asked, when the men had finished talking. She felt Curtis bristle at the question.

His attention shifted from the crowd and Sebastian, and focused on her. His eyes were particularly piercing as he assessed her, and then they lightened. "This is a celebration, Gwen. Why don't you enjoy your time and leave that mess for next week?" He smiled. It was an awkward, forced smile.

She watched as he smiled at her, but her gut feeling said he did know something. Something he wasn't going to tell her. Not now and not next week. She considered pressing him further.

"Leave it," Sebastian whispered in her mind, as his hand rested protectively on the small of her back.

She cut her eyes at him and frowned. "Of course. Enjoy yourself too," she said, and after they said goodbye, they walked away toward the games.

"Something is off with him," she said, and then tossed a ball, which missed the entire stack of bottles. The ball she threw hit the back wall with the force of her frustration and rolled back toward her.

"Focus, my dear," Sebastian said. "I felt your impression of him stronger than the impression he was putting out. That worries me."

"How so?" she said, and tossed another ball, missing again.

"I trust your instincts. If you don't like him then there is reason. I'm not saying it is anything other than the way he makes you feel judged, but I'd like to know what it is for sure before we write him off." Sebastian thought back to his past interactions with Curtis. He had never felt anything off with him. He never felt much of anything about him at all. He seemed focused and even-tempered. Except tonight. Tonight, he felt something. Curtis was nervous. That was uncharacteristic for him, even if it was very subtle.

"I wonder if I just have authority issues or if we just started on the wrong footing. Whatever it is, he makes me edgy. He has since the very start."

"No I agree, at least tonight he was cagey," Sebastian said, and paid for another set of balls. This time he tossed one and the entire stack tumbled down. He tossed the other two with the same results. "Pick your prize, love."

Gwen picked a big pink teddy bear, which he carried as they walked toward the rides.

"Did you want to go on any of these things?" he asked.

She could tell from his tone and the feeling he was sending out that he wasn't looking forward to any of them. She also knew that he would still go on any of them that she wanted to.

"What about the Ferris wheel? We could look at the whole town from up there. It would be like flying together."

He pursed his lips. Did he really want to be alone with her on top of the world with the stars as the backdrop? That could be romantic. He was finding it hard to keep his hand out of hers as it was. Had she not been so distracted trying to spy a killer, she would have picked up on how much he just wanted to be near her, and how conflicted that was making him feel.

"If you want to, then we can," he finally answered.

He was almost relieved that as they stood in line, Kathy and Trisha joined them. There was no alone at the top of the world. Instead, there was a lot of women who were happy to see the town from way up there.

They all found it magical to see the town from that vantage point.

He enjoyed feeling her thoughts as she relaxed, and the idea of this being her home gave her peace.

After they said goodbye to Kathy and Trisha they rode a few of the more mellow rides, the teddy bear making a needed barrier between them while he struggled with the intimacy of their connection and the urge to hold her.

"Are you going to the bizarre tomorrow?" Sebastian asked Gwen, as they drove to his house.

"The ladies would have my head if I didn't show up for everything. Besides that, so far it's been a nice distraction from all of the seriousness. I've enjoyed feeling mostly normal. Plus, my house needs some bizarre things to make it feel more me."

"I did like the shift in your thoughts toward the end tonight," he said, and held her hand in his.

Once they had run into Kathy and Trisha, she had stopped looking for killers in the crowd, and he felt her enjoy a little of the peace she gave to everyone else.

At his house she walked in with him, not really sure for what, other than she was enjoying his company and wasn't ready to be away from him just yet. They kept things light and she relaxed by the fire while he painted her. She was getting excited to see the results, especially because he was being very secretive with it while it was in progress.

"Did you want to stay here tonight?" he asked, as the night wore on and she started to look tired.

"I should go home. I am pretty good with some of the elemental stuff now. Water and fire at least."

"You are magnificent as I said. If you need anything, call the main house and Yardley will be there for you."

She sat up and looked around the room, making sure they were alone, then remembered she could just whisper in his mind. "Is he like us? I don't feel magic in him."

"He is not a magical creature, no. He is not a mere mortal either. What he is, is something you can count on if you need help. He is in my debt as much as I am in his. You can trust him."

The word something stuck in her mind. Not a mere mortal. Was he even human? "I am not going to ask. The last thing you thought I was better off waiting to know, I was better off waiting to know."

He smiled and then frowned. "Yes. Sometimes the illumination of truth makes things darker."

He offered her a place to stay again, and again she declined.

As she drove away, she tugged her shawl closed. The sensation of him being with her was still very strong and comforting as she pulled onto the dark road. There were still several hours of night and she was glad to be able to talk with him in case being alone ended up getting on her nerves. She might try to talk to him anyway, it would give her good practice communicating over some distance with him.

Since she was connected with him and her senses were keener, she felt Lewis as soon as she drove up. It wasn't the normal internal feeling she got from him. His presence bristled against hers as a strange outside force. She wasn't sure if she was happy or scared to know he was around.

"Lewis," she said as she stepped out of the truck. She let the thought drift on the air so that both Lewis and Sebastian could hear it.

Her eyes scanned the woods to either side of the house, looking for movement while she tried to pinpoint where his presence was coming from.

He stepped into the light. It startled her as he seemed to appear from nowhere. "Gwen," he said, his tone even.

"I missed you," she said, still standing beside her truck as she tried to get a feel for where his mind was tonight. That he called her Gwen rather than his witch made her feel sad. Didn't he feel like she was his witch?

"Did you?" he asked, feeling she was too afraid to even move. "That's not the impression you are giving me now."

"You didn't exactly leave here in the kindest manner."

"No. I guess I didn't," he said and looked away.

"Are you feeling better? Did you want to come in?" she asked, still trying, but unable to get a gauge of what he was thinking. The vibration he was sending out still felt like a mix of things. There was still anger. She felt that for sure. But there was also love, she recognized his love.

"Do you love him?" he asked.

"Lewis, what is going on with you?"

"I am asking questions now. Can you answer me?"

She felt herself getting a little angry. "Like you answered me about Fannie?"

"Is that why? You ran to his arms because I lied to you? Did he tell you about it all now?"

"No, we didn't even talk about it."

"Take off the shawl." His voice was still flat and firm as he made his demand.

She swallowed. "He wants me to take off the shawl," she sent to Sebastian.

"No," she got back.

"Why?" she asked Lewis. "He can't hear us. It isn't like that."

"Just like you and he were not lovers?"

"Lovers?"

"Yes, Gwen, I saw you in his arms."

"I don't know what you saw, but we are not and have never been lovers. What if we were? Seriously, you are going to pick my lovers now? Come inside and let's stop this silliness," she said, and started toward the door.

He stood in the path, watching her as she neared him. "Take it off. It reeks of him."

"No."

"No?"

"No, Lewis, you scared me. I don't know why you decided to behave that way, but I'm not sure I want to be alone with you."

"Fine, we will talk tomorrow in the crowd at the bazaar," he said, and shifted, flying away.

"He's gone," she said to Sebastian as she let herself in and pulled the door closed, locking it behind her.

"You can stay here," he said. Even with the distance, he could still feel a free flow of her thoughts and emotion, and right now she was scared.

"No, I'm going to lay down now. Sleep well."

"Sweet dreams," he said to her, and then walked outside to make sure Lewis had left the area.

Chapter Twenty-Nine

Gwen was contemplating a steam-punk lamp when she felt Lewis approaching. She expected him, or at least hoped for him to come, so she had left the shawl and charm in the truck for the day. She knew the shawl was useless during the day and didn't think she would need the charm, not yet, but she knew for sure, either of them would add to the already volatile tension between them.

"What do you think about this for the office?" she asked, and turned to see him standing just behind her.

"It suits you," he said. "I could see adding something pink to it though. Maybe paint this pink." He pointed to one of the gauges near the on/off switch.

She smiled. "That would be perfect. I'm sold." She made an offer and Lewis picked up the lamp for her. "I'm glad you came," she said as they strolled the vendors together.

"I wanted you to know that I know I shouldn't have behaved like that. I'm sorry."

She stopped walking and looked at him.

He did feel different today. There wasn't any anger.

Sadness filled her features. "I'm sorry I made you feel that way."

He shook his head. "It's not you."

"Yes, I've been as much a jerk as you were. You aren't just my teacher; you are my best friend. My first real love. That will never change."

"Something did change." He added her newest purchase to his load.

She fought back the pain his words brought on. The mirror she spotted for her bathroom would have been too much for him so she carried it and they walked the growing armload of things to her truck.

Once unloaded, they headed back to the bizarre again. She decided to try a fried candy bar and one of the hand-held pot pies from Mel. They stood in the very long line at Mel's food stand, and when they got to the head of the line, Mel beamed her usual hello.

"Oh, Gwen, who's your friend?"

Gwen smiled at her. "This is Lewis. We went to school together. Lewis, this is Mel, the best cook in Kansas."

Lewis also ordered a fried cake for appearances and after they walked away gave it to Gwen, knowing she was always up for extra desert, especially cake.

Hours later, with sore feet and more things to put away they headed back for the truck again.

"I would never hurt you, Gwen. I am in a dark place and I lost my temper, but I hope you know I will always love you."

"You are still feeling dark and betrayed? What can we do to fix this with us? How can I make it better?"

"I'm not sure we can. I need space, and time. I think you will be safe here with Sebastian." His voice reflected his sadness.

She sensed he thought a lot about it and this was his decision. "You are leaving me? For real?"

"Yes, for a little while at least. You can always summon me if you really need me. If you really need me."

She thought about arguing, asking, or even pleading with him to stay, but she didn't. She felt bad for making his life all about her. He needed this time, his time to feel what it was like to be him. She could give him the time and the space he needed. He would come back to her. She hoped he would. They were linked at a deeper level. They would always be together. Wouldn't they?

"Lewis, why did you take my hair?"

"I wasn't thinking clearly. I didn't do anything with it. I wouldn't. You know that, don't you?" Even as he asked he wondered himself. Would he, never? He had considered it. If he had stayed angry for just a little longer before his guilt raced in, he might have done something with it, might have taken it to Fannie.

"Of course, I know that. I hope you find your answers soon. I will miss you. I love you," she said and stepped to him.

He folded her in his arms. It didn't feel the same. It felt forced. Not dangerous like before but not comforting, not anymore.

After he left she put on the shawl and the charm, and headed back for the auction.

As night neared, she wanted to make sure that her and Sebastian had a table near the front for the auction. She had never been to an auction before and was looking forward to seeing how it worked.

They ended up front and center at the Yartists table, which suited her perfectly. Being with her friends gave her a sense of normalcy and having Sebastian there gave her the feeling that anything was possible, even normalcy, even with him at her side. She wanted to hold his hand but instead wrapped her magic around him as they listened to the auctioneer. The rhythmic sound of his voice as he chanted the prices relaxed her further.

She silently told him about Lewis and felt his tender magical embrace. "I'm sorry. I'm so sorry," was all he could offer. It wasn't something he could fix. It was something he could understand. To lose a magical companion, one that was connected with you like that, was a deep loss and one she would need time to get over.

She relaxed, enjoying the private thoughts and sensations they shared. For all the initial awkwardness, tonight she was glad for the free flow. She needed to feel his love, and gentle thoughts washing over her. She hoped she wasn't making him sad with her mood.

In answer to her thought, he squeezed her hand and gave her a reassuring smile.

When it came time for the blanket, she didn't realize how emotional it would make her. She fought back her tears and held her breath.

Sebastian's voice was gentle in her mind. "Are you okay? Do you want to get some air?"

"No, it's just, Lizzy made squares in that blanket. It was the last thing she was working on."

He felt her attachment to those squares, saw the memory of her holding the fabric in her hand, and knew what they meant to her. "I see," he said and raised his finger.

The bids went back and forth and everyone was surprised as it passed the hundreds and was now over a thousand dollars.

"Sebastian," she whispered.

He smiled and raised his finger, looking toward the man who was bidding against him.

The older man smiled at him, and raised his hand.

Kathy looked at Sebastian and Gwen and was about to suggest they make one for Sebastian if he really wanted one that badly, when she realized why he was bidding. She smiled and reached out, squeezing Gwen's hand. Had she thought about it sooner, she probably would have assigned those squares to someone else to redo and gave them to Gwen. Kathy hadn't been thinking too clearly herself, with the murder and upcoming festival as a distraction.

The other bidder finally gave up when Sebastian upped the stakes, taking the bid from two thousand to five thousand. The whole room hushed and he was counted as the winning bidder.

After the auction ended, he left her with the ladies while he sorted the blanket, and then they decided to go to her house so he could help her unload all the things she bought at the bazaar.

"Remind me what tomorrow has in store for us," he asked, as he walked in the last load of things. "You sure did find a lot," he added.

"Well I have a big place to decorate. Tomorrow is the livestock show. I am thinking I will turn up late, just long enough to say I did. We are both expected at the hoedown."

"Hoedown? Really, can't we find some other way to spend our night? We could have our own dance at the lake," he offered, and took her hand, twirling her once before pulling her close.

Her mind tried to respond, but as she stood so close to him, feeling him against her, feeling the way their connection pulsed and tugged, she couldn't. She hadn't been close to him with the connection as well, without her mind being distracted with sad things. The sensations were overwhelming. The draw to him was powerful. Her hands slid around his waist, sending waves of tingles racing across his skin. She tilted her head up and kissed his chin, her lips soft against him, burning hot with desire.

His eyes closed and he held her against him.

Her kisses trailed across his jaw and cheek.

When he felt her lips on his, one of his hands reached up in her hair, pulling her to him as he kissed her deeply. The heat of the kiss seemed to reach his soul and tug at a need he had been struggling to silence since she appeared in his world.

When they broke the kiss to breathe, their eyes locked.

He saw she had a desire that matched his own. He could feel it in her thoughts, feel it in the air. He could also feel doubt, and fear, which quickly reminded him that he was something to be feared, not something for Gwen. Something in her touch and kiss had made him forget his decision to be what she needed and not what he wanted, not even if she wanted it too. "I'm sorry," he said and stepped back. "It's been an emotional night and I shouldn't have."

"I think I got caught up in it as well," she said and blushed. If he knew the thoughts she had about him. She tugged off the shawl, realizing he could know those thoughts now.

He laughed. "It's okay. As you can hear, my thoughts have also been, well, let's get your things put away."

After they had things at least put in approximate places, she sat on the couch, holding the blanket. "This means more to me than you will ever know."

"I know. I felt it. It belonged with you." He took the blanket and stood up, wrapping it around her and tucking in the edges.

They sat on the couch and chatted while she had one last cup of coffee.

"I have a gut feeling that things are about to be over. Soon, maybe Monday, the detective will call," she said.

"What does your gut say about the end?"

"That it's going to get a lot worse before it gets better. I feel uneasy. I could just be worried about Lewis. Losing him hurts worse than I imagined it could."

"I'll be here and Yardley is also at your disposal. I'm not sure he would like a livestock show, but if you asked," Sebastian said, and gave a crooked smile.

She laughed. "I would never dream of dragging Yardley to a livestock show."

"No, but me and hoedowns are fair game?"

"You'll have fun. We'll have fun," she said, and leaned against him.

"I did say I would go anywhere with you," his voice sounded playful. "I should watch what I say."

She left the shawl on after he left and made sure everything was locked before she laid down. As she was starting to get sleepy she reached out and hugged him, again thanking him for the blanket that she snuggled under.

She contemplated asking him to come dream with her, but considering how the night ended, the kiss, and the uncertainty they both had, she didn't.

He heard the question floating in her thoughts and was glad she had thought better of it, because he wasn't sure he would have said no. He wrapped his magic around her as she slept and when he felt her starting to dream of killers, he shifted her thoughts to happier things.

Happy, peaceful things was what she deserved.

That's not you, he reminded himself as he pulled back a little, stopping the free flow of sensations.

Chapter Thirty

Gwen wasn't really into the livestock show, and was glad she turned up late. Mostly she just walked around, talking to the animals and waiting for time for the dance, which was actually a square dance, not a hoedown, not that she or Sebastian would know the difference.

"Who knew there was a difference," she whispered to the cow, as she stroked it behind the ear, looking into its big sweet eyes. She wondered if she had the right kind of land to rescue any of the cows she had been chatting with, and what it would take to make a suitable area if she did.

As she walked around, she thought a lot about the kiss they shared and wondered if it meant anything other than they had been through a lot and had an emotional day. There were still times she thought of him as a monster and could see him fanged in her mind. She knew in her heart he was a gentle creature, but that didn't change the fact he killed.

It wasn't really fair to him for her to kiss him and hold him that way if she knew she would always think of him as a monster. Did she? Would she? She certainly wouldn't ask for any more patience while she figured things out. He was a mentor, a true friend and she would be that for him. He needed that. He had lost his best friend just as she had. That was probably why they felt so close. Trauma had pushed them together from the start. Even as she told herself that, she knew that wasn't the extent of what was between them. She had felt pulled to him since the first day she saw him, before either said a word there was something.

Her thoughts were broken as Kathy came up and asked for some help with setting up things in the barn for the dance.

Gwen said goodbye to the cows and went with Kathy to get things arranged. By the time they were done, she felt Sebastian nearing. He walked in, catching several sets of eyes, wearing jeans, boots, plaid, and a cowboy hat.

"Dear god, do you always look sexy? I don't even like cowboys as a rule," she said when he walked over. While he might have been wearing the age glamour, it didn't change his underlying perfection.

He laughed. "I look old enough to be your grandfather. You however," he said, and spun her around, enjoying the way her jeans hugged her curves.

"Mind those thoughts. I can hear you," she said and tugged her shawl closed.

As she expected would be the case, Sebastian was swung from one giddy woman to the next. It was fun overall, even if it was a lot of exercise and she was tired.

She was stood, rubbing her feet and nursing a soda when Curtis walked over.

"You letting the old people out dance you, Missy?"

She laughed. "It would seem so."

"Let's go for a walk," he said more as a demand.

She fell in step beside him as they walked away from the barn. "Is everything okay?"

"No, Gwen, everything is not okay."

"What is it, did you find out who it is?"

"Would it matter if I said I did? Would you stop prying then?"

"Well I assume you would tell me, wouldn't you?" She kept walking beside him. "Wouldn't you?"

"What if I told you knowing wouldn't end well for you?"

"Is this about his brother? You found out about his crimes? He's wanted. Look, I know he is my uncle and I know he did some very bad things. I think they include killing William and Lizzy."

Curtis narrowed his eyes at her. "I wish you hadn't said that, Gwen."

She was about to ask why, when she felt a sharp pain from the back of her head and everything went black.

Chapter Thirty-One

"Wake up Gwen," a soft voice rang in her thoughts.

Gwen woke to a stabbing pain in the back of her head. She tried to think, but her mind was cloudy like she was ill and had been sleeping all day. The fog refused to clear as she tried to focus her blurry eyes. There was a soft hum and she felt movement that was making her nauseous. The slimy feeling of drool against plastic made her try to lift her head, but her effort wasn't rewarded with anything other than more pain.

She tried again to open her eyes. They hurt, the faint light that came in from the crack in her eyelids shot a fresh pain through her head. She closed her eyes and tried to communicate with Lewis. She got no response but assumed it was because of her headache breaking her concentration. As her mind started to sharpen, she remembered that Lewis was gone. The humming continued and as she laid there, it almost soothed her, reminding her of a lazy drive.

In a car, she was in a car.

"Don't make him angry," the voice said.

"Who?" she said as a whisper. She swallowed a dry lump and licked her lips. "Hello." Her voice sounded cracked and weak.

"Easy there, little lady, just relax, this will all be over soon," a different voice said.

Her mind struggled to place the voice. It wasn't the same voice that had woken her. Little lady. She hated that. Curtis?

"Curtis?" she asked.

"You're gonna be foggy for a bit, doll. You took a hard hit."

She tried again to open her eyes, ignoring the pain as the faint light of the moon shined in, feeling as intrusive as the noonday sun. Things started to slowly come back. She had been dancing. With Sebastian.

"Sebastian?" she said and reached up to her shoulders. Her shawl was gone. She turned her head to look around for it. The pain was making things seem like they were covered in a gray film. She realized she was in the back of his cruiser. She tried to sit up, but all that did was make her heave.

"Don't make sick in my damn car," he said gruffly. It was the first time she had ever heard any real emotion in his voice.

"I don't feel well," she managed as she tried again to sit up.

"Lay down and shut up then," he said, and she felt the tug of the car stronger. They were speeding up.

Grabbing onto the seat, she pulled herself up and saw his eyes in the rear-view mirror. Tonight they were dark, brown, with very little hint of the golds and greens she had seen in them before.

Memories came rushing back. She was dancing with Sebastian and then she took a break. Curtis. Curtis was angry, wanted to talk. She remembered walking away with him. "He was your brother?" she asked as it all started to fall together in her mind. "But why Lizzy? Why so many years later? Did she find out?" Gwen asked, more to herself than to him.

He didn't answer, just drove.

"He wants family. Use that to buy time," the voice said.

She looked to her side and saw a faint outline of a person. Lenny? It was Lenny. He was there to help her?

She felt herself start to hyperventilate. She had to make Curtis feel something for her. She knew from everything she had read and heard, that if a killer saw you as a person it would make it harder for them to hurt you. "You're my family, my great uncle?"

At that, he glanced at her in the mirror, then looked back to the road.

Her mind raced as fast as her heart. The sky started to cloud over and snow began falling. She struggled to reign in her magic, she knew she would need it soon. Her mind flipped between the thought that he killed Lizzy, to he was her only family. The two things wouldn't harmonize into one person in her head.

"Lewis," she called in her mind. There was no response. Maybe she could summon him when they stopped, once they were out of the car. Maybe, if he hadn't broken the connection. She looked out the window. Nothing looked familiar, it was like any other snowy wooded back road. She sensed Lenny was still beside her.

"I've been looking for you. I wanted to know you," she said. Her mind still wasn't as sharp as it should be, but she was trying to make herself sound tender and sincere. She had wanted to know him. Mostly, she wanted to know how or why he could do what he did.

His cold, suspecting eyes watched her in the mirror and then he looked back at the road. The car turned and the new road they were on made for a bumpy ride as they drove deeper into the woods.

She wasn't sure how long they drove when they stopped.

He walked around and opened her door. "Get out," he said, and yanked her arm.

She got out and stood on shaky legs. "Where are we?"

"End of the road, little witch."

"Run, now," Lenny said.

His words barely registered when she felt a rag over her mouth and blackness washed over her.

When her eyes opened again, she was looking at a wooded area. She tried to move but couldn't and struggled against restraints. Tied to a tree. Dear god, he was going to burn her alive too, just like Lizzy. Did he know they were witches? For real? She could smell a strong odor.

Gasoline.

"Uncle Curtis," she screamed. "I'm your niece, please."

"Now you will burn, witch," he said, and laughed a crazed laugh.

She wanted to understand why, wanted to know what had happened between her uncle and grandfather, but first she needed to stay alive. She screamed in her mind for Lewis and felt him wrap her thoughts as the fire lit.

The flames grew quickly and she was greeted by a familiar scene. She hadn't been pulled in the past before, she had been seeing the future, seeing her own death. She had to do something now before the fire took her away to blackness.

Her mind drifted to the lessons she had with water, and started pulling from below. She didn't have time to direct it as the heat started to push at her. She pulled, imagining it pool at her feet and wrapping around her.

There was cursing and she felt a wet splash on her. It wasn't water, it was more gasoline. The smell made her sick and she started to gag. If he lit that now she was done.

"Lewis!" She summoned him with her full intent. She knew she needed his power boost to hold the water and fend off the flames.

She felt as he neared, perched above her and she pulled again, this time causing a flood of water. She saw Lenny manipulating things and blowing out the lighter each time Curtis struck it.

"Please, Curtis, don't," she begged.

"Witch, monster." He dropped his lighter. He reached down and pulled his gun, his finger flicked the safety off.

She closed her eyes and imagined the gun red, melting, hot. It was the first thing that came to her mind.

He dropped the gun, his hand throbbing in pain and started toward her.

Gwen needed free, she called up vines, calling on earth elements for the first time. The vines crawled under her bindings and tore them free. She covered herself in water and stepped through the flames.

Curtis looked at her, dumbfounded. "My father destroyed the witch. William should have never brought more witches into our lives." He started toward Gwen, his eyes insane with hate.

Gwen realized what he was saying. His father, the scene of the murder when the two boys were orphaned. He killed their mother because she was a witch.

Curtis must have some innate power to recognize his own kind, a kind he hated, something that let him sense Lizzy was also a witch.

"You burned Lizzy." Gwen saw red hate flash before her eyes. "You took my family."

Vines came up from the ground and wrapped around his arms and legs. They jerked him to the ground, flat on his back. Gwen watched as they tugged, and rubbed her fingers together to tighten the grip and pull at his limbs. She heard a pop as his shoulder dislocated.

His screams filled the air.

She felt Lewis at her side and opened her eyes to see a wolf quickly clearing the space between the woods and Curtis.

Lewis reached out, and held her in his arms.

She pulled back and looked over his shoulder when she heard another scream.

Curtis was covered in sweat.

She pushed out of Lewis' arms and twisted her hand again.

"Don't," Lewis stepped in front of her. "You will never come back from it if you do."

She felt her hate tug at her to let the vines rip him apart. "He killed her, he killed them both."

Sebastian walked over and looked at her with serious eyes.

Her eyes flicked to him. "I can't let him live."

"You can, your heart demands you do. I will take him and I will make him suffer." Sebastian left her with Lewis and walked over to Curtis.

Lewis reached out and put a hand on her shoulder. "Let him do it."

"No, he's right, my heart says no. Curtis is my uncle. My only family." She let her attention turn to Sebastian. "Stop, don't."

Sebastian turned to her voice, his snarl now just a tight-lipped frown. Could he let this man who had killed Lizzy and tried to kill Gwen breathe one more breath, even if it was her wish that he did? His rage boiled under the surface as he tried to control it.

She stepped away from Lewis, walking toward Sebastian, her eyes locked on his. "Mi bestia, por favor, no."

Lewis was behind her, edging closer, feeling the tension in the air easing.

Sebastian reached down, snatched Curtis up by one arm, and drug him to the cruiser. The door was still opened and he tossed him in the back before slamming it shut.

He walked a few steps back to Lewis and Gwen, laying his hands on her. She felt his magic rush over her. She tried to step back but he pulled her close.

He needed to know that no part of her was hurt.

"I'm fine. Sebastian, I am fine."

He ignored her as his hands searched for any injuries. While he searched, his eyes narrowed at Lewis. Lewis should have been there faster, should have done more. Curtis shouldn't have been standing by the time he got there.

When he felt the knot on her head, he took in a breath and exhaled sharply. "You are not fine."

She felt warmth replacing the pain in the back of her head.

When he was sure that was the only injury that needed his attention, he pulled her to him and wrapped her protectively in his arms. His eyes met with Lewis again. "You comfort her while I finish with this unpleasant monster."

"No, he is…" Gwen started to say.

"He killed Lizzy. He had the same in mind for you," Sebastian said.

Gwen nodded. "Justice is not to be had by killing him."

"It would be a start," Sebastian said.

"I agree," Lenny said, his form faint and off to the right.

"He's right," Lewis said. "The lunatic was seconds from burning you alive."

"No, Lizzy wouldn't want blind vengeance. We don't even know why he hated witches."

Sebastian's eyes flashed black as he felt rage welling up again. "I don't care why. He was going to burn you alive. Leave me with him. I will make sure he feels regret in his black heart."

"No, I am calling the police," she said. "Please Sebastian. Leave this."

Sebastian paced a few steps away and made a sound that startled both Lewis and Gwen, it was a cross between a howl and a scream, pure anger, agony, sadness all wrapped in one.

Gwen hugged tight to Lewis as she felt the weight of the night and all that happened come crashing down.

"Give me a boost, this is too much for him." she said.

Lewis looked at her concerned, what she had intended to do was evident, but he wasn't sure she was ready to take on such emotions. Regardless, he infused her with everything he had and shifted so that he had more to give.

Sebastian felt her step closer, he felt her hands on him, felt her magic. He turned to look at her, his eyes black as rage washed over him. He started to shake his head no, but she gripped him tight on his wrist with one hand and held her other hand toward the open sky.

Before he could take his arm away, he felt his rage being sucked from him. For a second he panicked, thinking she would drown in his anger, but he saw a white streaking light flowing from her open hand. It sparked and popped with electricity and cracked like thunder as it was released.

His eyes returned to blue, his mind calmed, and she let go, falling into his arms. He held her close to him, not wanting to ever let her go again.

Lewis walked over, standing beside them. "We need to do something with him."

Sebastian called the police and waited with Gwen while Lewis sat perched overhead.

Curtis confessed to everything.

Gwen assumed he was terrified either of her or Sebastian, or both, as she listened to him speak with a shaken voice. When she looked closer, she saw what had Curtis shaking. Lenny was beside him, a dark, menacing form, not the friendly vision she had of him. She thought that was good for Lenny to have his own justice for the time he lost. Her and Sebastian would release Lenny from the summons after his own death and wrongs were righted.

Chapter Thirty-Two

"What are you doing here, Sheriff Dillon?" Gwen asked as she walked out the prison toward her truck.

Dillon tipped his hat and smiled, winking at her with his sharp green eyes. It was his usual greeting. "Monday, always seems some paperwork or other such unpleasant task awaits me on Mondays. What about you, any joy this week?"

"No," she said and looked down at her sneakers.

She came every week, Monday and Friday, and every week Curtis refused to see her. She came anyway, he needed money added to his commissary funds and she felt one day he would want to see her. They were the only family each other had left.

"Chin up. Frowns don't suit that pretty face. Meet me at Mel's in an hour or so and I'll buy you some pie. Pie always makes things better." He smiled again, this time the dimple on his right cheek showing.

"You like pie. I like cake."

"Pie and cake, it is. See you soon," he said, and walked off.

She watched him walk away.

He was initially sent as a temporary sheriff, but fell in love with the town as she had. Since he took over as sheriff they had become friends of sorts, having an instant common ground as two city kids who were now living in a small town, but that was all it was.

They often met for meals and conversation at Mel's. All the yartists had read much more into things, but Gwen was still struggling to place where her heart belonged.

Lewis took a part of it when he left. She knew she would always love him and there were still times where just the sight of a bird flying overhead would make her cry.

When the nights felt long she was often tempted to call to him, but each time she remembered him asking her only to call if she really needed him. While she really wanted him at times, need was still something she struggled to define.

There was a part of her heart that also belonged fully to Sebastian, even though they had both pulled back from that and had been tiptoeing around anything that might be even remotely intimate. They each had their own reasons for not exploring the deeper connection they seemed to have from the start, but that didn't change the fact that it was there. When the conversations ended, the painting stopped, and the room went silent, they always struggled to stay out of each other's arms, thoughts, and hearts.

She knew how he felt, it was in each painting he finished. He painted her as if she were a goddess. Her favorite painting, the first one he did, was hung in the main room above the fireplace. It was her in the snow, trees in the background with snow tipped branches. There were small pearls of white throughout her hair, and at her side was a beautiful blue eyed wolf.

"You okay sweetie?" Mel asked, drawing Gwen's thoughts away from Sebastian and Lewis.

"Oh sure, I'm waiting on Dillon. Can I get a coffee?"

Mel went to get her a coffee and Trisha walked over, hugging her and startling her at the same time. As soon as Mike was released, she had returned to her flamboyant happy self.

"How are you?" Gwen asked.

"Good, I've been struggling on the new pattern. Did you have any problems with the stitches slipping off?"

Gwen pursed her lips together. "I did. I switched to plastic needles, they grip that yarn better."

"Oh, I never even thought of that. I have some too. Thanks. Mike wants to see you too. He says you are helping with something on his family tree stuff and he had something for you to see."

"Of course, I'll call him after I eat," Gwen smiled as she walked away.

Things with her and Mike had smoothed out once he was cleared and his mom explained to him Gwen had been the reason for that. She wouldn't exactly say they were friends, and the older librarian lady still said her name like it was a dirty word, but she at least felt okay enough around them to go get books.

Dillon walked in, took his hat off, and ran his fingers through his curly blonde hair as he walked over and sat across from her.

"Sorry, that took longer than usual," he said.

Mel came over and they ordered pie and cake. "You kids should eat real food too," she said as she walked away.

"Small towns, it's the equivalent of having twenty mothers always watching over you," Gwen said and sipped her coffee.

"Yeah, I wouldn't trade it for a city with a million strangers always watching over you though."

"No, me either."

"Speaking of small towns and gossip, did you ever get a handyman to help you around that place?"

She laughed. "I just started looking. Wow gossip spreads fast. Maybe that will work in my favor. Mostly I want someone to help with heavy chores. I enjoy doing the housework and yard-work."

"Well I may know someone. Kid of one of the men. I say kid but he is probably over twenty. I'll give him your cell if you want."

"Sure, thanks."

They both stopped gabbing while they made fast work of the desserts.

Dillon's radio crackled and came to life. A voice came over, calling him back to work.

"See you soon I hope," he said, walking over to settle their bill, and flipping his hat on as he walked out.

Gwen spent the rest of the day knitting in her recliner. Since it was Monday she wasn't surprised to feel Sebastian come in. He always came by on Monday's to see how it went, and make sure she wasn't too sad or disappointed. The shawl was resting on the back of her chair, she hadn't realized it had gone that late as her mind drifted.

"It's always nice to see you relaxing." He walked into her craft room.

"It is always nice to see you," she said, and watched him walk over. His gracefulness still captivated her.

He could tell by her lack of excitement that Curtis had refused her again. "I'm sorry."

"Yeah well, one day he'll come around."

Sebastian was never sure how he should feel about that. He was glad the psycho hadn't wanted to see her, but on the other hand he was unhappy that it made her sad. That, and the continued absence of Lewis played heavy on her heart.

"It's stunning at the lake tonight. You want to go for a walk?"

She agreed, pulled on her shawl, and they made their way to the lake.

There was never a time they had been there that she left feeling sad. They both stood silently, watching the moonlight dance on the water. It seemed like it was so far away from the first time they came there together. This had become their place.

She could feel him relax, feel his love, feel the perfection of the connection they had. Being with him was easy. Once they stopped trying to fight the flow, it had become a natural feeling that she missed during the day. He made her feel whole.

"You complete me too, beauty."

She leaned to him, and rested her head on his arm. Had they been anywhere but the lake, this would be the time one of them pulled back.

Instead, he put his arm around her and tucked her close at his side.

She felt his uncertainty start to drift in as it did whenever they found peace together.

"We'll figure it out, together." She nuzzled against him and enjoyed the feel of his magic blanket as it wrapped around them.

The end.

Sort of… read chapter one of part two, Burning Captivation on the next page.

Burning Captivation:
An Elemental Witch Trials Novel Book Two
Chapter One

"THE PLEASURE IS mine, Master Dmitry." Gwen kept her eyes down as custom dictated. She focused on the tips of her shoes while she fought the urge to look at the monster.

"Is the council sending me a snack as some sort of bribe?" Dmitry ignored Gwen's address and looked at Nikolay, who stood beside her.

"She is the new envoy," Nikolay said.

"Envoy? A human?" Dmitry's tone carried disbelief.

She could feel him circling her, feel the cold death he radiated, and smell the damp mustiness of wet earth that trailed him and filled the meeting room.

"They decided an ambassador was still unwise, all things considered. This is simply a formal introduction," Nikolay said.

Gwen noticed his voice sounded nervous in the presence of Dmitry, she understood why. Her eyes drifted to the carpet with its intricate swirls. It made her wonder how all the pieces actually fit together.

Don't alter human and vampire relations, the instruction played again in her head. Since the witches did not bother to fill her in on any specifics of that relationship, she took her cues from Nikolay, the vampire ambassador living at council who they partnered her with.

Dmitry snorted. "Unwise indeed. Perhaps humans can be taught after all."

"Perhaps. Unless there is business you need me to take back to the council, we will not disturb your night further, Master."

"Envoy? To what end? I need no help to navigate this simple realm. Certainly not from a girl witch. Isn't that what you are for?" he asked, and started to circle Gwen again. He ran his fingers across her hair, gathered a lock, and twisted it between his fingers.

She shivered at his touch, but managed to keep it internal. She knew how vital it was to not appear weak to these predators. She wanted to address him again, but Nikolay stressed to her the importance that with the master she didn't speak unless asked a direct question. Since even Nikolay offered that respect to Dmitry, she took it serious as well.

Dmitry sniffed her, paused and sniffed her again a few times. "You are bonded with one of us?" He tilted her head up to look at her eyes.

She caught a brief glimpse of his solid black eyes, before they flashed green and she looked away. "Yes, Master Dmitry, I have a magical bond with one of your kind." Her voice still sounded sure, due to the bond and the extra support she received from Sebastian.

"Magical?" He leaned close, and breathed in again.

She watched him puzzle over what he smelled. When he looked at the shawl and wrinkled his nose, his lips pulled back to show fangs; she looked away.

"A mutt. Bonded with a mutt. I'm not sure if I should be amused or insulted at this choice." He spoke in a tone that reflected the face he made.

"I'm certain they meant no disrespect, Master. If she displeases you, I will inform the council of their error." Nikolay stepped back from the two of them.

Gwen remained silent; she wondered if him upset would end the whole charade and allow her to return home. She did not want this appointment, not even as a cover, as it were. She heard a sucking sound as he ran his tongue along his teeth. Since she knew his fanged sneer would unravel the false bravado she barely held on to, she kept her eyes averted. Looking toward the ground again she saw him rub his long fingers together, the pale gray skin, and thick, yellowed nails startled her.

Her eyes darted away from his fingers. The room looked like any other meeting room she ever visited. The large wooden table with several chairs and various stacks of papers took up the center of the floor, and even though it was sparsely decorated, each item fit perfectly together to complete the formal, yet decadent business appearance.

"Leave us," Dmitry said to Nikolay.

"Master?" Nikolay said, his voice rang as both unsure and hurt.

"I said leave us. I will not be questioned or repeat myself again."

Gwen heard Nikolay's footsteps as he walked out and the noise of the door when it closed behind him.

Her heartrate picked up. Alone with the monster.

"Look at me," Dmitry said as a demand not a request.

She slowly looked up. The risks of getting caught in his gaze only slightly under weighed the risk of annoying him. She knew most vampires could entrance a human with a mere glance and could only imagine what a master vampire could do.

Sebastian reacted to it badly when she told him where the council wanted to assign her, and indicated that a master vampire, or any royal vampires near her could spell trouble. His warnings filled her mind and she pushed them aside.

For a second Dmitry's appearance terrified her while his form wavered, his whole body appeared gray with thick and hard skin. Wings with dark, pulsing gray veins in them stretched behind him. The long and pointed chin of his face made the fanged mouth seem mammoth.

In a flash it all changed and he looked harmless, good-looking even, just a tall sleek man, no different to any other man. His long black hair and piercing green eyes complemented his sharp features and white smile. The image flickered as she looked at him, the monster hiding under the pretty face wavered in and out while his shift took hold.

Dmitry watched her reaction to his wavering form.

She guessed from his confused look that humans didn't usually see, or react to the monster hidden under his glamour.

He narrowed his eyes and then entranced her with an effortless glance.

She stood frozen, held captive in his eyes as he reached out and touched her face.

The confusion on his face grew when she didn't mentally recoil. He smiled as if he found it all amusing and curious. His hand reached around her and with two fingers he lifted the shawl off her shoulders.

She struggled to keep her fears under control when he flicked his fingers, and it dropped to the floor.

He gave her another curious smile.

She assumed he found her courage new; she found it miraculous. His intense green eyes held her frozen or she would have returned the smile as bravely as possible. If this meeting happened before she lost her whole family, before she tracked down her murderous uncle, before she escaped being burned at the stake, and before Lewis, her familiar, abandoned her, she would have cowered at his feet. She wasn't that scared witch anymore. She was an elemental witch, a survivor, in charge of her own fate.

As she reached out with her magic, he cocked his head, the edges of his lips twitched while he held back a smile.

She assumed he felt it and pushed a little more.

This time he smiled.

"This is going to hurt," he said, and his gaze intensified.

Coldness came at her in painful flashes as she felt him enter her mind in cold threads. While he searched her memories and looked for what he needed to know, she continued to feel nauseating pain.

Quickly she pushed any connection to Sebastian away, she didn't want Dmitry to access him via her. The cold threads tightened into a solid cold pain.

No matter what she tried to pull up to help her, nothing happened.

3

The longer and deeper he probed, the harder she found it to even form a coherent thought. All she saw was gray, all she felt was cold pain, and the scent of decay became overpowering.

The pain left and she felt the threads unwind. Her head felt like it did after drinking a milkshake too quickly. The gray started to retreat. The scent of decay remained.

Dmitry used a white handkerchief that he pulled from his suitcoat to wipe under her nose.

She watched, still unable to move as he took the bloody cloth and raised it to his nose.

He turned from her and took a few steps toward the head of the table.

As soon as he released her from the trance she reached up and rubbed her head. Did she dare retrieve the shawl? Would he consider that rude? Not ruder than his invading her mind so violently.

"You may have a seat." He gestured to the chairs and watched as she walked to the one closest to him, her head still down. He gave a half-smile in approval that she didn't sit as far away as possible.

She pulled out the chair and sat down.

He remained stood. "You understand that a man in my position must know with certainty those who serve him are actually in his service. That puts you in awkward place." He paused, his eyes studying her. "I appreciate your council needing spies in the halls, nonetheless to bury you in my ranks was unwise." He paced a little, and stopped behind her. "Your unique power makes you a superior witch, and your connection with Sebastian has added to that power. I see your dedication to him and require no less. You will submit to me tonight, or you will not leave this room."

Fear started to take a grip of her. What did he mean submit? How could the council send her to him? They knew about vampires; they knew she could not defend herself against the master monster.

She felt the chair slide out.

He made no sounds of effort, the chair glided across the carpet as if she didn't weigh anything. "Get up, look at me."

Gwen stood and looked at his face again, glad his human form held, since her shawl rested crumpled and useless on the floor. Did she dare try to call up magic before he entranced her? Could she win? Vampires moved faster than the eye, would a master move even quicker.

He watched as she considered her options. "You realize you are mine regardless of how you decide the roles play out? Dinner or diplo-mat. Do you submit or die?"

Did she say yes? What would that mean? She knew she couldn't ask

4

him. Not now. She kept her eyes steady, slowed her breathing and al-lowed her heartbeat to smooth out. She would not die, not there, not like that. "Yes, Master Dmitry." The words filled the air with a certainty that sounded foreign to her.

"Before you are welcome to my circle of service, there will be a test of your devotion. Upon completion, you will be honored with my mark and protection. In the interim, you are a member of my tribe and will bear that mark. Sit down." He watched as she sat and then he walked back to the head of the table, leaned on it with both hands, and rapped his fingers. "Things in this realm are as they should be. They are to be left as they are, unless I tell you otherwise. The other tribes will ask you to make changes no doubt. Changes will result in great loss of both human and vampire lives. No changes. Do you understand?"

"Yes, Master Dmitry." She looked at the wood grain on the table as she tried to reason out what she agreed to. What did it mean to be a member of his tribe? She should have asked Nikolay a more questions before they left.

"I do hope it will prove to be a worthy sacrifice, this missing witch, for your subjugation to the monsters you despise so. It is curious you love such a monster. Sebastian will need to make his own submission. Not today." The smile on Dmitry's face said an unpleasant day awaited her and Sebastian.

Gwen didn't see Sebastian submitting to anyone.

He reached out and took her hand. "Look at me."

She looked up from his mouth to make direct eye contact again. "This too will hurt. Hurt is part of my kind, your kind, welcome to the tribe, Gwen." His voice sounded anything but welcoming.

She didn't have time to pull her hand back, not that she would have tried, when she felt his nail break her skin. She kept her eyes on his as she felt him drag his nail across her hand. After the initial cut, the pain dulled to a sting. Her eyes remained on his, in her peripheral vision she saw his finger raise to his mouth, his tongue flashed, licked the tip, and then she felt the wet finger on her hand. The sting intensified and she looked down to see a small scar on the back of her hand. It looked like the letter 'c' with a squiggly line through the center. She felt the sting of her skin break-ing, and knew it should look much worse, but assumed his saliva healed it already.

She looked away again. Her attention focused on the wood of the table as she tried to maintain her fear level and not think about what just happened. She didn't have much of a choice. Join his tribe or die, her magic wouldn't have stopped him. He would have seen it in her eyes and drained her dry before she even focused her intentions.

He watched her a moment longer. "Come, I will return you to Nikolay and your mystery solving."

She looked up at him, and pushed aside the rules, worried he might blow her cover to Nikolay.

He paused, turned his head and raised an eyebrow. "Forgiven, this once." He pointed down. When she looked away he continued. "Fret not, we all have secrets that need keeping. Don't forget your blood token."

She reached down and gathered her shawl, but did not stop to put it on as she followed him out of the room and down a corridor.

They entered a small room where Nikolay paced in front of a fireplace.

"I trust you were fed well," Dmitry said as they entered. "She can live, for now. Will you be parading her before the other two?"

"It is customary, Master, at least until things are settled," Nikolay said, and took a step back as if he expected a thrashing.

"I suppose it is. Do report to me the reactions to our little muddled envoy," he said to Nikolay, and then reached out to lift her chin. "Should I summon, you will come immediately," he said to Gwen.

"Yes, Master," Gwen and Nikolay said in unison.

With that Dmitry left them. When she felt him leave, she let out the breath she held, and pulled her shawl tight over her shoulders.

Nikolay laughed at her sudden change from brave to relieved. "You are a skilled facade builder."

"Maybe it wasn't false bravado." She ran her fingers over the fabric of the shawl as she thought about Sebastian. Her time with him, his lessons, and his guidance helped her grow so much. With his mentoring, she blossomed from a scared child into a powerful witch. A witch who just submitted to the master vampire. She sighed. That could complicate things.

Nikolay nodded. "Are you up for another master tonight, or do you need time to regroup yourself?"

"Are they all going to be deciding if I can live?" She tried to laugh it off, but her laugh sounded anything but amused.

"Sweetheart, I am still deciding if you get to live." He turned to look at her sharply. His tone, his eyes, and the chill in the air as they walked to the front door served to remind her that master or not, Nikolay was still a monster as well.

Out of habit she looked away.

"They will not be as, dominant, as Dmitry," he answered as they stepped into the crisp night air.

"Why is that?" She hadn't really found much of a chance to talk with Nikolay at the council manor. After they informed him of her new title, he spent his time behind closed doors with the head council members until just moments before they left to meet Dmitry.

"The tribe they are masters of are not the ruling tribe."

"Isn't that being disputed?" She looked up to see his black eyes glare at her. "I mean isn't that what the unrest is about in your realm?"

"It isn't a matter you would understand. They are masters of lesser tribes and will fall under general rule. Dmitry is the master." His words sounded hard.

"We may as well save it for another night. I have a lot to consider." Her tone reflected that she wanted to go home. When she looked at him, she saw a soft smile and a kind face. It unnerved her how the human glamour they created didn't fool her anymore. "What does it mean for a human to be a member of a tribe?"

He stopped walking and yanked her hand up into the moonlight so he could see the mark. His snarl made her step back. "You don't deserve this mark."

She felt his hate so thick it raced across her skin and her thoughts.

"Stand your ground." Sebastian whispered in her mind.

She let her eyes trail up to his and fixed her lips in what she hoped looked like a challenge. "That is for him to decide. I only bear a tribe mark. Apparently, I will have to earn the other mark. You can tell me what it means or I will find out elsewhere."

Nikolay laughed. "It means you don't die tonight. Sister. Be warned it will offend even his own tribe, should he choose to mark you as his inner circle. While you will have his protection, you will find you need it."

"Do all tribe members have this mark?" she asked, rubbing the scar. It didn't hurt and looked like it had been there forever.

"No, we are members of his tribe by birth. Marks are only needed for other species or slaves from other tribes. It will scent you, and the scar will end any doubt who you serve." He lifted her hand to his nose and frowned. Now she smelled of an odd mix of Dmitry and Sebastian.

He watched her and wondered what the council had in mind with the new envoy, and why Dmitry had taken to her so much so that he marked her as tribal. No issues in either realm required attention. He proved himself as more than capable of being an impartial representative to both the humans and vampires, and as far as he knew they both respected him.

It felt like a slap in the face, or at the very least a step on his toes. He bit back his frustration as he thought about how adamant the council had been about having an envoy work with him.

As a rule, vampires were territorial, and the seat at the table of the council and with the tribe leaders had been his territory. His and his alone. If she got in the inner circle before he did, or even after, he would kill her himself. No human was marked with a master's personal mark. Very few vampires had the honor. Why was she even being considered for that? He couldn't question Dmitry.

He would have to rip it from her mind.

Later.

"Serve?" she asked, after waiting and watching as he clearly thought about things, getting unhappier by the second.

"Yes, serve. I need to feed. Have you managed to still your fears for the moment?"

"Yes, thank you. Will you need me to take you back to the council tonight, or will you make your own way?" She asked, sensing again that he didn't care for her, regardless of how nice or brave she had been.

"I will need some alone time, sweetheart. Unless you want to provide me a snack?"

"No, I will see you tomorrow night then? To meet the other tribe leaders?"

"Suit yourself. I would have only had a taste." He walked away so quickly she found herself looking at the empty place he just stood.

She didn't want to be alone on Dmitry's grounds any longer than she had to. The air seemed to be scented with death and decay. The cool feeling vampires put off came from all directions and made it hard to determine if any were near, or if so many of them walking around had left cold trails in their wake.

She took the black stone from her pocket and held it in her hand. Her palm warmed up the stone. She had brief lessons on using the shadow stone at the council before they left for tonight's meetings. While it was a new skill to walk in one shadow and emerge in another, the most unnerving part was when she had to take Nikolay with her. Not only did she have to let him in her mind a little to give her an image of the location, but she had to hold his hand to take him along.

Finding a shadow of suitable size under the billowing trees on Dmitry's property was easy. She looked around, getting a good image in her mind of the place, in case she needed to return. In case he summoned.

Once she stepped in the shadow she felt a slight tug and appeared in the room she had been given to stay in at the council. She didn't bother to take off her shoes or clothes before she crawled in the bed and closed her eyes, reaching out to Sebastian.

"That was awful. Can you please take away my fear so that I can sleep?" she whispered to his mind.

"Of course, mi belleza. I felt how scared you were, and then I lost you. I'm glad you are safe now."

"I had to push you away. For your own protection," she said, and then told him about the night and what happened. She could feel his worry across the miles. He wanted to see her, but she didn't think it was a good idea, not yet. She didn't like the way Dmitry hinted that Sebastian would be drawn into this at some point.

It was only supposed to be a cover so she could investigate a missing witch. In one night, things had gotten way out of hand. She would find out what happened, and get home, hopefully without another scrape with Dmitry, and certainly without involving Sebastian.

When she couldn't allay his concerns, they decided that after she drifted, they would have a dream walk, a gift the shawl allowed and one they only used once before. It would let him step into her dreams, see she was okay, hold her, and hopefully set both of their minds at ease.

As she drifted off she hoped she could refrain from falling into his arms. They were off limits. They were where she wanted to be. More than anywhere.

LUCRETIA STANHOPE is the award-winning author of The Elemental Witch Trials series, featuring witches and vampires in an eternal struggle for power. She also writes horror, and paranormal romance.

Say hello on Facebook https://www.facebook.com/diana.stanhope to connect and keep up to date with new releases, crochet projects, pets, random musings, and whatever else has her attention on any given day.

Made in the USA
Lexington, KY
15 December 2017